*Adult Fiction*
*Romance/Drama*

# A Taste of BitterSweet Fruit

## The Novel
&lt;Raw and Uncut Version&gt;

## Kharisma
"Kharisma"/D. L. Miller@2006

Printed and Edited by: Miller Publishing Enterprises
Miller_publishing@yahoo.com

*\*Disclaimer: A Taste of BitterSweet Fruit is raw and uncut. If a novel could have a rating, it would be Rated R. It has some components of sex, profanity, and violence in its contents. If you are particularly sensitive to this subject matter, this novel is not for you.*

This is a work of fiction. Names, characters, places, incidents and dialogues are the products of the author's imagination, or are used fictitiously, and any resemblance of actual persons or events, living or dead, are entirely coincidental.

Published by: Miller Publishing Enterprises
www.millerpublishingkharisma.com
miller_publishing@yahoo.com

ISBN 13: 978-0-9818915-0-7
ISBN 10: 0-9818915-0-0
LCCN: 2008906459

Editing:   Miller Publishing Enterprises
Consulting: Renee Bobb of R.B.I. Enterprises

Book Layout: Northlight Publishing
Cover Design: Marion Designs

Copyright@2006 by D.L. Miller
All Rights Reserved.
No part of this book may be reproduced
without the written consent of the author.

# In Dedication

For my dearest family and friends with love.

And for the ones who have inspired the words of this text, the warmth of my soul, and the rhythm of my heartbeat I thank you all.

Kharisma

# Acknowledgements

Although I have never been a very religious person, I would first like to say thank you Lord for bringing me through this book, and through every other challenge I have faced in my life. There have been many of them through the course of this book, and I expect there will be many more in the future. Please continue to stand by me.

I want to thank my family; my mother, father, sister, and my grandmother (RIP) as well. Even though they knew little about the existence of this novel, they have always supported me in what I have done, and told me exactly what I needed to hear.

I have to send out thanks to my close friends and associates; Monica, Sharlene, Trina, Charita, Keisha, Oliver, Lamont, and many, many others. And I must thank my enemies as well. It was actually my ex-boyfriend who helped to inspire the creation of this novel.

To my future business associates; publishing companies, editors, agents, artists, photographers, and anyone else who will help to see this book develop and grow into a mature flower. I thank you.

If your name is not mentioned here, please don't take it personally. Just know I didn't think enough of you to mention it here. Just playing! I know I'm evil, but you still love me though! lol

## Kharisma

## Characters/Setting

### Characters

- D.C./Dion Curry- 26, Khailas boyfriend, Veys brother
- Cocoa/Cofina Harris- 35, Reeses wife, mother of Reese Jr./ Shayla, Khaila/D.C.s neighbors
- Fefe/Feyona Jackson- 20, ex-girlfriend of D.C.
- Jy/Jyree Williams- 24, D.C.s best friend from high school
- **"Khai"/Khaila Roe- 23, D.C.'s girlfriend. Tracie/Keyon's sister**
- Q Quiante Shaw- 21, Tracies boyfriend, D.C.s friend
- Mr/Mrs. Roe- 52/ 49, Khaila/Keyon/Tracie's parents
- Reese Harris- 36, Cocoas husband, father of Reese Jr./Shayla, Khaila/D.C.s neighbor
- Shante Brown- 23, Khailas best friend
- Tonda Davis- 21, Fefes best friend
- Tracie Roe- 20, Khailas younger sister
- Vey Curry- 29, D.C.s older brother
- Wanda Freeman- 42, Reeses co-worker

### Setting

- Place: Khailas new apartment in South Richmond, VA.
- Time: Thursday, June 8, 2004, 4:00 am.

# Her obsession comes from pain, and with Her obsession She brings vengeance!

ᵋKharisma

# Prologue

"Yo man, this shit has gone too far. Let's go!" Jy's voice was almost trembling.

Q noticed Jy's nervous state, and picked him apart, "Look, yo' bitch-ass can go 'head and leave then. I'm staying right here with my boy 'til we finish teaching this ho' a lesson."

"I'm telling you man we need to go…now." He pointed towards the bedroom window frozen like ice.

We all turned facing the window, noticing the all too familiar red and blue lights. It was the po-lice! Q and Jy looked at each other both with fear in their eyes. I imagine in those lights they saw flashing images of their soon-to-be fate. They both knew they couldn't afford another trip to jail. We had all done time before and knew the deal. Lockdown was no joke for real. Bad food and lack of freedom were the least of our concerns. Jail meant living in a jungle full of rapist and murderers. The same method of the street, also dwells in the jungle. You had to get "broken in", because you were "fresh meat." And unless you had peoples on the inside that gave a fuck about you, you were destined for the initiation process. Q stood to lose the most inside the jungle with Virginia's three strikes law in full effect. He knew more than any of us that he couldn't go back to jail. My boy could possibly get a life sentence with no chance of parole.

Before I could even say, "hold up," my so-called boys made a dash for the back door, while I stayed behind. I had unfinished business to take care of. I stood face to face with my enemy, and I had to finish what I had started.

Without a blink or a sigh I stared down at my victim, and said, "If we ever see or hear from you or your friends again, a court order will be the least of your worries. Do you hear me?" I approached closer hovering over the bed and said, "I promise you I-WILL-KILL-YOU-IF-I-SEE-YOUR-FUCKIN-FACE-AGAIN. You can quote me on that. Right now I don't give a fuck, and I ain't got shit to lose! I'd suggest you find a new place of residence….."

# Miller Publishing Presents.....

# Kharisma
### New local author from Richmond, Virginia

As a young child, this Richmond native demonstrated her passion for writing through journaling and short story writing. As time progressed her love grew and expanded to develop her own personal poems, soap operas, and television scripts.

By her senior year in high school, she was ready to serve as a school newspaper journalist. It was at this time she realized her raw talent in writing/journalism, although she decided to pursue other career areas first.

In college, she majored in Psychology, (Bachelor's of Science) and Rehabilitation Counseling, (Master's of Science), and went on to counsel youth in her community.

It was not until a failed relationship in 2001 that Kharisma was inspired to write her first fictional romance novel. She started writing little by little until it was finally completed in 2006. Thus A Taste of BitterSweet Fruit was born!

Kharisma is currently self-publishing her first novel. The bound copy is raw and uncut, and has been released to locals in her hometown. The finished copy is expected to be released this fall.

## HERE ARE JUST A FEW OF THE RAVE REVIEWS:

U. Baskerville from Richmond, VA writes...
"This book kept my interest all the way through.
I think we can all relate to the situations that take place in the book.
I can't wait to read the sequel. In my opinion, you are up there with some of the best authors,
(Eric Jerome Dickey, Nikki Turner, Terry McMillian, etc.)

E. Mcgee from Ettrick, VA writes...
"This book was very exciting to read and it kept me on my toes the whole time.
Drama after Drama....I'm placing my order for the sequel now."

C. Wiggins from Richmond, VA writes...
"The novel you wrote was very exciting, dramatic, and a little bit sweet.
It kept my mouth open from beginning to end. I'm looking forward to reading Part II of your novel."

**For more information, please contact Kharisma via email: miller_publishing@yahoo.com or via web: htttp://www.webspawner.com/kharisma1/users/index.html
A free preview of the novel, A Taste of BitterSweet Fruit, can be promptly emailed to you at your request**

## Chapter 1

## *Khaila*

"Damn, baby! You know we need to argue more often!" I screamed out in ecstasy, pulling D.C.'s long, smooth locs until he moaned painfully.

"Naw we don't! Let go of my head girl. That shit hurts." He replied while rubbing his sore scalp with his fingertips.

"I'm sorry boo, you know how I get when we make love....."

D.C. licked his luscious full lips and told me, "Yeah I know. That's why we don't need to argue. It leads to this violence." My 'violence' had interrupted our beautiful rhythm to allow him to massage his wounds.

D.C. whispered sweet things in my ear, and gently kissed each lobe. I slowly and passionately stroked on top, all the while screaming his name. He palmed and savored my brown apple bottom, moving it up and down to his cadence. He looked at me as if he could eat every morsel of my sugary caramel. I could tell he was ready to explode. He began to thrust harder and faster to complete his mission.

"Slow down baby. Let's take our time. I'm enjoying every minute of this." I said, trying to savor another dose of D.C.'s good loving. Everything was so sensual and beautiful. I wish I could have preserved the moment forever. I was completely taken in by the sweet aroma of vanilla-scented candles lingering in the air, as well as the smooth sounds of contemporary jazz in the background. As I licked him from head to toe, I could taste the salt on D.C.'s skin. His sexy, smooth chocolate frame, a sculptured work of art, was perfect in every way. The feel of his warm moist body next to mine was like bathing in smooth buttermilk. I would have to be crazy not to be totally drawn into his presence.

I laid softly on D.C.'s chest biting hungrily on his neck. I could tell D.C. wanted to ask me to stop, but it felt so good he couldn't get the words out. He knew he would pay for the love bites later, with the stinging sensation and purple bruises he would usually endure. He told me over and over, he didn't like passion marks, but he knew I couldn't help it. He finally gave in and decided to stop complaining about it.

I could tell he loved me every time I saw his face. The love was overflowing from the warmth of his embrace, the width of his broad pearly-white smile, and the intensity of his big brown eyes.

He used to tell me all the time he wanted to marry me, but he felt he had nothing to offer a wife. He constantly dwelled on how he had no car, no place of his own, nothing but a high school education, and a "sad excuse" for a job, as he put it. He figured his "sponging" off me needed to stop and soon.

D.C. startled me back to reality. "Baby, you alright? You got quiet all of a sudden. It's not like you to be this quiet."

"Yeah. I was just thinking about how good you feel."

"Uh-huh, whatever girl. I know something's not right with you."

D.C. knew me like the back of his hand.

He knew I was concerned about him, and his inner struggles, which usually involved money. He felt he was useless in my life. I would always tell him everything was going to work out, and I would always be there for him. I loved and respected D.C., even if he did not have much, because he always worked hard to make it. I knew about his grim background, and understood why he struggled so much. His family lived in Bronx, New York, poor and unhappy, until his mother died in 1999 of lung cancer, at the early age of 55. D.C. was very close to his mother. He loved her more than anyone or anything else in the world.

His father, who still lived in Brooklyn, New York, had always been in and out of D.C.'s life since the beginning. His parents never married. D.C.'s father always had a couple of girlfriends at a time, which he usually used for money and shelter. He never did stay in one place long. His father was just a "rolling stone" as the Temptations would say. Although D.C. would never admit it aloud, he wanted to have a stable relationship with his father, and it hurt him that his father was barely ever there.

His older brother, Vey never was the supportive type and was rarely there for D.C. when he needed him. Needless to say, they were not close emotionally, even living together as roommates for almost five years.

My distant thoughts were interrupted again when D.C. remarked, "Everything will be alright as long as you're here with me, Khai. So stop worrying about me and get back to business woman." He said jokingly.

D.C. flipped me over and began to thrust deeply inside me again. I was enjoying every minute of his good loving, and forgot where my mind had gone for the moment. I quietly moaned, gently biting my bottom lip. Then he hit my spot.

"Aw, shit!!!! Keep going, baby! Ok, I'll deal with you later, I ain't gonna' forget what we need to talk about though! Ummmhmmm....."

"After I work yo' shit out, we going to sleep. A'ight?"

D.C. joked, but he really wanted me to forget what I was preoccupied with. Discussing his problems was not his forte', only if I brought it up would he open up to me. He believed his issues only brought my spirits down.

In pure heaven, I told him, "Ummmm, baby! That was good. You really worked me out." Then I teased him a little, "A'ight, we can go to sleep now. I'm done."

I started laughing out loud. He hadn't noticed I had my second orgasm while he was talking.

"Aw, no you don't!!! I'mma get mine!!!!! I never did think it was fair you get four/five shots to my one."

"Cause you got it like that boo!"

He asked me, "And you don't?"

"You know I do. We can go another round, if you can hang. I'mma work your shit out after this......"

"I'm.........out for the....ughhh......count after this......... Awwww, shit!!!!!!! Mmmmmm!" D.C. said barely holding on to consciousness. "I'm out for the count baby ............ goodnight."

He softly rested his head on my chest.

I said to myself, *goodnight? Huh?*

"See how you do? Talking about me!" I said giggling.

He was good and sleep, before I could say another thing. Then it dawned on me - D.C. had slipped out of consciousness to avoid talking. I guess it was a good thing anyway. I thought about it, *why ruin an otherwise pleasurable experience?* Eventually I fell asleep myself, very content and satisfied.

## Chapter 2

## *D.C.*

"Ain't no sunshine, when she's gone......," blared on the radio alarm. Set to my favorite station the Kiss, 105.7 FM. It was during the "flash to the past" morning music hour. For a young kat, I really did love my old school music, probably more than hip-hop. Got my good taste in music from moms.

I woke up to Khaila's terrible sing-along, and a pleasant smell of cheese eggs, pancakes, and turkey sausage cooking on the stove. I crept out of the bed and down the stairs to see the most gorgeous vision in my kitchen. A caramel brown, petite beauty cooking breakfast half-naked, wearing only Vickie Secret lingerie and a pair of slippers on her feet.
I snuck back to the bedroom and got back in the bed. I pretended to be sleep, so I could be "surprised" with my breakfast in bed. This was not a usual thing. Breakfast was usually at the neighborhood, Chicken and Waffle Hut or Mickey D's, especially during weekdays.

A few minutes later, Khaila walked in quietly with my sweet-smelling breakfast in her hands.

She said with pride, "Hey baby, I got something for ya'."

I could hear her struggling with the door and the food.

Eyes still close, I mumbled, "Huh?"

"Open your eyes and sit up, baby."

I opened my eyes wide like I was shocked, "Ahhhhh, you cooked breakfast? How sweet. Thanks, boo."

"You knew didn't ya"? With yo' fake ass."

We both chuckled at that one.

"Yeah, I smelled the food and heard your *lovely* singing about ten minutes ago. I didn't want to spoil your surprise."

She slapped me on the forehead, punishment for making fun of her singing voice. She sat the tray on my lap, and waited for a reaction.

"Well, what do you think?" She asked while I tried the cheese eggs.
"Deellliicious!!!!!!!!"

"I'm glad you like it."

She grinned so hard it made my cheeks hurt.

"Where's your food?" I asked her.

"Not eating 'til lunch. I'm trying another new diet, Carol at work told me about it. I've gained ten pounds, D.C.!"

"Wow, ten whole pounds!" I said trying to be funny. Khaila Roe was always worrying about something petty. She really needed to get a grip, before she lost grip of reality.

"Stop! Don't you think that's kinda' weird, gaining ten pounds in a month and a half? I'm getting fat."

"What are you talking about? Baby, you look good. I don't care how much weight you gain. You've gained it in all the right places anyway."

I gave her a hard smack to the ass, so hard that my hand stung. We wrestled on the bed a few minutes. Some kinda way I got her in this weird pretzel position. Made me horny. I was hard as a rock. She was getting hot too. I could tell by the way she played with her hard nipples.

While tonguing my ear, she whispered, "Boy, you know what happens when we wrestle, and you know I need to get to work too. I've been late to work every day this week, thanks to your horny ass."

"How about a quickie?"

"A'ight, just five minutes!" She said excitedly. It didn't take much convincing to get her butt naked. Those early morning quickies always turned us both on.

I didn't even eat the food still sitting on the dresser. We had about fifteen minutes of wild, banging ass sex. Then Khaila jumped up immediately after we finished to get ready for work. Most weak-minded niggas would've taken offense to that, but I understood.

"A'ight D.C., I gotta' jump in this shower, get dressed, and get the hell out of here- fast!" She ran off to the shower with clothes in hand. Like usual, she came out the bathroom a few minutes later, fully dressed, running around like a chicken with her head cut off. Knocking shit over in the process.

"Shit!" She screamed as she stumped her toe on the dresser. "I don't feel like going to work today." Khaila hopped over to the bed in pain.

While I rubbed her aching foot, I told her, "Baby, you know I want you to stay here with me, but you running late...."

I got a half smile out of her after massaging her pain away. She was finally ready to leave for work.

"A'ight Khai, go 'head and get yo' ass out of here. Here, take your purse and your bag. I'll see you, when you get back."

It was an everyday thing for me to help her get her self together for work. She was always running late, but somehow she usually managed to get to work on time, or delayed by no more than ten minutes.

My girl was all that. To me she was like a real-life version of superwoman, who could make anything possible if she put her mind to it. I was proud to call her wifey. She never got a big head about her accomplishments, and never made me feel like I won't worth shit, 'cause I didn't have many accomplishments of my own.

"Damn the way you rush me out, I'd think something was going on." Khaila said heading for the door, with all her pearly whites shining.

Ignoring her little comment, I told her, "Gimme' a kiss." She gave me a quick peck on my lips, and was on her way to the car before I could blink good.

She yelled back, "Bye, Baby. I'll see ya' at five-thirty, ok?"

"A'ight, see ya' then."

## Khaila

I drove zooming in and out of traffic like crazy to get to work on time, which gave me only about ten minutes.

I liked my job at Makalin, Makalin, & Associates, a small law firm in downtown Richmond, VA. I had been working there for about three years as a legal secretary. I was single-handedly responsible for answering phones, maintaining and reviewing case files, scheduling appointments, and many other miscellaneous duties. I always complained to D.C. and my friends about the stress of the job. Sometimes, I felt overworked and under-appreciated, but at the same time I still loved it.

I attended Richmond City College, twice a week in the evenings. Majoring in criminal justice, I had aspirations of one day becoming a lawyer. I really looked forward to graduating with a Bachelor's-degree in Legal Studies by May of 2006. I was hopeful that after graduating I would then be able to advance my career working at the law firm.

I ran in the office halfway out of breath, seven minutes late for work. My supervisor greeted me at the door with a frown and arms folded across her chest.

"Morning, Khaila." She said in her serious-I'm not in the mood-tone.

"Good morning. I'm sorry, I'm a few minutes late."

"It's been this whole week, Khaila. I'm gonna have to start docking pay for this excessive tardiness."

"I understand I will work harder to be prompt."

"You will or it's your job!" She raised her voice, a couple octaves.

"I know, I understand I will be on time from now on...."

"Yeah, I know, 'cause it'll be your ass...."

Mrs. Brown-Schafner couldn't finish talking, because she was laughing so hard. I started laughing as well, though I was a little confused of the reason why.

"I'm just joking, Khaila. Lighten up. I just got to work myself, and you know I was supposed to be here an hour ago." Then she whispered in my ear, "Don't tell ole' Makalin though." We both giggled to each other.

"Your secret is safe with me." I whispered back. I still felt the need to explain. "It's just that I'm usually on time. I don't know what has come over me this week. I've been so absent-minded lately. I think I may need a vacation."

"Ok. You got it. You have been saving up your vacation time ever since you started here three years ago. It's time you used it. When do you want to take off, next week?"

"That would be good, because I haven't been feeling well lately. I need the rest."

"Then, it's done. You're off next week...."

"Thanks." I interrupted her, feeling overjoyed about my unexpected vacation.

Mrs. Brown-Schafner continued, ".........and you know what else, you are due for a raise too. You're a hard worker, perfect attendance at work, and a lifesaver in an emergency situation. Let's discuss your raise at the end the work day."

I sighed in shock, "I really don't know what to say, Mrs. Brown-Schafner. This news is right on time!" I said excitedly.

She was a pretty cool boss for a middle-aged white woman. I figured she must have been in a very good mood though. I wasn't usually treated that well, or appreciated for my hard work. In one day, I was offered a vacation and a raise. *What in the world is going on?*

During my break, I called D.C. as usual to wake him for his part-time job at Dickie's Record Store. He was a stock clerk and sales associate.

"Boo, guess what???" I blared into the phone. I was so excited I thought I would pee on myself.

"Huh? What's up?" D.C. said startled from his sleep.

"I got vacation time and a raise."

He replied with slurred speech, "Damn, baby, that's great. That's real good. I'm proud of ya'."

My success always reminded him of his personal failures. He wasn't very enthusiastic when he responded, and I knew the reason why. It wasn't that he didn't feel happy for me. He just felt he should have been the one calling home, with news of a raise and vacation. D.C. always believed the man should provide for the woman, and treat her like a queen. I did feel like a queen each and every day I was with him, but he didn't feel much like a king.

I asked him, "D.C., baby? You ok? You don't sound very happy."

"I'm happy for ya' baby. I just wish I could help out more around here. I've been looking for a full-time job paying some good money with no luck. I'm holding you back, Khai. You and I both know it. I have been eating your food, practically living off of you, and all I can contribute is grocery money. I have to pay my brother Vey, $400 a month for rides to work and a room at his place, and I hardly even stay with him. I'm usually staying with you, being a bum...."

D.C. was rambling on and on again, so I had to stop him. He was stuck in his self-pity mode again, and I needed to help boost his ego.

"D.C., why don't you just come live with me, and pay me what you can afford? Save up for a car or whateva'."

" I don't want to continue sponging off you."

"You're not sponging off me, baby. I told you that. You do help me a lot with paying some of the apartment bills. I don't know what I would do without your part."

"I know, but...."

"But nothing. Come live with me. Like you said, you're here most of the time, anyway. I'll get you a key made, and we can move your clothes and stuff here over the weekend."

"A'ight. It doesn't look like I have much of a choice. Thanks, sweetheart. I'm gonna pay half the bills, naw fuck that, all the bills when I get a better job. I've been applying to this technical school, Delta Tech in the West End. I wanna' study computers, 'cause you know computer engineers get paid!"

"Yeah, I know." I was so proud of his enthusiasm, I was smiling from ear to ear. He truly wanted to better his situation. It was really turning out to be a great day.

D.C. interrupted my pleasant thoughts to say, "Hey let's go out tonight and celebrate your good news. We can have dinner or something, my treat."

"Ok, that would be nice baby."

"You eat lunch yet?"

"I drank some Slim and Trim for lunch." I realized I made a big mistake the moment the words left my lips.

"I told you about that Slim and Trim shit! That mess will make you jumpier than your usual nervous self."

"Well, yeah I'll probably be a little jumpy at first, but I need the energy anyway. I've been so tired lately with all this work I have to do." I could feel I was getting a bit defensive. I had to take a deep breath to keep from getting upset. He always fussed with me about dieting. What was the big damn deal? I was just trying to look good for him.

"Khai, you know that stuff ain't good for your system. I want you to stop dieting, fo' real. You look good just the way you are."

"Whateva, D.C. I'm grown. I do as I please."

"Yeah...well... Anyway, let's change the subject. I don't feel like arguing. When it's too hot in the kitchen get the hell out, right?" D.C. joked. We both laughed.

"You right about that. A'ight, D.C. let me get back to work. I'll see you tonight." I said quick, fast in a hurry. I was more than ready to leave the conversation.

"A'ight baby. See you tonight."

I hung up the phone, but something told me it wasn't quite over yet. D.C. always told me he wanted me to put on weight, because I was "as skinny as a rail," as he put it. His "treat" probably involved taking me out to some soul food restaurant for fat backs and pig feet, so I could get "phat in all the right places."

I giggled to myself, just the thought of it. At least he put a smile on my face for work, which I wasn't in a hurry to get back to.

## Chapter 3

# *Khaila*

"Glad you're home, boo. You ready for dinner?" D.C. eagerly greets me at the door, with a big, goofy chester-chettah smile on his face.

"Let me jump in the shower right quick. Give me fifteen minutes, baby."

"That's fine Khai, take your time."

I ran back to the bedroom, grabbed some underwear, my new red dress, and my hot ass red and black designer pumps. I got those pumps for a good deal at Red Hot Shoes, a new hat and shoe boutique in Carytown. I threw my things on the bed, and went straight to the bathroom for a quick shower.

When I got out the shower, my stomach was feeling some kinda queasy. I didn't feel like eating anything, but D.C. was so excited about going out. Thinking to myself, *I guess I'll just get a salad or something small, nothing too heavy*, I got ready to go out with my man for the night. I fixed my hair real quick, and put on my clothes in a rush. I misted my clothes with strawberry scented Vickie Secrets body spray, glossed on my best shade of lipstick- mahogany brown, and made sure to wear my favorite sterling silver earrings to accentuate my outfit.

By the time I finally came out the bedroom, forty minutes had past. I could tell I took way too long primping, because D.C. drifted off to sleep on the couch. I hesitated waking him, but I nudged him in the shoulder anyway. He was so cute lying there, sorta' balled up like a kid. Not to mention the fact that I didn't feel like eating anything anyway. I should have left him alone.

He woke up quick and went to freshen up. So now I was waiting on him an additional ten minutes. I kept thinking the whole time, *are we ever gonna to make it to this damn restaurant?* At last, he came out the bathroom ready to go.

"D.C. can you please drive like you got some sense tonight?" I said handing him the keys.

"A'ight, but you won't be able to see how I'm driving, 'cause I'm blindfolding ya'."

He grinned a silly grin and put a black scarf tightly around my eyes. Then he led me slowly to my silver 2003 Nissan Maxima. I wasn't too sure about him driving, because he always drove like a maniac.

"D.C. where are we going?"

"It's a surprise. Just hold tight we'll be there in a short."

I sat there patiently wondering where we were going. I was trying hard not to think about my stomach the whole time, which was turning more than a washer during the rinse cycle. It didn't help with D.C. weaving in and out of thick, downtown traffic!

So I said, "D.C. slow down! We ain't going nowhere."

After about twenty long minutes, we finally stopped. D.C. got out of the car, opened my door, and led me to the restaurant. I couldn't believe he didn't take off the scarf until we were inside.

"I look real crazy D.C. Un-blindfold me!"

I was dying to know where we were. He finally broke the suspense and took off the scarf. Now I could finally see.

We were in a very classy, Italian restaurant called Bella's, in the heart of downtown Shockoe Bottom. I had heard all about the restaurant before, but it was the first time I had been. It was so classy, I just knew we couldn't afford the menu prices.

The restaurant had a beautiful deck outside, and I could hear Italian opera music playing in the background. There were huge chandeliers in the high ceiling and expensive furniture in the lobby area. It was really impressive. I thought to myself, *how did D.C. find this place, and more importantly, how the hell is he gonna pay for this dinner?* I was in total awe of the whole experience.

I exclaimed, "Ohhhh....D.C! This is really nice!"

The host of the establishment greeted us at the door and asked D.C., "Do you have reservations?"

"Yes, we have reservations for two. Curry's the name."

After the host checked for a minute, he said, "Ah, yes, sir. I see you have reservations for two, follow me please."

"Can we have seats on the balcony?" I asked the host, since it was such a beautiful, warm evening.

The restaurant had a beautiful view of city lights and tall buildings. Right around the corner on Canal Street was a romantic spot called Brown's Island, which overlooked the James River. I even considered us taking a walk down the cobblestone streets to enjoy the scenery. I figured we would probably need to walk off our big meal afterwards. The host replied, "Sure, that can be arranged." He led us upstairs to the balcony area. We were then seated and given menus to look over. I was so busy looking around the restaurant, I didn't stop to check out the menu. I was totally mesmerized. It was the classiest place I had ever been in my life. Right there in my own hometown.

"You like it, don't you?" D.C. said proudly.

"I love it, D.C. This place is so classy and romantic."

"And I have more plans for us unless you gotta' get back home."

"Naw, I'm yours for the night."

I was starting to feel a lot better, and I was so excited about his next plan for the night. The word "proud" minimizes how I felt about my man planning such a special date for us. He always did sweet things for me, but never to that magnitude. I fought back the tears, because the whole thing was so overwhelming for me.

"So you're mine for the night, huh?" He said smiling real devilish like.

"I'm yours every night baby, but you ain't getting none though." I burst out laughing embarrassing myself. People close by glanced our way.

"All this money I'm spending, that ass is mine. You betta' believe that's right, " D.C. was having me practically in tears laughing at him.

"Oh, I gotta' pay for fun nowadays, huh?"

"You know I'm just fuckin' with ya' boo."

Pointing to my coochie area, I said, "You know 'cause I'm running all this up in here." We both laughed out loud, again turning heads. I thought, *Forget them.* I was out having fun with my man for the first time in a very long time.

The waiter came to take our order. We still hadn't even looked at the menus, with all that talking and laughing we were doing.

"Oh, I'm sorry, sir. We're not ready yet," I said.

"Yes, ma'am. I will return shortly."

"I guess we need to check out the menu instead of each other, D.C."

I looked the menu over for the prices. They were outrageous but what did I expect in a nice restaurant like Bella's. D.C. had to have saved up a couple paychecks to prepare for our night out. I knew it would probably set him back financially for a while. He was so determined to show me a good time, so I just went along with the flow. It must have been my lucky day. I got a raise, vacation and a nice time out, all in one day. It was better than hitting the Virginia lotto!

"Order what you want. The sky's the limit, babe." He told me in a serious tone.

"I'll just get the chicken quesadilla appetizer and a salad."

"Come on now, Khai, you can do betta' than that. You order some real food girl, a full-course meal."

"A'ight, a'ight. How about the chicken marsala? It comes with a baked potato, mixed vegetables, and bread."

"Good, get that. I don't know what I'll get. The sirloin steak with mushrooms sounds good."

"Yeah, it does. I'mma try some of yours," I joked.

"I ain't sharing. Eat your own food, what you t'inkin' 'bout mon'?" He said with a Jamaican accent.

"I'm thinking 'bout eating your food, and I'm 'bout to eat some of yours."

"Um-hum, we'll see about all that."

D.C. grabbed my hand and gently kissed it, which really surprised me. How romantic! I didn't know what that was about, but it was nice. The waiter returned, and we placed our orders. We were sitting there just looking into each other's eyes. There was kind of an uncomfortable silence between us. D.C. had such a serious look in his eyes, like he had something on his mind.

I guess he noticed me noticing him, and he broke the silence and said, "So, how was work?"

"It was nice, especially with the raise and vacation I was offered."

"How much of raise and vacation time you get?"

"I got a 10% raise! My boss told me I could use all my vacation time saved up, which is enough for three weeks, but I'll just use two weeks for now."

"What you gonna do with your vacation time?"

"Well, I would like for us to go to Florida or the Caribbean or something, but there isn't much time to plan that now. We can easily get a hotel room and stay in Virginia Beach or D.C."

"A'ight, when we doing all this?"

"My vacation starts next week, so ask off as soon as you can. If you can't do a week, a couple days would be cool. We can plan the big vacation for Christmastime."

D.C. said, "Ok, I'll try to take off next week. Hopefully I'll be able to." We both knew with D.C.'s job, he probably wouldn't be able to take off a whole week.

"I'll call them tomorrow and request off for the week of June 15th – 22nd. The worst they can say is "no." Once I get this computer thing off the ground, I'll have a job with better pay and benefits, and we can go on vacation wheneva'."

"Ok, boo. It don't matter as long as you with me." I whispered affectionately across the able.

He shocked me again when he slid over and gave me a little unexpected tongue action. We kissed so long we didn't even notice the waiter back with our drinks.

"Mhhm!" The waiter cleared his throat with a look of disgust on his face. "Your drinks."

"Um, I'm sorry. Thanks for the drinks." I said nervously. I was kinda embarrassed we got caught kissing in such a classy restaurant. D.C. didn't care, as evident by his next comment.

He mumbled, "Yo' fuck him," and he kissed me again. "It's just about me and you tonight girl."

"Stop D.C.! You're embarrassing me in this nice place," I said grinning, because deep down I loved the attention.

That Negro took offense to what I said, and yelled out, "Oh, you embarrassed to be out with me now???"

"No, I didn't say that. What I said was, 'you're embarrassing me in this nice place.' I'm not embarrassed to be out with you."

"Whateva, Khai! You're ashamed of the real me, monitoring what the fuck I do, how I act, shit most of the time how I dress." He was yelling so loud other people could hear him across the balcony.

*Damn D.C. Don't start making a damn scene in this place,* I thought to myself. Then I thought, *he thinks I'm a control-freak, which definitely I am not.* The people on the balcony started staring at us like before. They were probably thinking "somebody please get these 'ghetto' Black people out of our classy restaurant."

"Oh, so you feel like I'm controlling you?" I said on the verge of tears. I had been so emotional lately, and D.C.'s petty debates didn't help any.

"Now, baby girl, don't cry." He handed me a linen cloth napkin to dry my eyes. "I'm sorry…. let's just drop it, ok?"

"You think I'm controlling you! Well leave my controlling ass alone then, D.C.!"

I was getting ill. It was my guess my stomach probably wouldn't make it through dinner. I ran off to the bathroom, where I vomited up my Slim and Trim diet drink. I looked in the mirror feeling like shit and looking like it too. My eyes were all sunken in and they had bags under them. I did the best I could with my hair, but it looked like hell too.

I said out loud, "What's wrong with me? Throwing up, crying all the damn time, getting fat...."

"Girlfriend, you pregnant!"

This large middle-aged lady, who was in great need of the fashion police, came out the stall behind me. The whole time I thought I was in the bathroom alone. *You can't even get privacy in the bathroom*, I thought. *Wait a minute, what did she just say to me?*

"Huh?"

The lady visually inspected me from head to toe.

"Uh-huh. Without even knowing your business, I can see a baby glow in your face, you're a little pudgy around the middle, and your hair is brittle. Sure signs of a baby coming." The lady said nonchalantly, like it was no big thing.

I thought a second. Then it registered. *What!!! Pregnant?*

When she said that I really started bawling and screaming like a baby. "Nooooo!!!!! Noooo! I can't be! Not now! Shit!"

The lady gave me a look like I had completely lost it. I guess I was freaking out too much. She held open her big arms to comfort me with a hug. I thought it was nice, because most people wouldn't even care, especially a perfect stranger.

"I could be wrong but you show all the signs. You're as skinny as you can be, except in the face and belly. Don't worry. No one is ever really ready for this you know. You'll adjust. Shit, I thought I was through having kids at 40, 'til last year. I had my fourth boy, Shawn. I got five kids altogether, four boys, one girl. They are 1, 10, 15, 19, and 20. I didn't expect none of 'em, but they my babies. Even that big 20-year-old baby I got. He's in college. He'll be a senior next year...."

As the lady rambled on about her kids, I thought about what it would mean to have a baby at my age. At 23, I hadn't even finished college or started a real career yet.

D.C. knocked on the door of the women's bathroom to see if I was

ok. "Khaila, you in there?"
"Yeah."
"You coming out baby, so we can talk. I'm sorry."
"Give me a minute, ok?"
"A'ight," He left to go back to our table.
I leaned over and cried in the sink. *What am I gonna do?* I thought to myself. My mind was racing a mile a minute.
"You gonna tell him?" The lady asked me handing me a paper towel.
"No, not now. Not 'til I'm sure. And even then I won't know how to tell him. If I am really pregnant, how will he take it?"
"He loves you, don't he?"
"Yeah." I smiled an uncomfortable smile in the mirror.
"I'm sure he'll be thrilled, although it will be hard at first, y'all will manage. At least it's two of y'all. I'm raising five by myself."
"I don't know. I'm scared."
"You betta' get back out to him before he get suspicious, and starts asking questions," the lady winked at me. It lightened the mood.
"Yeah, I know. Thanks for listening."
"Look, give me a call if you need anything, baby." She hands me a beauty salon business card with her name and office number.
"Thank you," I said with desperation in my voice.
The lady left me alone with my thoughts. *Damn I can't believe this!!!! What am I gonna do?*
I started crying uncontrollably in the sink, real pitiful like, when two other women came in. They tried to ignore the bawling, and desperation in my eyes, and kept going for the stall.
*A'ight, Khaila get yourself together!* I said to myself. I wet a paper towel and wiped my face, fixed my hair a little, and applied some make-up. *I'm ready now!* I left the bathroom with a fake persona, smiling real pleasant like.
D.C. looked up at me with his concerned face and said, "You ok? You were in there a long time boo."
"Yeah, I'm fine. I'm sorry for acting stupid." I smiled at him, hoping to hide any sense of concern on my face. If he saw that, he'd question the hell out of me the rest of the night.
He said loudly, "You won't acting stupid, I was. I apologize for starting some dumb shit with you."
"That's alright, just lower your voice, baby."

He mumbled, "See there you go again."

"What?"

"Nothing, your food is getting cold. Just eat."

"You don't tell me what to do D.C."

His attitude was getting much colder than the food. I had had enough of his shit by that point. He was messing with the wrong sista' that night.

"Let's go Khaila, 'cause now you making a scene." He signaled for the waiter to bring the check.

"Whatever, let's go then!" I played like I was tough but I really felt like crying again.

D.C. paid the waiter, and said, "Let's go."

"No, D.C.! I want to take my food home." I turned to the waiter, "May I have a box to take home please?" I was stalling time to piss him off even more.

"Yes, ma'am. I will return shortly." When the waiter went back to put my food in the box, D.C. really started trippin'.

"What's your problem Khai????" He yelled out.

"Nothing. I'm just fine!" I said sarcastically. The waiter returned with the food, we tipped him, and left without another word.

The car ride home was quiet. I stared out the window, thinking about my potential situation. I was cool, calm, and collected on the outside, but I was a complete nervous wreck on the inside.

D.C. and I didn't talk for the rest of the night either. We slept with our backs to each other.

I got up early the next morning to vomit in the toilet. This time, D.C. heard me yacking from the bedroom.

"What's wrong with you, baby girl?"

"I think I got the flu or something." I had to stall him as long as I possibly could, at least until I got my head together first.

He told me, "Call in sick."

"I can't call in sick. I want to take a vacation next week, remember? That's too many days out."

"But you can do that, Khai. You have plenty of vacation and sick days saved up." He held me close to his chest. "I want you to go to the doctor today, you don't look good at all."

"Oh....thanks!" I said with a giggle.

"I'm for real. I'll call your job for you. Don't worry about it. You get ready to go to the clinic."

"A'ight, D.C. I'll go for you."

"Good. That's the end of that. And I'll take you today, 'cause I got the day off."

Little did I know, D.C. had a lot of time off, because his job was cutting back on hours. They would have him coming in a few hours here and there, but whenever they needed him he needed to be available to work. Which didn't make sense to me, because business had been really slow at Dickie's lately.

"I can go to the doctor on my own. You go ahead and sleep in."

I really didn't want him going with me, and risk him finding out about my possible pregnancy. I wanted to break it to him when I was ready.

"You sure? "

"Yeah, I'll be fine."

## Chapter 4
## *Khaila*

I left out for the doctor's office at nine am, right when the office was due to open. I had to wait two hours to be seen since I came in without an appointment. With all the suspense of waiting, the black, female doctor finally confirmed the news. I was eight weeks pregnant and didn't even know it!

My new obstetrician discussed all of the pregnancy options with me. I knew in my heart and soul, I didn't have any options. I was not giving up my baby for adoption or abortion. I didn't care how things went between D.C. and me, I was still keeping my baby.

All that time I thought I was just stressed out or sick, I was actually pregnant. I couldn't believe I was one of those young, irresponsible, unmarried girls I often talked about. I promised myself I would never be one those girls. I was one of those girls, and it was stressing me out to no end. What was I gonna do? I wasn't ready to be anyone's parent.

I guess my pregnancy was bound to happen eventually. I never used birth control pills for protection, because I didn't like the possible side effects. D.C. usually wore condoms, but in the past six months we had a few "accidents" with those. We were so unprepared financially and emotionally. But like the lady at the restaurant said, at least our child would live in a two-parent, two-income home. I knew a baby would definitely complicate things, but the more I thought about it the more excited I became too. I was actually gonna be a mom!

*Now how was I gonna tell D.C.? And when? And my mom, oh God, how am I gonna tell her?* That was the million-dollar question. I started thinking a mile a minute while the obstetrician was reviewing "my options."

She gave me prenatal vitamins, set my next obstetric appointment, and told me how to properly care for my unborn baby and myself.

I drove home creeping, trying to figure out what to say to D.C. I decided to take a detour to my best friend, Shante's house. I figured she would be at work, but sometimes she worked nights so I thought I would check to see if she was home. I lucked up, she was.

Shante was home watching TV., eating a late breakfast. I came in, sat on the sofa, and didn't say a word. Of course, she knew something was not quite right with me by the funny looking expression on my face. She probed and probed for answers.

"What? You and D.C. get into it again?"

"Yeah, but that's not it. I don't know what to do Shante."

"Well, what's wrong?" She asked with irritation.

I didn't answer. I just stared at the floor, looking and feeling ashamed.

"Is he cheating on you girl? 'Cause if he is I'll kick his ass for you."

"Naw, you know that ain't it...."

Shante interrupted, "Then what is it Khai? Spit it out!"

She said, 'spit it out,' so I did just that. "I'm pregnant, Shante!"

I couldn't believe the words I was saying out my own mouth. I looked like a little lost deer in headlights, still in shock of everything that was going on. Warm tears started streaming down my cheeks, and my nose was running like a leaky faucet.

Shante handed me a tissue box lying on the dining room table. She didn't know how to react. My girl just stood there over me with her mouth hanging open. After a few seconds went by she finally blurted out, "Oh my God, Khaila! Oh- my- God! You're pregnant!"

With a scared shaky voice, I replied, "Yeah, I'm gonna be a mother...I'm really scared, Shante."

"Girl, are you for real? So you're saying I'm gonna be an auntie soon?"

"No. You're gonna be a Godmother. If you would do the honors."

"Of course, but I'm not sure if I can be a good Godmother." Shante said with apprehension.

In a way she was sorta like me when it came to worrying about things. Not quite as severe though.

"I don't know how to be a mom either. This is all new to me too, you know."

I held my head in my hands. I could feel a painful headache coming on.

"How you gonna tell him?"

I shrugged my shoulders. "I don't know. And I have to tell my parents too. My mama's gonna kill me, and daddy will be so disappointed."

"Why? You grown."

When Shante said that, I realized why she was my girl and why I loved her so much- she always kept it real. She was my rock through a lot of hard times, times I could never had dealt with alone.

Shante and I grew up together, best friends ever since we were in middle school. She was there for me when my first boyfriend dumped me to be with this nasty-I will take your man and hers- neighborhood hoochie. Shante was gonna fight the girl for me, but I told her it wasn't worth it. I never was much for a lot drama or confusion, but Shante didn't care. My sister, Tracie was even worst. When those two got together, I was usually missing in action to avoid the madness they were bound to get into.

Shante was the same age as myself, 23, and was also unmarried, and childless. That was about to change, since I had a man and was currently carrying his child.

Like myself, Shante was always looking for the family-life. She loved falling for the wrong kind of men- who consisted of money hungry drug dealers, spaced out weed-heads, bums who lived with their mamas, cheaters with wives and girlfriends, and ruthless woman-beaters. I used to always tell her to stop looking for men and concentrate on her future. She would usually get defensive and tell me not to worry about her future or the poor excuse for a man she was dating. I always valued our close friendship, so on many occasions I decided to keep my mouth shut when I probably should have said something.

She learned the hard way, when the last guy almost killed her. First beating her ass to the ground and then putting a switchblade to her throat. She was lucky her male neighbor came outside to save her, serving dude a nice old-fashioned ass whipping.

Coming out of my trance, I remarked, "But my parents will be so upset with me."

Shante shot me a glare across the room that said, "Grow up. You not a kid no more."

I whined in response, "I ain't married, Shante."

"And? As long as you take care yourself and that baby. Who cares? You don't have time or energy to be worried about what your parents think, Khai."

"I know but I'm scared Shante..." I couldn't finish talking with my continuous streaming tears and trembling voice.

I couldn't pull it together at all that day. Shante held open her large arms to comfort me.

"Come here," she said as she hugged me tightly, "You're gonna be fine. You always work through things, and you'll work through this too. And don't forget I'm here for you, as well as your family, and D.C."

"I think I'll tell him tonight after I make dinner."

"That's a good way to break it to him."

"Well, let me go. He's probably wondering where I am. I was supposed to be back from the doctor's by now"

"A'ight. You need me, I'll be here."

"Thank you girl. You're a good friend."

I waved goodbye to my best friend, and walked to the car. I sat there behind the wheel, staring in space. It took me about a minute or so to start the car. With a deep breath, I mustered up the courage to go home. I had to face D.C. eventually, so I said *to hell with it* and drove off heading towards home.

## *D.C.*

I was good n' sleep on the living room sofa when Khaila walked in. Although I was asleep, I could still hear her going straight to the kitchen, fumbling around with some pots and pans. I got up and went straight upstairs to lie down in the bedroom.

I really needed some peace and quiet before work, and all that unnecessary noise was not helping me any. I had called my job earlier that morning requesting to pick up a few extra hours. Lucky for me someone had called in sick.

A few minutes later, Khaila followed me upstairs and backed that thang up right up against me. She smelled so good with her strawberry fragrance, and felt even better with her warm body against mine. I held on to her tight around her waist.

With her back to me she said, "Hey." Her voice sounded dull like something just wasn't right.

Barely conscious, I could only mumble, "Hey baby."

Then I nodded off to sleep, and Khaila followed suit, after shedding quiet tears in her pillow.

I knew she had been crying when I woke up to another damp pillow where Khaila slept. I wondered what she was crying about this time. She was really turning on the waterworks lately. I had to get myself ready for work, so I didn't have time to investigate the issue.

Twenty minutes later, I rushed downstairs to a mixture of smells. The aroma filling the air smelled some kinda good, and I was ready to eat. My baby had meatloaf, baked potatoes, and mixed vegetables cooking for dinner. She was even in the cooking mood enough to bake my favorite cake for desert, strawberry cake with vanilla icing.

I just had to ask, "What's going on in here Betty Crocker?" Aren't you supposed to be getting well, and I'm supposed to be taking care of you? Look at you, sneaking out of bed to cook." I paused before asking, "What did the doctor say?"

"I'll tell you after dinner, D.C."

I was thinking to myself, *what the hell she gotta' tell me after dinner for? She has to be really sick to be so secretive.* I didn't ask any more questions, I figured she would tell me sooner or later. I'd just have to worry through dinner.

A few years back, Khaila's mom was diagnosed with ovarian cancer. She recovered from her illness, but I was really buggin' out thinking maybe the same thing could happen to Khaila. Cancer ran in her family, kinda like it did in mine. With my mother's sudden passing, I didn't need to lose another person I loved to cancer.

My mother's death was a complete shock. She didn't tell me or my brother she was sick, until she could no longer work. The only reason she told us then was because she needed us to help cover the bills. That shit made me so mad that she would hide something like that from us for almost two years. I guess she called herself protecting our hearts, but all she did was break mine. My brother and I really didn't have much time to say goodbye, before she was gone. Four months to be exact. Khaila wasn't going out like that without me knowing about it. I would make sure I was there for her. I'd see to it.

"Sit down, Khai. We need to talk." She kept trying to set the table for dinner to avoid talking to me. She knew I knew something was wrong, and I was serious about finding out about it.

"I'll set the table, Khai. You sit down."

"But I gotta' get the cake out the oven and ice it."

"I can do that. What you think I don't know nothing about cooking?" I laughed to lighten the nervous energy in the room. She laughed a little as well.

I glanced at the clock. It was already four-thirty. Making it to work wasn't gonna happened, so I called into work again. I had to obligate myself to work a full shift the following weekend to have the evening off. I traded shifts with my boy, Rayshaun.

After hanging up, I served Khaila food, and then watched her pick at her plate for a half-hour. She hadn't been eating right lately, and I was really concerned about her health. Like her, I hadn't touched my food, even though it looked good. I just stared at Khaila- thinking, while she stared at her plate- thinking. Probably could have burned a hole through her if I had tried.

"You gonna eat?" She asked me.

"Yeah, I just wanted to make sure you were straight first. The question should be are you gonna eat? You're just playing with your food."

"I'm fine. I'll eat…. don't worry. You know I'm lucky to have a man like you, looking after me like you do." She smiled barely looking up from her plate.

"I know! What can I say?" I said imitating J.J. off of Good Times trying to lighten the mood. Khaila giggled so I guess it worked for a minute. Then she got quiet and looked down at her plate again.

"D.C.?" She said so softly I could barely hear.

"Huh?"

"I got something to tell you."

"It's about your doctor's visit, right?"

"Yeah, I don't know how to explain it." She looked around at the walls, avoiding eye contact.

"Just tell me please."

The suspense was killing me. I thought I was ready for what she had to say, but her next words would change my life forever. It was like she was saying them in slow motion.

Barely above a whisper, she said, "Well…. you know how I have been sick lately and gaining weight out of no where."

I nodded still looking and feeling confused.

"Do you know why?"

"You sick like your mom?"

"No, D.C.!" She sighed out of frustration. " Men are so dumb about women things…"

"Well…. what is it? Just say it already."

"We got a baby on the way, D.C." When she said that- time stopped for a minute. If I wasn't already sitting, I swear I would have hit the floor, and hard.

I had to ask to make sure I heard her right, "What??? We what?"

"I'm pregnant D.C."

There it was in plain ole dummy terms, straight up, no room for confusion or mistake, Khaila was pregnant! I couldn't say a thing in complete shock. Khaila just kinda stared at me waiting for a reaction.

"D.C.?"

I surprised myself when I yelled out, "Damn, I'm gonna be somebody's pops! Oh…shit! I'm really gonna be a dad, for real?"

"Yeah."

"I'm so happy, boo!" I jumped out of my seat and walked over to touch her stomach. It was round and much harder than usual. Damn, I was stupid. I hadn't even noticed the difference.

Still concerned about what I thought, Khaila said, "So you mean you really are happy about this? You know, this will mean that things will be hard for us, and money will be tight. How you gonna go to school like you planned? How will I finish? What will we do about…?"

I stopped her rambling to say, "Don't worry about a thing baby girl. Everything is gonna be fine. I got interviews coming up for nice full-time jobs like Morgan Corporation. Once I get a full-time job, we will be set. I'll start evening classes in a semester or two. I already applied for financial aid. So yeah I am very happy to hear we will be parents soon. Aren't you?"

I gently touched her face to help soothe away her nervousness, but that was an up hill battle. Khaila feared everything in life. She had real and unreal concerns, which she probably should've considered looking into.

"That's all great news D.C., but I'm still scared."

"But there is no need to be scared baby."

I kissed her lips and held her tightly in my arms.

Then I said with much excitement, "Well you had a big surprise for me, so I got one for you! Close ya' eyes, no peeking. Matter of fact, I'm gonna use that scarf again."

"Oh, no. Not again." She finally gave me a little smile. Deep down she loved surprises. I took the scarf from my head and secured it tightly around her eyes.

"Ok, I'm a little excited about this. What is it D.C.? What is it?"

I loved how she giggled like a little kid when I surprised her with things. I knew my surprise would be the surprise to beat all surprises.

Her cute laugh reminded me of how much I loved her, more than any other female I'd ever been with before. I'd planned to pop the question, but I didn't know how. I saved up for months for her engagement ring, and I finally got around to buying it for her a month prior. I was gonna wait to propose to her on her birthday a few weeks later, but I decided it was perfect timing with the baby coming.

I went to my hiding place in the bedroom. Under the bed, I hid my gift inside of an old shoebox. By this point, I was more excited than Khaila. The anticipation was intensifying as I returned with my surprise.

When I came back down the stairs Khaila was still in the same spot, with the scarf around her eyes. She looked so scared and defenseless. It was really quite pitiful. I quietly bent down on one knee in front of Khaila like they usually did in the movies. I pulled out the smaller box inside the shoebox, revealing a petite, diamond-cut engagement ring.

"Take off the scarf, Khai." She did as I requested, and she finally saw what I knew she had been waiting for. Her face glowed with excitement. Her mouth hung open, but no words came out. So I decided to do the talking for her.

"Khaila, I love you, and like I told you before I want to marry you. This is the perfect time with your big announcement for us to do it. Marry me, Khaila Shea Roe. I need you in my life, and you are so important to me. Please do me the honor of being Mrs. Dion Curry...."

I know it sounds corny but, I couldn't continue because I was getting so emotional. I had to pause before I said, "Will you marry me Khaila?"

I shocked myself getting so emotional with my voice shivering and flowing tears falling from my eyes. So you know the whole scene blew Khaila away.

"Of course, D.C. I will marry you."

I was so happy that she said "yes", it was my turn to be speechless.

"The ring is so beautiful, D.C. I don't even want to know how you got it. It looks expensive."

"I've been saving up for it about a year now, making monthly payments. That's why I was always broke."

"You didn't have to...."

"Yes, I did. You deserve this and more, Khaila, and I *will* give you more when you're my wife."

"I know D.C. I appreciate everything you've done for me. You are a good man, and I'm lucky to have you. I love you so much."

My reality set in when she said that.

"I haven't given you much of anything. How are you lucky to be with me, Khai?" I replied in a depressed tone. Looking back I know I put a damper on our happy occasion.

"Yes, I am lucky. You have been there for me through thick and thin. When my mama was sick, you were there for me the most."

"I know, but I couldn't really help you with your bills, or buy you nice things."

"So, that wasn't what I needed then and it's not what I need now. I need you for emotional support now more than ever."

I thought for a minute. She was right about that. Khaila really did need me for emotional support. She would never make it through her pregnancy sane without me. Like I said before, she was an emotional wreck most of the time.

I picked her up from the chair. I thought, d*amn she's heavy*. I took her to the bedroom and placed her carefully on the bed. I took off all of her clothes and put her under the sheet.

I leaned over and asked her, "Is this ok, in your condition?"

'Yes." She said with happy tears in her eyes.

I began to gently kiss and lick her entire body from head to toe, until she couldn't take it anymore. She was giggling and squirming all over the bed. Out of old habit, she reached to the nightstand, grabbing for a condom. Then she stopped herself, I guess she figured it was too late for that.

We usually tried to use protection every time, but we made a few mistakes obviously. There were times when either the condom broke or we didn't have a condom available, and just did it anyway. You know Khaila didn't like me "pulling out" without a condom, but it had worked for us before.

Without saying another word, we made love slowly and constantly through the night. It was Friday night and we both had free time to enjoy each other's love juice all weekend long. If Khaila wasn't really pregnant, she would've been after we finished sexing each other all weekend.

\*\*\*

## D.C.

We both woke up around noon. I sat up in bed about to go to the kitchen, when Khaila opened her eyes.

"Go back to sleep baby. I'll be back."

"Ok."

She quickly drifted back to sleep. I went down to the kitchen to cook breakfast, when the phone rang.

I was hoping it wasn't for me. Barely awake, I knew I was not up for any conversations.

"Hello?"

"Hello. D.C.? Can I speak to Khaila?"

It was Khai's mom. She was a little snappy. Khaila's mom liked me, but she wasn't too crazy about her daughter shacking up.

"She's asleep, Mrs. Roe. Can I take a message? I'll give it to her as soon as she wakes up."

I started thinking about what Khaila would say to her mom when she did wake up. I wondered what her people would say, especially her mom, when she confessed the news about her pregnancy.

"That girl gonna sleep her life away. It's noon and her ass is still in bed. Tell her to call me when she wakes up." Mrs. Roe said in a disgusted tone.

Her negative attitude about Khaila really pissed me off. She was always saying that Khaila was lazy. If she only knew how hard my baby worked everyday. How stressed out she usually was. I didn't feel like Khaila's mom ever gave her credit for her accomplishments. I have never heard her say she was proud of her, not even for going to school or having that nice job at the law firm. So I knew she thought I was an underachiever for sure, or should I say a bum, since I hadn't accomplished half of what Khaila had accomplished.

Fuming, I tried to disguise how I felt by keeping the conversation short and sweet. "Ok, Mrs. Roe, I'll tell her to call you. She should be up soon."

We ended our call, and I went back to cooking. As I put the grease in the pan, I came to the realization that I would be a dad soon, seven months to be exact. I wondered how I would deal with fatherhood. I also wondered if it was healthy for Khaila to be eating fried foods. Shit, I figured it wouldn't hurt the baby just one more time. I would make sure she was on a strict diet for the rest of her pregnancy. She'd hate me for it, but it was for her own good.

Twenty minutes passed and Khaila got up to the smell of turkey bacon, eggs, and French toast. I planned it that way. It was her favorite meal for breakfast, lunch, or dinner.

"Who called earlier?" Khaila mumbled.

"Your mom called. She wants you to call her back as soon as you get a chance."

"Shit!!!!! What am I supposed to say?" She paused a moment in deep thought before she said, "I ain't telling her nothing 'til I give birth. I really don't feel like hearing her mouth!"

"Khai, let's be real. You might as well tell her now, she gonna find out sooner or later. If you want, I'll go with you to tell her?"

"Naw, I don't suggest you do that. My mama will beat you down D.C."

Her remark about her mother beating me down really cracked me up. Khaila was too frantic to notice I was laughing at her. Her anxiety fits were really quite comical at times.

She said, "I'll tell her myself."

"A'ight, you on your own. The quicker you tell her the less you will have to worry. You don't need to be stressed out through your whole pregnancy."

"Ok, ok. I'll tell her today."

"There you go brave pregnant woman."

I smiled and kissed her forehead. She relaxed a bit and sat down to eat breakfast with me. Afterwards, she got dressed and left for her mother's house. I felt a little nervous for her as she pulled off slowly from the curb. I thought to myself, *maybe I should have gone with her.* Too little, too late, right?

# Chapter 5
## *Khaila*

I was terrified the entire ride to my parent's house. I prayed to the Lord above that my mother was the only one I had to tell the news. I figured I could knock out a lot of birds with one stone by telling her. I knew she would tell everybody else. The easier route would have been my sister, Tracie, to be the reporter, but she was usually at one of her men's houses. I didn't see Tracie's car, so there went that idea. I saw both of my parents' cars in the driveway, so I knew my daddy was home too.

I opened the door with my key, and took a deep breath. *I can do this,* I repeated to myself over and over in my head.

"Mama? Mama, where you at?"

"In the kitchen. I called you earlier. What were you doing sleeping 'til noon, girl?"

I didn't know if I wanted to face her, so I stayed in the living room. Her tone was always so firm and intimidating.

"I just slept in mama. Dag, like you never slept in before."

She ignored my smart comment, and got back in my shit, "You feeling alright? It's not like you to sleep so late. Khaila, are you pregnant?"

"Huh?"

She raised her voice and said her words nice and slow, just in case I had a temporarily case of hearing loss. "Are…you…pregnant?"

There was a minute of silence, which felt like hours. It was the moment of truth. I don't know how she knew I was pregnant, but all I had to do was confirm her suspicions.

"Answer me Khaila! And come in this kitchen now. I need to see your face."

I took that trip to the kitchen at a snail's pace, thought about taking a detour instead out the front door. I finally got there, never looking up.

"Yeah, mama. How you know?"

She replied, "I'm your mother that's how. I knew something won't quite right a couple weeks ago. You were getting fat and you looked a damn mess."

My mother never was too tactful, especially when speaking to me. She would never talk to Tracie like that, 'cause Tracie would probably cuss her out. My sister was always very disrespectful to my parents. I never took it there with them, 'cause I got my whippings very early on. My sister on the other hand was spoiled rotten at an early age. So she was destined to be rotten as an adult. A mistake I swore I'd never make with my kid. I never understood why my mother treated me differently, but whatever the reason, it caused us not to have the typical mother-daughter bond.

"Damn, mama. You sure know how to make me feel good." I said sarcastically.

"Well.... you do look a mess. That's exactly how I looked when I was pregnant with you and your sister. A mother always knows. Mine did."

"For real ma? Grandma knew you were pregnant? Did she know before you knew?"

"Yeah she knew first, and then she told me. I didn't have a clue what was going on with my body."

I was surprised at how calm my mother was. I figured if I focused on her pregnancy stories, I could avoid talking about my new situation. Then I thought about it, *why didn't she tell me I was pregnant, like grandma had told her?*

So I said with much curtness in my voice. "You know I had to find out from this woman at a restaurant the other day. Then I went to the doctor yesterday, and she confirmed it for me. Why didn't you tell me you thought I was pregnant?"

"Because you made your bed, now you must lie in it. You're grown now. It was your responsibility to find that out. Which you finally did."

My mom was really cold-blooded sometimes, I swear. I was disgusted with her attitude, which was so ironic because I expected her to be disgusted with me. She wasn't supportive like most moms would be in this circumstance. It was a good thing though; at least she didn't break my neck!

"You're about to turn 24 soon, you can handle this."

"Yeah, but I still need you too mama. I don't know nothing about taking care of a baby."

"Well...you can forget me babysitting every time you want to go out or something. My children are grown. I'm through raising kids."

"But you'll watch my kid sometimes, right?"

"We'll see." Her mom said with a hidden smile. Deep down my mother liked the idea of having a grandchild. She just wasn't going to admit it.

"You gonna tell Tracie and daddy for me."

"No, that's your job."

"Please.... at least tell dad for me."

I knew my dad would be disappointed and upset. He thought of me as the Virgin Mary. He had hoped I would wait until marriage to even have sex.

"Alright, I'll tell your daddy. You can tell your sister."

"That's a deal." There was a brief uncomfortable silence that lingered in the air. I had shut down for a moment. Without thinking I said, "I'm scared Mama."

"You can do it. I'll help you."

"You betta' or you'll get full custody of the baby." I said in joking manner.

"Oh, no I won't! You gonna take care of this baby. You wait 'til I notify your grandma. She's the one you need to worry about." My mom said in a serious tone.

She was really weird. At first, she wouldn't tell my dad for me, but just couldn't wait to tell my grandma the news. My mother was a very irrational person, if I had ever met one.

"You gonna tell grandma on me?"

"I sure will. You can't keep hiding this, Khaila. I'm really surprised you finally told me. I was just sitting back waiting to see how long it would take you to confirm what I already knew."

"Well you can also tell her I'm getting married to the baby's father."

I displayed my beautiful new diamond-cut engagement ring. My mom was in complete shock, with her mouth hanging open. She couldn't say a word. Sorta what I did when I first saw it.

My cellular displayed D.C.'s seven digits, and I quickly answered on the first ring. Before I could say hello he said, "Khaila, you not dead yet?"

It was obvious he was really worried about my mom's reaction. I was gonna have a little fun with him.

I moved swiftly to the living room for privacy.

"No, she actually took it pretty well." My phony voice turned serious to say, "…but you're dead D.C. She said, you knocked up her innocent child, and she coming after you or something like that." I fought back the laughter, my eyes practically in tears.

"She did? Damn. I'm not coming over there for a while! I'll just lay low."

"D.C., she didn't really say that. She's still cool with you. Her reaction surprised me today. She was calm through most of it, because she knew I was pregnant a while back."

"She what? Why didn't she tell us!"

"I said the same thing. That Gina Marie Roe is crazy. That's why. I betta' shut up before she hears me." I lowered my tone to avoid being heard.

My nosy mother had bionic ears and I just knew she was listening to my conversation in the next room.

"When you coming home babe." His voice was a little more relaxed.

"In a few sweetie."

"Hurry up, Khai. I'm bored like crazy. I thought maybe we could watch a good movie tonight.'

"Ok, D.C. I'm coming now."

"Don't cum without me."

His sex jokes really cracked himself up. They usually made my eyes roll in the back of my head, and I don't mean in a good way.

"Stop pervert, that's why we are in this situation in the first place! Now get your horny ass off the phone, and get the movie ready. I'll be there in a few."

We hung up.

I headed to the kitchen again to say goodbye. Of course my mama had one of those funny looks on her face, the one that says, "Khaila, you could be doing a much better job with your life. Or "you really disappoint me, with all of your potential." She wasn't the only one who gave out funny looks. I shot her a look that said, "Damn, you are so negative and judgmental all the time. Get a grip." Before those looks could turn ugly, I told her goodbye and headed out the door.

# Chapter 6

## *Fefe*

  *D.C.'s gonna be surprised to see me. It's been more than two years since we've seen each other, and I know he still wants to be with me.*
  I had just pulled up to D.C.'s place. According to my girl, Tonda, D.C. was probably still living on the Northside with his brother, Vey. The scoop I needed didn't come easy at first. Tonda felt she needed to lecture me first, talking shit 'bout I needed to move on with my life. She told me, "Get over him girl…he's over you." After I told her ass off, she finally told me what I wanted to know. I think that skank was jealous, and just didn't wanna see nobody happy 'cause she won't. What they say, "misery loves company." Well I'd be damned if I was gonna be miserable in her company.
  D.C. and me had our rough times, but I still loved him and I knew he loved me, too. We did everything together. D.C. and me used to hang out smoking bud, sexing each other all night long, and every now and then we'd make time to catch a flick at the new movie theater in Short Pump. We were only together nine months strong, but we went through a lot together. The whole time, I had to fight to keep my man, but I never gave up the fight. I had to beat a bitch ass every other day, and I almost went to jail for one of 'em, but that's a whole other story.
  A couple months after we broke up, D.C. was trying to play both sides of the field. Like most men, he was trying out his options. He'd mess with me, get mad, screw her, get mad, then mess with me again, you know how it goes. The continuous love-hate cycle. The madness had to end so I told him he had to make a decision- her or me. He couldn't decide, so I did it for him. I told him to kiss my black ass. I left him alone for almost a whole month. When I started missing him, I decided to call to get back together. He completely went off, calling me nasty names like "crazy bitch" and "stalker." I knew he was listening to what his new ho' was telling him to do. Poor thing was pussy-whipped

real bad, whining 'bout how much he loved his new girl. I hung up in his face. Who did he think he was anyway?

I never believed that's what he really wanted, but he hurt my feelings, so I said "ta' hell wit' it." I left town a few months later to go to this Technical School back home in Newark, New Jersey. I got a lot of family out there. I stayed with an aunt here, a cousin there, and whoever else would keep me.

I had to do what I had to do, 'cause I didn't have a job or a place set up when I left. That's the kind of drama love brings. But like my dead grandma used to say, "You gotta' take the bitter with the sweet baby. The bitter is what makes the sweet taste so good." I know that's right. I knew I had something real sweet coming, 'cause it had been all bitter hell ever since me and D.C. broke it off over two years ago.

I thought to myself, *D.C. and me are gonna have a real nice reunion. It's gonna be real nice. Yeah, he has that bitch who been hanging around since we broke up, but I can take care her ass real easy. I think she's just a rebound girl anyway. She don't have what I got, he need to finally realize that. That little yella girl, ain't got nothing on D.C.'s smooth chocolate. Matter-a-fact, he used to call me Mocha. But that ho' slipped in right when D.C. and me were on the downslide. That's cool, because now it's my turn to do some slipping.... Slipping right into some Vickie Secrets.*

* * *

After about fifteen minutes of stressing what I would do next, I went up to the door ready for whateva'. Vey never did like me and I never liked his ass either. I wasn't there to see him anyway, so it didn't matter to me how he felt.

Walking up to the stoop, I remember thinking to myself, *whateva you gonna bring motherfucka, then bring it. I'm down for whateva.* I thumped on the door with much aggression, letting Vey know exactly what time it was- I won't to be fucked wit'. Bam. Bam. Bam. No answer. I knew he was inside, probably peeping through the peephole grinning at me. The thought really pissed me off, so I knocked harder and quicker than the first time. He opened the door looking like the living dead. He apparently just woke up from his "ugly" nap. 'Cause it damn sho' won't no beauty nap!

He came out his smart mouth with spit flying, "What you want Fefe? I'm trying to rest before I go to work!"

"Where D.C. at? I need to talk to him!" I went straight to the point, what the fuck did I care about his rest. He gave me a funny expression, almost made me laugh, that said, "*bitch you must be crazy!*" So I shot him a nasty look of my own, with my hand on my ample hips, waiting for his next response.

"He ain't here Fefe. Now take yo' ass on."

He must ain't know who he was messing with. I could make his life a living hell.

"Where he at Vey? I ain't leaving 'til you tell me!" And I meant that shit! I was on fire at that point, steam was practically coming from my ears. The look in my eyes could have pierced a hole through his forehead.

He gritted his teeth and replied, "You wanna bet on that one. Get out of my fuckin' doorway Fefe!"

He pushed me out the doorway, and closed the door in my face. I knocked and knocked for at least thirty minutes straight. I think at one point, a demon possessed my body, 'cause I was kicking the door, and screaming at the top of my lungs. Some nosy people across the street started coming out their doors looking to see what was going on.

You know how I do it, I yelled out, "mind your own fucking business," to a couple of skank hoes staring.

I just knew Vey had lost all of his senses, because just about everybody around the way knew about me. I could have him "taken care of" before he could speed dial 911. He didn't really wanna try me for real.

See back in the day, Vey ran the streets, and he was a force to be reckoned with. I guess he was trying to do the legal 9-5, leave-all-his-past–behind-him kinda thing. If I couldn't hurt him physically, I definitely had enough old dirt on him to mess him up mentally for a lifetime.

I decided to go back and chill in the car for a minute, to see if Vey would come out or if D.C. would come home. I thought, *Shit I didn't come all this way for nothing.*

I was feeling some kind of hype by the time I got to the car. I felt like I was on some kinda stake out or something. I didn't have anything to do anyway, so why not scope out D.C.'s world for a minute? Tonda told me he still lived with his brother, but he stayed over his skank's house a lot. The way I figured it, he would have to come home for clothes and stuff at some point. I waited and waited and waited. I can't even remember how long, but long enough to have a hot, steamy dream about making good, good love to D.C. Just like the good ole days.

## *D.C.*

Vey called me in frantic mode, yelling, "Your old girl, Fefe, just came around here looking for you, son. I'm not having no stalking bitches coming around here like that duke. You need to handle that 'D, because..." I could tell Vey was mad as hell 'cause his old New York accent had come back for a minute.

I loved my brother, but most days he irked my nerves big time. He acted like I hadn't paid rent to live there for the past five years. I just kinda let him rant and rave about Fefe disturbing his sleep for a while, until I had had enough.

"Listen man, I can't control what that crazy girl do. If she does it again, handle your business and call the po-lice or something. Is she still outside?" I could tell Vey had not thought about the fact that Fefe could still be outside waiting. I personally knew her better. He put the phone down for a minute, and then came back to the phone.

"Naw, I don't see or smell her skank ass."

"Well what did she want?"

"I don't know what she wanted, I didn't wanna deal with her like that. That's your business. All I know is she looking for you. She beat on the fuckin' door for twenty, thirty minutes straight. She done lost her marbles, son."

"Damn she gets on my nerves, man. She's gonna 'cause problems for me and Khaila, I just know it!" I was getting heated.

Fefe had literally been crazy over me for years. Even though she had been gone off the scene for a couple years, I knew she was probably lurking around like a snake ready to strike.

It was evident my brother could care less about my new found drama. He nonchalantly said, "Since I can't get my sleep before work I might as well get ready. Holla at you later."

Dial tone. Vey never said goodbye before he hung up the phone. A few minutes later, he called back talking 'bout, "When you coming to get the rest of your shit?"

"What do I still have over there?"

"You left some clothes and a watch is lying on your dresser. I think that's about it."

"Well, can you drop it by the house on your way to work?"

"Naw, man I'll be late for work. I gotta' get dressed, man. Damn!"

He was really getting on my nerves, with his bitch fits. He acted just like a female sometimes.

Vey had always been the most difficult person I knew, but you can't pick your family. As for close family, he was all I had. My father – was just that and nothing more. It's cool though, because I have learned how to be a good man without him, thanks to Vey's many lessons. Most of which he learned in the streets. Vey had always protected me, especially from family who were still in New York. He would often refer to them as "snakes." Vey knew what he was talking about. He had endured more years of the phoniness, fakeness, lying, stealing, and cheating from people we called family. I guess that would explain his cold attitude and abrasive personality.

I tried to rationalize with the man, "Come on, Vey, you're right down the street from me. Drop the clothes by here on the way to work."

"A'ight, but you need to get your shit out my car when I blow the horn."

"I'll be out there as soon as you pull up."

Vey hung the phone up in my face again as usual. It was something he'd do to purposely get on my nerves. Ten minutes past, and I decided to wait by the window; because I knew he would drive pass my house if I took too long to come outside.

## *Fefe*

D.C.'s dumb ass brother led me directly to D.C.'s new place. I figured he would, especially after I made my surprise visit. Vey didn't have a clue I was waiting outside and following closely behind him. He was in such hurry he didn't notice my Dodge Neon trailing behind his old beat up Toyota.

Vey laid on the horn for about a half-minute straight. Then, D.C. came out looking all good and sweating after rushing to the car. Vey handed him a trash bag of stuff. That's when his bitch, Khaila, came out to wave hello to Vey. I guess he didn't care much for her either, 'cause he pulled off burning rubber when she came outside. I covered my mouth as I laughed under my breath. I wanted to make sure I didn't blow my cover.

I watched the two of them all hugged up in front of their apartment, and I could feel the anger and jealousy growing inside my body. I couldn't control it when it came to D.C. Despite the bullshit D.C. told me in the past, I was determined to break up the "happy" couple if it was the last thing I did. D.C. and me were meant to be- not them. I sat in the car for a while thinking about what to do next. I figured I had to get inside Khaila's head- bad. Bad enough to make her leave for good.

The threats and harassment were not enough, so I knew I had to up my game. Especially since the bitch tried to file a restraining order against me a couple years ago. She had no real proof of emotional, verbal, or physical harm, so she really just wasted her time. I never got physical with her anyway. I only did minor things like flatten her tires. Just enough to get her attention and let her know it could get worst for her. She called the po-lice on me after that, but I denied the shit and I was let go. They told me to leave her alone, but I would do no such thing. D.C. was always like some kind of drug I just couldn't kick, and like most junkies I would do anything for a "hit." Word on the street was that Khaila's sister, Tracie, was supposed to kick my ass, but the shit never happened. Good thing she didn't step to me, 'cause I'd hate to put a hurting on folks who didn't have nothing to do with nothing.

Khaila and D.C. went in after a few minutes of making out. I decided to leave shortly after. As I pulled off, I remember saying aloud, "I hate that skank ho and when I catch her alone, I'mma kick her ass!" I knew where they lived now and that information was more than powerful!

## *Khaila*

I was lying there in bed with D.C., watching this new reality show,

"My Other Husband." Both of us eventually dosed off in the middle of the show, because it was boring as hell.

Half sleep, I heard a faint crash outside. I didn't pay it no mind, until I distinctly heard the sound of glass breaking. So I jumped up, walked over the window squinting to see what was going on outside. My car passenger window appeared to be smashed in, but I wasn't sure. I poked D.C. in the side to wake him out of his deep sleep.

"D.C.!!!! D.C.!!! Wake up!"
"What? What is it?" He said slurring his speech.
"Get up! Look outside!" I got no response. Nothing. " D.C.!"
"Huh?" He said sitting up slowly in bed, and then he rubbed his eyes.
"Look out the damn window!" I said gritting on him.

He finally opened his eyes halfway, and staggered to the window. Then he said, "What? I don't see nothing."

"Open your eyes, D.C., and look at my car!"

His vision was much better than mine, so when he finally did open his eyes he saw what I thought I had seen earlier. He couldn't believe it. I could tell by the way his mouth practically hung open to the floor.

According to D.C. there was no one that he could see within armslength of the car.

After staring at the car for a while, we finally decided to check out the damage close up. We both went outside in our nightclothes, t-shirts, shorts, and slippers. Not only did we see all four windows smashed, but all of the tires were slashed as well. The sides of the car were keyed really badly. The words, "IT'S OVER BITCH," was deeply etched in my hood.

There were four spark plugs in the floor of the car. I assumed they were used to break the windows more quietly than a brick or a rock. D.C. explained it was common for car thieves to use them in order to break into cars without being noticed. It just so happened that I was startled awake by the noise.

I just couldn't believe my eyes. I cried on D.C.'s shoulder for at least ten minutes straight. I sobbed so loudly my next-door neighbor, Cocoa, turned on her lights and peeped out the window to see what all the commotion was about. I ignored her, and kept crying feeling sorry for myself.

Cocoa and I had been close associates for about a year, not quite at level of being friends, but close enough to have concern for one another. I knew I would probably be telling her the story later on anyway.

"I can't freakin' believe this D.C.! This will jack up my car insurance rates. I can't pay out of pocket for this. Well actually I can pay for it, but I don't want to spend our vacation money..."

D.C. interrupted, "I'll pay for the trip, Khaila. I just wanna know who did this shit to you. You got any problems at work?"

"No, I've been getting along with everybody." We walked over to the driver side of the car to examine it more. There was a small, white note taped to the driver window. I snatched it, and read it aloud. *"Yeah, I'm back Bitch. You thought I was gone for good, didn't you? You thought you got rid of me. I don't hardly think so! I'm your worst nightmare. You betta' leave D.C. the fuck alone or there will be serious consequences for it. -Signed, Your worst nightmare."*

Right at that exact moment, a car came speeding pass and screeched around the corner. It didn't take a genius to figure out the person in the car, probably wrote the note and damaged the car. I was still clueless of who it could be. I started reading the note again to try to decipher it's meaning.

D.C. screamed out, "Fefe!!!!!! That's who the fuck it is!"

"Fefe? Your crazy ex.? I thought she left for Jersey a couple years ago."

"Like she said in the note, 'I'm back...' Hell yeah she wrote it! I'd bet you all I got she wrote that note." D.C. examined the note closer, and said "Yep, it looks like her handwriting. And you know what? The car that just sped pass us looked just like Fefe's!" D.C. was fuming more than I was. The anger in his eyes scared me for a moment.

"What's her problem, D.C.?"

"Obsession. She's crazy Khai, but I'm crazier."

"How did she find out where we live?"

"You know earlier today, Fefe knocked on Vey's door looking for me. I didn't think nothing of it. She probably followed him over here."

My blood pressure was rising, and I was getting madder. "Why didn't you tell me D.C.?"

"Cause I didn't want to worry you. You get upset so easily. I didn't think she would act like this. I figured she would be over me by now. I thought she just wanted to holla. Say "hey" or something. I should have known better though after the way she acted before she left town," he paused, "I'll take care of it babe, don't you worry about it."

I wanted to slap him right that second. I had to worry about it, my car was passed messed up, it was close to demolished. I was looking at least $3000 dollars in damage. 'Don't worry about it.' Y*eah right,* I thought to myself.

"How am I supposed to not worry about it? Look at my car!"

"I told you I'll take care of it. I know where her best friend, Tonda stay, and her people stay. I'll catch up with her."

"D.C. please don't get yourself in trouble messing with her dumb ass. I'll just call the police again. Matter-of-fact I'll call to report a vandalism incident now."

"And what's that supposed to do? She'll just keep getting away with this shit, if we keep letting her. You should get Tracie's ghetto-ass to put a hurting on her." D.C. laughed.

I didn't see shit funny at that moment. I gave D.C. a nasty look that could kill.

"Don't call my sister ghetto, D.C. She's just a little angry. She has an anger management problem."

"Naw, she's definitely ghetto, Khai." He smirked, a very annoying smirk. "And she could help you out with this. You are not a fighter, especially with the baby coming. Tracie is a fighter and she'll take care of this for you."

"I don't want her involved with all this D.C. So don't say nothing to her, ok?"

"A'ight. Go 'head and call the po-lice, and you'll see what'll happen. Nothing."

"I will, and something will happen. We have past complaints against her a mile long. And now we have even more proof. Your brother saw her earlier, we saw her car speed off from the apartment, and she left a note on the car. Open and shut case."

I really did believe we finally had her cornered.

She'd made our lives such a living hell two years ago. Especially mine. The price to be with D.C. was pretty high, but I stuck through it. Then she finally left town. You talking about somebody was happy, I was ecstatic. I thought her days of wreaking havoc were finally over. Little did I know she had really just gotten started. It was way overdue for her madness to be put to an end.

## *D.C.*

Khaila called the police station as soon as we got in the house. She talked to the police sergeant of Third Precinct, and told him all the details about Fefe. The sergeant told her he would be recording their phone conversation for records, and he would personally come out and survey the scene. Surprisingly, he did come out to investigate the scene and took a thorough report. He also said he'd have more neighborhood patrol. I knew that was bullshit as soon as he said it. I also knew the police were not going to resolve the shit 'til something tragic happened. I decided I'd handle the situation myself some kinda way. *But how?*

## Chapter 7

## *D.C.*

The next morning, Khaila decided to go to an early church service. She felt that maybe she needed to get some more religion in her life and everything would be ok. It was funny, because she actually believed God was cursing her for not serving Him the right way. As innocent as she was compared to me, she was the one being "cursed."

Khaila was paranoid too. She said she had a weird feeling that Fefe was watching her, and would try to follow her to church.

I guess Khaila was a little psychic. 'Cause almost the moment she drove off in the new rental, Fefe was knocking on the door like a crazed lunatic. I tried to ignore the persistent knocking, and prepare for work, but it was hopeless.

I yelled at the door, "Who is it?"

"Open the door and find out baby," Fefe said in a soft, feminine voice. She was putting on a fake persona. 'cause she never spoke sweetly unless she wanted something.

"Fefe, I don't have time for this."

"I wanna talk to you D.C."

I waited a few minutes by the door, looked outside and she was still out there waiting. So I went to the bathroom to shave thinking she'd eventually leave. The bitch was still out there when I came back.

Defeated, I finally opened the door. She just stood there in her gray sweats and Nike tennis shoes looking real dumb. All of my hostility for her started rising to the surface when I saw her. I started to slam the door in her face, but I felt I needed to get her straight first.

"We don't have shit to talk about, except why'd you fuck up my girl's car like that. That's all we need to discuss."

If I had my way, Fefe would have been a dead woman.

"I don't know what you are talking about D.C. I wouldn't do nothing like that. You know me better than that."

She was so nonchalant, and smiling like she was innocent. Like she didn't screw up Khaila's car the night before.

"That's exactly why I know you did it, 'cause I know you well. Plus, the note you left was in your handwriting...that was real smart, Fefe."

"Whateva, D.C. Can I come in? You looking real good in those boxers."

She giggled, and then tried to feel me up through my boxers. I grabbed her wrist, letting her know I wasn't for her bullshit.

I gritted at her and came back with, "Hell, no! We ain't on it like that no more Fefe. Now take your trifling ass on!"

She tried to force her way into the apartment, but I grabbed her again and pushed her through the door to the front yard.

At the same moment, I noticed Khaila pulling up, and she was watching us make a scene outside. I figured she came back to get something. I wasn't sure how long she was watching, but I knew things didn't look good. Holding my right hand up in the air, I motioned for Khaila to stay in the car. She didn't need to get in the middle of drama especially carrying my child. She must have gotten the message, because she stayed in the car. It must have really freaked her out watching the whole thing unfold.

Fefe got up, and turned around noticing Khaila sitting in the car.

She yelled out so Khaila would be sure to hear, "I'mma call the police, D.C.! You can't be beating me down and getting away with it!"

She looked back at Khaila again for dramatic effect. My facial expression had to be classic. I looked at Fefe like she had totally lost her mind.

I barked, "No, I'm gonna call the police if you don't get the fuck away from my apartment!"

She got up off the ground and started to walk towards her car. At the same time, Khaila got out her car heading to the apartment. Khaila and Fefe traded evil looks in passing, but neither of them said or did anything.

"Come on baby. Don't worry about her." I said to comfort her.

Making sure she was loud enough for Fefe to hear, Khaila replied to my comment, "Oh, I ain't sweating her, D.C. I just need to be concerned about our baby coming."

Fefe was sitting in her car with the window down listening and watching everything.

I must say I was very proud. My baby was finally standing up for herself. I knew it took a lot courage for Khaila to get out of the car right after Fefe had just acted a fool on the front lawn. Khaila has never been the confrontational type, at least not since I'd known her, but she wasn't backing down this time.

Fefe yelled out the car window, "I'mma have his baby too, after what we just did a few minutes ago! I got your man boo."

She laughed out sadistically, and pulled off.

I didn't need that shit, for real. Khaila wore an expression I'd never seen before. It was a look of hurt like she had heard her mother had past away or something. I felt guilty and couldn't say a word, even though I had done nothing wrong.

Khaila said after a moment of thinking, "What is she talking about D.C.?" She was mad as hell. I guess her mind was playing tricks on her, because she was actually believing Fefe's lies.

"Come on, Khai. You were only gone fifteen minutes tops. And I know you saw me push her ass to the ground just now. I don't want her. And she's lucky she's a woman, otherwise I'd be kicking ass, for real! I'm serious Khai. That bitch is psycho."

"You know better than to put your hands on a woman, D.C. No matter who she is.".

"I know. I didn't wanna have to put my hands on her, but she left me no choice. I had to be forceful to get her out of our apartment. Besides she's a strong girl."

I started walking inside and Khaila followed behind me. I tried to calm my nerves, so I could put Khaila's mind at ease.

It was hard though, 'cause I really wanted to kill Fefe- literally. Thinking about all the shit she put us through in the past really made me want to hurt her. I was determined to prevent Fefe from ruining our future like she had in the past, by any means necessary.

Khaila called the police again and I let her. She wouldn't listen to me, so why fight it. She told them all about Fefe's performance on the lawn, and reminded them about all the other shit she'd done before. The police told her she had reason to file a restraining order. Like we hadn't tried that before.

The next morning Khaila went down to court building once again to file a restraining order, just like the police told her. I had to go to work, and wasn't about to take off for some bullshit that won't gonna make a difference anyway. Of course Khaila was upset with me for not going, but even she knew it was bullshit they were feeding her.

When I got off work, I found out it would take months for the court to hear our case. Khaila was willing to wait. I was hoping, Fefe wouldn't try anything crazy in the meantime.

Khaila confided in our next-door neighbors, Cocoa and her husband, Reese about the court case. She didn't feel she could talk to me about it anymore, because we didn't see eye to eye. I was from the streets so I knew no restraining order would tame a hood rat like Fefe, only punishment would.

# Chapter 8
## *Reese*

"I heard the whole thing yesterday Reese..." My wife dramatically replied. She was telling me about our neighbor's business again, during my thirty-minute lunch break. Like I had nothing better to do with my break time.

I loved my wife a lot, but I hated the fact that she was so nosy. I could care less about the latest drama in the neighborhood. I was all about making money and catching up on our house bills. I worked hard as a maintenance supervisor at Reynolds Metal, an aluminum factory in the West End.

Cocoa, on the other hand, was supposed to be taking care of home, but she had much too much time on her hands. She should have been tending to our two young children, Reese jr., age two, and Shayla age three, a lot more than she actually was. Let her tell it, the kids were such a handful especially on those days I worked overtime. I knew better though by the way the house and the kids looked when I came home. She paid more attention to the neighborhood scoop than our kids.

We already had Child Protective Services, (CPS) investigate our home a few months prior, due to a reported incident of neglect. She left the kids home alone sleeping for twenty minutes while she went to the corner store for cigarettes.

Now Cocoa explained the kids were locked inside sleeping during their afternoon nap, so they were fine. I understood what she meant, but CPS won't trying to hear that shit.

The day after we were investigated, Cocoa confronted the woman across the street face to face. She accused the woman of jumping to conclusions and reporting lies to CPS. Cocoa was all up in the woman's face about to fight her and everything. The woman just looked her up, down, and sideways, denying everything she was being accused of.

Cocoa continued with her gossip, "…Yeah Reese this what happened. You know Khaila next-door right? Well her man's ex-girlfriend came over unannounced yesterday...they were arguing….then her man, D.C., pushed her on the ground….Khaila showed up out of nowhere…I tell you it was a mess…and then….."

She must have heard me snoring because she started blaring in my ear, "Reese are you listening to me??? Huh? Wake up!"

"Yeah, babe." I answered clearing my throat.

It was quite comical, because Cocoa just continued where she left off like I really was listening to her story.

"Uh-huh….Khaila told the girl she was pregnant. I thought she was pregnant all along, 'cause she was gaining weight all of a sudden you know…."

"Um-hmm. Yeah, right. Anyway, Cocoa I gotta' get back to work. Tell me the rest later on."

"A'ight baby. I can't wait 'til you get home, I got a surprise for you."

I knew it had something to do with sex. Cocoa was always into lingerie, sex toys, and other exotic things. I was usually too exhausted to even enjoy the goodies by the time I got home. She usually drained me further when she started getting all freaky in bed. She had to understand I was really working while she was laying around the house on the phone gossiping.

"I hope you cooked." I knew she hadn't, but I wanted to question her anyway. "It's been weeks since you cooked a descent meal. At home *all* day doing nothing."

"Whatever, Reese." She paused like I had broken her spirit. Then all of sudden she said excitedly, "You'll see what's up tonight baby."

"Alright, alright. I should be home about eleven tonight. Tell the kids that daddy loves 'em, and kiss them goodnight for me."

"You won't be home 'til eleven, Reese?"

"Yeah, that's what I said. You know I have to work late on Monday and Wednesday nights."

I knew I was being nasty towards her, but I was so disgusted with her continuous nagging and complaining. I never meant to upset her, but lately she was really starting to get on my nerves.

"A'ight, Reese. I'll see you then." She said in a disappointed way.

I believe she thought I was cheating, when I actually worked late nights at the plant. That was why she always had a surprise for me almost every night. It was attempt to keep me home more, but it didn't work. I really had to work those 12-14 hour shifts in order pay the bills. While her ass was on the sofa watching soaps, I was busting mine at work. I admit, I had considered stepping out on her more than a few times before. With all the accusations and other bullshit I needed the emotional support and relief.

    I arrived home at 11:10 pm., tired, feet hurting, head throbbing, accompanied by a very nasty attitude. I was not in the mood for Cocoa's wild late night rendezvous.

    She greeted me at the door with her usual red lingerie and bright red high heels. She fixed her long hair into a beautiful up-do and her nails were done up real nice too. I had to admit to myself she looked real pretty, but she ruined it with too much make-up and perfume. The strong scent of her perfume was giving me an even worse headache than before.

    On the dining room table was a place set for dinner for two by candlelight. Soft jazz was playing on the stereo. The ambiance of the room was real nice.

    If I wasn't so exhausted I probably would have appreciated her effort for a romantic evening. She took off my jacket, and told me to kick off my shoes and relax on the couch. She went to the kitchen to chill the red wine, completing our late night meal. Dinner would have been nice idea, if I hadn't already eaten during my lunch break, a couple hours before.

    "What is all this, Cocoa? I'm tired as hell. I don't have time for this tonight."

    "Reese just relax baby. Sit in your favorite chair, until dinner is ready. It's almost done." She hollered from the kitchen with much enthusiasm.

    I was trying to be understanding, but my patience was wearing thin.

    "A'ight, but I'm hitting the sack in a few."

    "You damn right you are." Cocoa said real sly and sexy. It wasn't doing anything for me. Only aggravating the hell out of me at that point.

    She came out the kitchen a few minutes later with pot roast, potatoes, and mixed vegetables in hand. She had even baked my favorite for desert- chocolate cake. We sipped red wine and ate our food in silence.

    I eventually warmed up more to her "surprise" after I stuffed myself with the delicious meal. I glanced across the table, looked into her eyes, and just melted like butter. Though I wouldn't admit it then I wanted her so bad I could taste it.

"That was real nice Cocoa. Thank you."
"There's more…" She said seductively.
"I don't have the energy for anymore baby."
"You will sweetheart. Go upstairs and get comfortable. I'll be up there after I put the food away."

I couldn't grasp the concept that she was actually cooking and cleaning. I was in complete shock and disbelief.

"Ok."

I slowly made my way upstairs to the bed to lie down. I didn't fall asleep though, because I was so curious to find out what she had in store for me next. Cocoa came upstairs a few minutes later.

"Reese?" She whispered warmly in my ear, which was a serious turn-on.

I sat up, and she proceeded to strip my clothes, one article at a time, until I was totally naked. Though I was exhausted, I enjoyed her incredible performance from start to finish.

Cocoa lit the vanilla scented candles, cued up my favorite jazz compilation CD, and pulled out the warm lickable massage oil. Then she began to massage my entire body, head to foot. I was even more turned on by the effort Cocoa had put into our special evening. Especially the cooking part. She didn't ask for anything in return as I had expected. I guess because it was my night, and she knew I was tired as hell too.

I know she wished I was more of a romantic, but I just didn't have the energy most nights after working. The only day I had to myself was some occasional Sundays, every blue moon if I didn't have to work overtime, and you know what I did on those Sundays. I watched Sunday night football with the boys to detox from a week of hard work. All men need a moment to themselves, or a moment with their boys, every now and then.

Even still, I promised my self to one day make Cocoa feel as special as she had made me feel that night.

We made love, not "banging it out" like usual, for about four hours straight. After my late night shift I expected to be asleep many hours before. I was rejuvenated with all the exciting things Cocoa threw at me, in and out of bed. She was gentle and passive at first, but by the second hour she was riding me like a wild stallion. Cocoa even pulled out some sex toys for us to play with. We did some freaky shit I know we hadn't tried before. At least I don't remember anything that wild since we had the kids. Oh and get this, she had even arranged for the kids to sleep at grandma's, while we had our fun!

The next morning when I woke up the fun was officially over. I jumped up and looked at the clock. Blinked a couple times to make sure I was seeing right.

"Damn, Cocoa! I'm late as shit! I knew we shouldn't have been up 'til five in the morning. I should have went straight to bed like I was trying to when I got here."

I was yelling and bumping into stuff trying to get ready for work as fast as I could. I was supposed to work a 8 – 8 shift, but I was already thirty minutes late. There was a possibility I was going to be written up for being late, and I knew I'd definitely be working 'til ten pm or later that night to make up for it.

"I'm sorry, Reese. You did have a good time though, didn't you?" She was asking me all seductive again.

She was only pissing me off for real. I couldn't believe her. There I was totally losing my mind, and all she could do was think about sex. If I were the abusive type, I would have backhanded her ass right there.

"Having a good time doesn't pay the bills, Cocoa!"

"Look, I try to do something special for you, and you wanna be all nasty towards me the next morning. Go straight to hell Reese!"

I was like, *so what if she's pissed, I'm passed pissed.* At least she could sit on her ass fuming all day. I had to go to work in a pissed off mood.

Preparing for work, I laid my clothes on the bed and rushed the bathroom in a hurry.

I hollered, "Whateva, Cocoa! I don't have time. I'm already late for work from messing with your ass last night."

I went into the bathroom and slammed the door behind me.

Then I yelled out, "Cocoa, call the job and tell them I'll be late."

"Call 'em your damn self!"

I swear, sometimes I felt a man should be able to legally kill his wife under certain circumstances. She had the nerve to get sassy with me, after she made me late for work.

After I calmed down I thought about what I said to Cocoa, and I genuinely felt bad about it.

I told her, "I'm sorry. It's not your fault I forgot to set the alarm. Please call the job for me."

Although I was sincere in my apology, I also needed her to call while I got in the shower.

"I ain't trying to hear that Reese. You don't appreciate me, and we both know why you're apologizing."

"Just forget it then."

I took a quick shower and shave, and came out about fifteen minutes later. I was wearing a towel, still dripping wet. I know Cocoa wanted to jump me again, but her pride wouldn't let her say so. She played mad and upset, and tried to give me the silent treatment. She laid back down in bed and turned her back to me.

I ignored the bullshit and childish games, and called my boss dressing the whole time. He wasn't too upset with me, though he stressed I would be making up for lost time.

By the time I got off the phone, Cocoa was busy pretending to be asleep. I kissed her on the cheek as part of a truce, and left without a word.

During my lunch break Cocoa didn't call like usual. I knew she was still mad at me. She did little petty shit like that when she got upset with me, usually about something stupid. I called the house. No answer.

I started thinking the worst. I was hoping she hadn't left the kids alone again. We couldn't afford CPS to pay us another visit. They would probably award the state our kids if we had another incident reported.

By my next break, two hours later, I was really bugging out. She still didn't answer the phone. *Where could she be? She should be home with the kids*, I thought. I worked the rest of my shift worrying, not even focusing on my work. I didn't even make my work quota.

I later found out what really happened. Cocoa was in one of her depressed moods again. During those times, she would be sleeping the day away. Meanwhile the kids would be going crazy in their rooms, hungry and bored. I've come home a number of times to Lil' Reesie's unchanged, funky ass diaper. The last thing I wanted to deal with after work was changing diapers, cleaning rooms, and feeding kids. I have to take the slack when she got like that.

Soon as I stepped through the door, Cocoa and me had our second argument of the day. The kids were in their room throwing toys and jumping on their beds. I had to get their rooms clean, give them a snack, bathe and dress them for bed. You know I was red hot at that point.

Cocoa followed me around the apartment making excuses for her oversleeping, saying our previous argument stressed her out. I wasn't trying to hear it. After about an hour of a continuous debate, I went to the bathroom to shower and more importantly to get away from Cocoa's whining.

She was yelling through the door, "I'm sorry, I'll do better." I didn't respond. I had heard it all before. What she said next was new and unexpected.

"Baby, I been thinking 'bout getting some help."

*What the hell?* I remained quiet, still wondering what she was talking about. She finally said, "I think I need a counselor or therapist or something...."

I interrupted, "Cocoa, stop it! There you go making this about you again, when you should be focusing on our family."

"I mean we can get a family counselor too, but I think I *really* need help. I don't want to risk losing the kids again."

"Cocoa, all you gotta' do is get off your ass and raise our kids. That's it. No counseling required."

I immediately regretted it when I said it. She started sobbing so loud, I could hear her through the bathroom door. Kinda made me feel bad. I never could stand a woman's crying.

I came out of the shower ready for bed and prepared to console her next. I did the damage, so I knew I had to fix it.

I held her for a minute or so before I asked her, "Are you feeling ok?" "Have you eaten today?"

"No, but I fed the kids a late lunch earlier today."

"It's after eleven, baby. You didn't feed them dinner? They told me they were hungry before I put them to bed."

"I told you Reese I drifted off. I had to lay down; my head felt like it was about to explode. The kids kept hollering and screaming. I just couldn't take it, especially after our argument."

She started sniffling again.

"Your mother is retired, call her over for a few while you rest. You can't be stressing yourself like that."

I couldn't believe the words that were coming out of my own mouth. The bullshit you'll say to get on your wife's good side.

"I know. That's why I need some help." She was really quite pitiful. Something had to give.

"Sit up, Cocoa. You still in your night clothes from this morning."

I took her clothes off, and escorted her to the bathroom for a bath. I bathed her in her favorite milk bath. When I was finished, I dried her off. I walked her to the bedroom, and sat her on the bed. She was still bawling. I pulled out a comfortable silk gown and dressed her. I told her to lay down and watch television. Then I went down to heat up some leftover pot roast and mashed potatoes from the day prior. While I was fixing her dinner, I remember thinking, *what am I going to do about her?* She was on the verge of a nervous breakdown.

She only ate half her dinner very slowly. Just because I forced her to eat. I knew she didn't feel like eating, she really just felt like sleeping her life away. I had to make her eat; it wasn't healthy to skip eating the whole daylong. I cleaned up after her meal, and when I returned she had fallen asleep again. I held her there tightly while she nodded off.

"I'm sorry I hurt you today." I said unaware she could actually hear me.

She mumbled, "I know. It's not your fault. You were right."

"It was my fault for reacting that way, and I'm gonna do something about it."

Her facial expression told me she was wondering what the hell I was talking about. I didn't have the energy to discuss my plan with her that night. I told her we would talk about it the next day. I drifted off to sleep a few minutes after the Late Show went off.

## *Cocoa*

For the first time in a long time, I couldn't sleep. After Reese fell asleep, I started thinking about what he said. What was he talking about? Would he put me in a mental institution or something? Was I really becoming a nut case? Just the thought had me on the verge of tears again.

I didn't want to lose my husband, my children, my freedom, and my mind. I knew I was missing something in my life, but I didn't know what exactly it was.

I knew my bouts with depression were brought on by me feeling so unfulfilled in my life. I felt I had no real purpose. Yes, I was a mother and wife, but I had nothing else going for me. I had little education, no job, and very few friends. I had little to do to unwind, beyond occasional family functions.

I had thought about going back to school before, but how was I going to get there? Reese had the only car in the house and he used it for work. Who would watch the kids? Was I ready mentally and emotionally for school? My emotional health and mental health were both gradually deteriorating away.

## Chapter 9
*Cocoa*

After holding a conversation with myself for hours, (in my head of course), I finally drifted off to sleep. When I woke up, Reese was still lying next me massaging my head.
*Why wasn't he at work?*
He was acting strange, taking care of me and giving me extra attention. You know what they say about men who start pampering their wives out of nowhere, but I wasn't gonna start accusing him like I had done in the past. I was determined to try being more secure in our marriage.
My baby was a fine specimen of a man, any woman would feel insecure in my shoes. Six-three, 210 pounds, washboard stomach, sun kissed skin, and a smile that makes my panties melt every day I saw him. Besides all of that, he was a really good man, a provider, great father, and an incredible lover. Sometimes when I woke up next to him, I would blink a couple times to make sure I wasn't still dreaming.
I glanced at the clock on my nightstand and it read 12:06 pm. I looked at Reese like, *oh shit does he know what time it is? Not this again, he'll be blaming my ass for being late.* He was supposed to work an 11-11 shift.
Before I could say anything, I guess he read my mind and said, "I took the day off to look after you. I think we should go to the clinic to make sure everything's ok."
"I'm not crazy, Reese!"
"I'm not saying that, I just want to make sure you're ok. I think you have some serious issues going on Cocoa. You have been sleeping too much and eating too little lately. You're not caring for the kids like you

used to. The first time you went through this phase of yours, we ignored it, and the kids suffered for it. We almost lost the damn kids for God sakes!"

"I went to the store, Reese. I just left to get the kids lunch."

"Cocoa, come on now. They're only two and three. You suppose to take them with you. And I thought you said you were out getting cigarettes."

He had a point. I wasn't thinking clearly that day, and I was out getting cigarettes. Anyway, I had to defend my position.

"They were napping, Reese. Why wake them, when I can run up the street, get the food and stuff right quick?"

I was getting defensive as hell having to explain myself on some old shit. I'd made a mistake I promised myself I wouldn't let happen again, but he wouldn't let it go. He could tell I was getting heated.

He said, "It's ok Cocoa. Just calm down." He was talking to me like I was a nutcase, like he was afraid I'd breakdown right in the middle of our bedroom floor.

"I already called Mental Health and they set us up with an appointment."

"I'm not a nutcase Reese. I'm just a little stressed right now. I need to get counseling, not to be fucking committed!"

He was stressing me so bad, I felt I was really having a breakdown.

"What are you talking about baby," he held my hand tightly, "I'm not trying to put you in the crazy house. I need you more than the kids do. I'm just trying to make sure you're taking care of yourself so you can properly take care of our family."

He held me close to his chest with a lot of love and tenderness. I truly believed he was concerned about my well-being and the children's as well. I could understand why he didn't wanna risk leaving me alone with the kids, until he was sure I was "ok." The word "ok" was another way of saying "sane."

So I was like, *fuck it! I'll go just to get our household back to normal.* I really missed making love to my husband without arguing afterwards. I also missed playing with my children and taking care of them like I used to. The more I thought about it, the more I agreed with Reese about making the appointment.

I got dressed quickly, while Reese called my mom over to watch the kids. I really wished I had called instead, 'cause Reese told her everything about me being depressed. My mom knew about my past issues, she really didn't need to know the latest. Of course she was more than ready to watch the kids, while I got my head examined by the state.

My mother was on early retirement from being an elementary schoolteacher. She continued to work part-time at a small grocery store as a cashier. My stepfather had recently past, so I knew she welcomed the kids' company.

I never knew my real father, who left my mom and me shortly after I was born. It was always weird to me that I had a whole other family I didn't know anything about. It didn't matter though, 'cause I didn't want a family that didn't want me anyway. Especially when I had my own family to deal with.

We arrived at the clinic and sat in the crowded reception area for close to an hour before being seen. I had to fill out so many damn forms I thought my hand would fall off right there. Finally we met with the clinic counselor. She quickly reviewed some of the forms I filled out. Then she briefly explained the nature of their services and policies. The counselor asked me if we were getting couple's counseling. I explained that I only wanted individual counseling. She then made it a point that Reese could not stay because of confidentiality. Didn't make much sense that my husband couldn't stay in the room with me.

"Why can't I stay with my wife? She needs me here!" Reese was becoming irritated, raising his voice. The counselor probably thought he needed the services instead.

"Mr. Harris, I'm sorry, but I'm going to have to ask you to leave. You can wait in the waiting area for a few minutes. The intake won't be much longer."

That poor little white lady didn't know what she was in for with Reese. He was staring a hole through that women's forehead. He wasn't gonna leave without a fight, so I decided to help her out a little.

"Go 'head Reese. I'll be fine." I gave him a reassuring look, and grabbed his hand to let him know everything would be fine. "I'll be outta' here soon."

He finally left giving the counselor a look of disgust on the way out the door. Reese was always very protective of me. It was kinda cute and pathetic at the same time.

I must say I was just as curious to know why he couldn't sit in on the intake. There must have been a special reason the counselor didn't want him there. I didn't ask though. I just sat there in suspense and waited to find out what was coming next.

"Ok, Mrs. Harris, now we can begin. I must videotape my intake interviews and review them with my supervisor. Please sign this waiver form, which states you approve videotaping of all counseling sessions."

I quickly signed the waiver, without really reading it. I didn't care about videotaped sessions, as long as I got the help I needed. Avoiding the mental ward of course.

"Ok, Mrs. Harris, would you like me to call you by your first or last name?"

"I usually go by my nickname 'Cocoa', but you can call me Cofina if you like. It really doesn't matter to me."

"Alright, Cocoa it is. By the way, I'm Michelle McMillian. I'm going to ask you a series of questions for the intake interview. After I obtain the necessary information, I will turn in the information for immediate processing. In a couple weeks, you will be assigned an outpatient therapist, and given the date and location for your individual sessions."

"Oh...so you won't be my counselor?" I was quite confused by that point of the session. I figured she was going to be my counselor, especially after she made such a big deal about my husband leaving the room.

"No, Cocoa. I'm only here for the intake interview. I'll then refer the paperwork to your future counselor.

"Oh, ok."

What else could I say? I really didn't have a choice in the matter.

Ms. McMillian asked me a thousand and one questions. I just knew Reese was freaking out by this point, yelling and making a scene. I giggled to myself, thinking they'd be putting Reese's ass in a straightjacket, instead of me. I figured my giggling looked quite crazy to the head shrinker.

She proceeded to ask me questions about my past and present life circumstances, my childhood, friendships, relationships, and other personal information  I personally felt some of those questions were just plain nosy, but I answered them willingly. I hesitated on answering some of those questions.

She would ask me shit like, "How many times a week do you have sex with your husband?" That ain't none of those people's business, but I told her the truth.

I said, "Lately it's only been like....once a week, if I'm lucky."

"Well, how often did you have sex before that?"

"It was like once or twice a day." I smiled at the thought. She smiled too. I guess she had thoughts of her own sex life. She then changed her line of questioning, which took me completely off guard.

"I remember reading in your screening that you felt you were depressed a couple years ago. Were you ever diagnosed?"

I got really choked up out of nowhere, and starting crying. Ms. McMillian handed me a tissue and patiently waited for me to gain my composure. After a few minutes of silence, I was still getting myself together.

"Cocoa, I know this is a sensitive subject. You don't have to answer that question right now, if you don't feel comfortable."

"No, I'll tell you, Ms. McMillian. I was really depressed about two years ago, when my stepfather was shot and killed in a store robbery. He was only 59 when he was...." I could feel I was starting up again. I was crying a waterfall; the tissues couldn't come fast enough. I was still hurting, because me and my step-dad were really close. He was my real dad in my eyes. I still couldn't believe he was gone, and his killer had gotten away with murder scott-free.

"I'm really sorry to hear about your dad's death. I lost my father as well, when I was quite young."

She helped me to open up more when she told me about her father's death as well. I started explaining the whole tragic story to her. I told her about how supportive Reese was during that period in my life. How I still wasn't myself, and had taken it so hard. I told her no one could fill the void for me, not even my husband and kids.

A year after my dad's death, I was at an all time low. I even quit my job, and started being a full-time homemaker. With a 14-month-old baby, and one on the way, it was especially hard to go back to work. It was hard to get my life back on track period. I'd just accepted things would never be the same again.

I depended on my dad's love and support the most, and he always gave me the best advice. He was there since I was three years old, so he was the only dad I'd ever known. He was the greatest, and although I wasn't his biological daughter he always showed me the most love, unlike his other four biological children.

He rarely saw his other children, 'cause they were living all the way in South Carolina with their mother. I have two stepbrothers and two stepsisters I have never met. All older than me, except for a brother who was the same age as myself. You do the math on that one. My mom never wanted to talk about the affair. It didn't take a genius to figure out why my step-dad wasn't close to his children. They hated him because he cheated on their mom. I never thought less of him for it. Call me selfish, but it only affected me in a good way.

I told the counselor, "....I guess I'm still healing from that. It has been two years since he past away, but it still hurts. I miss him so much. You know my mom and I were never all that close, and she's blood." I giggled a little.

The counselor wasn't quite sure if it was safe to share a laugh after our serious talk. I was always the type to dodge a serious discussion with a joke or something to avoid feeling uncomfortable.

"Cocoa, I wouldn't expect anyone to heal right away from losing a loved one. It's been over twenty years since my father died of heart disease. I still miss him very much, and it hurts that he is gone." She paused taking a deep breath to compose herself. "You're probably gonna go through the normal stages of grief. Most people go through the grieving process when they lose a loved one. There is denial and disbelief, bargaining with God, anger, blame and acceptance. A lot of people go through these stages repeatedly over a long period of time, and they may even occur in a different sequence."

As our session came to a close, I didn't want to leave. It was a breath of fresh air to have an outlet to talk with someone who actually listened. I got a lot of things off my chest during that session, and I couldn't wait for the next one.

She gave me the information I needed for my next session with my new counselor. I still didn't like the idea of talking to another person about my issues. I was even more concerned with re-opening an old wound in reference to my father, which I thought it had begun to heal. My dad's death was too painful for me to think about. I hadn't made the connection that my depression had anything to do with him, but I guess it did. It was a combination of things that were revealed to me.

# Chapter 10
## *D.C.*

That stalker bitch showed up at my job Monday afternoon. I saw her ass sashaying towards Dickie's through the store window. Enough was enough. She had taken stalking to a whole other level. She had to be stopped. I truly believed the only way to stop her was to breakdown her pride and make her fear me.

I told my boy, "Rayshaun, hold my register man. I'll be back. I gotta' handle some business."

"Fo' sho' handle yo' business, son. I got this." Rayshaun had a strong New York accent and style that never left him the five years he lived in Richmond.

"A'ight."

I stopped her ass before she could touch the door handle. It didn't look good the way I manhandled her and pushed her away from the store to the back parking lot. But I really didn't need her showing her ass in my workplace. I needed my job especially with the wedding and baby coming. I needed it more than ever.

"Fefe, what do you want from me man?" That was a dumb question, 'cause I knew exactly what she was gonna say.

"I want you."

"I DON'T WANT YOU, FEFE! DO….YOU…..UNDERSTAND? I am in love with my girl. She will be my wife soon. Even if she won't in my life, I wouldn't want your ass now. Leave me the fuck alone before I do something I'll regret!"

"Ohhh....testy! I like it when you're rough like that. I remember when we used to fight like this back in the day, and make up later. Let's make up, D.C. I still love you, and I know you still feel something for me too."

I was thinking, *yeah I feel something for you alright, pure hate.*

She smiled at me and tried to hug me, but I jumped back from her like she had a contagious disease. Which was actually possible with the way she got around.

"You just don't get it do you?"

I didn't know what else to do or say at the point. She was mental. I tried to keep it cool and talk logically to her, but you can't rationalize with a nutcase. I was losing my self-control, but I thought about the repercussions. I didn't want to go jail without seeing my first kid born. I was thinking, *maybe I'll play the nice route, and she'll listen.* Crazy thinking, but I was desperate. Nothing else was working so I had nothing to lose.

"Fefe, look it is possible we can be friends one day, but you really need to chill out." The more I talked the dumber I felt. *Friends? We damn sure couldn't be friends. The bitch was crazy!*

"Ok...I'd like that."

I realized that I had made a dumb move, because now she had an opening to call me and shit. She probably figured if we became friends again, we could eventually be together again. Too late to fix the damage, it was done.

"A'ight Fefe, I gotta' get back to work now"

"Ok then. I'll come to see you later boo."

"You can't keep stopping by my job, Fefe. I'll lose my job."

"I won't come a lot."

"Whateva, Fefe. I'm gone."

I turned a cold shoulder to her, and headed back to the store. I had wasted ten minutes too many talking nonsense.

Fefe returned to her car, probably feeling on top of the world. Thanks to my stupidity. I decided to stop beating myself up for the mistake, because what was done was done. I just needed to figure out what to do next to get rid of Fefe.

When I got back in the store, I told my boy Rayshaun about what happened.

He was like, "I would have kicked her ass by now. If I were you, I wouldn't have a problem right about now."

"Yeah man trust me I thought about it, but my girl don't want no violence. She thinks the police gonna handle things. Them motherfuckas won't do shit unless something tragic happens first. My girl would be dead before they even make any real moves. I can't watch it happen. She's pregnant with my kid man."

"Um...you gotta real problem on your hands, son. What if someone else took care of the situation for you?"

"Been there done that. I told Khai's sister one time before to take care of her. Her sister is a lot crazier than Fefe ever was. She was gonna do it for me. Khaila found out, and told her sister to mind her own business and stay out of it. They got into this big argument about it. Now they don't even talk like that no more."

Rayshaun couldn't really relate, because he took care of his business violently. I know one time his ex-girl got jealous and vandalized his car. Fucked it up real bad. Rayshaun beat the hell out that girl. Bruised her face up real bad and knocked out a tooth. His girl was a dime piece before he did that to her, took her right down to a nickel piece. She kept messing with him anyway. Craziness. I never respected him for that, 'cause I didn't believe in beating women. I kinda understood where he was coming from, ever since Fefe started tripping again. I guess some women could push you to the point of no return.

We stood there in silence thinking for a minute, before Rayshaun said, "well maybe we could get somebody Khaila don't know to kick Fefe's ass."

"Still, Fefe will become more violent towards Khaila if we do that."

"Yeah, you right. What if we hooked her up with a man."

We both started cracking up. A customer who was browsing the CD's was trying to figure out what was so funny.

I really thought maybe that shit could work. It wasn't like I had a whole lot of other ideas to work with.

"Maybe Ray, but how we gonna find someone to deal with her ass. I mean, you know she off her rocker son, she done let herself go, and she don't have nothing a man would want."

"Well.... you wanted her."

"That was years ago. Fefe kept it tight back then. She looked good and she knew what she wanted. Since the break up she went straight downhill. Fefe looks and acts like a damn crackhead. Actually crack would explain her stupidity."

We laughed, but won't shit funny about Fefe's craziness. I was joking about the crackhead thing. I mean, I doubt if she was on drugs, she was just plain mental. There was no other reason for her obsession. I mean, Rayshaun and I both knew crack doesn't make you stalk people, just more crack.

Rayshaun said, "I know a dude who wouldn't give a fuck, as long as she gave it up. And we know she would give it up. She would definitely give it up." We high-fived on that one. One of the reasons I broke it off with Fefe was because she had a reputation on the streets that had skank written all over it. I was beginning to get excited about our plan. I figured it just may work if done correctly.

Khaila walked in the store at that moment. It was our usual time to have lunch and I had lost track of time. Khaila was on her two-week vacation, and it was her second day off.

Our vacation plans were still in works for a quick trip to Virginia Beach for a few days. I had taken off and everything for the following week. Khaila wanted to spend more time on vacation, but we couldn't do it with Fefe's drama. Khaila and I decided that Fefe wasn't gonna ruin our plans. We were getting a rental car and everything else ready for the trip.

She greeted me with a kiss to the cheek. "Hey baby. What's going on?"

"Nothing baby, nothing." I was kinda out of it, plotting on what to do with Fefe.

I guess she could sense it. She said, "What's wrong, D.C.?"

"Everything's cool, Khai," I turned to Ray and said, "Ray, I'mma take my lunch break now. You take yours when I come back, a'ight?"

"That's cool man."

We went across the street to our favorite lunch spot Angelina's for pizza and pasta. We picked that place 'cause we wouldn't waste time traveling to some spot across town for lunch. That way we would always get our maximum amount of time to chill with each other.

During lunch, Khaila made sure to question me about our vacation. She was such a planning type. I was more a just-go-with-the-flow type.

"Khai, don't worry about a thing I'll get the car and hotel ready for our trip."

She gave me a look like she was concerned about me setting things up. I always did stuff last minute. I was more concerned about paying for it. I had made a promise that I wasn't even sure I could keep. I still owed Vey $400 for my part of last month's rent. Vey wanted his money immediately, especially since I'd left to move in with Khaila. He really couldn't stand Khaila when I decided to move in with her, and he was gonna be extra nasty with me because of it. Vey knew he would have problems paying his rent without me paying my part.

Khaila said, "Can I at least pay for the food and stuff like that?"

She knew I couldn't really afford to pay for the entire trip. But my mind was made up. After Fefe made her dreadful appearance to town, I wanted to go on vacation with Khaila more than ever.

"No, I got it Khai. Once you have my baby boy, you won't be able to travel much."

"Your baby boy. How do you know it will be a boy?" She smiled, and started eating her Caesar salad.

"Because my sperm can only make boys."

I laughed, but Khaila got serious. Gave me one of her funny looks. She was getting to be so emotional ever since the pregnancy.

She replied, "How you know, you got some kids I don't know about?"

"No. What are you talking 'bout? I was just trippin' with you babe."

"Oh, I thought…. Never mind, how was you day?"

"You be getting so sensitive 'bout stuff lately. Khai, you don't have nothing to worry about. I don't want anybody else but you. You don't have to be concerned about Fefe's stupid ass or any other woman taking your place."

Khaila didn't have any reason to be insecure. I believed she compared our relationship with all her other relationships. Men had constantly hurt her in the past, cheating, lying, and even stealing from her. She had never been with a man she could trust, and she believed I would eventually do her the same way. I reminded her that she had to trust me especially since I was going to be her baby's father and soon to be husband. Khaila had to know I was different from the other dudes, by the way I treated her like the queen she deserved to be.

After a long silence, Khaila said out of nowhere, "I know I be saying stupid stuff sometimes. What I said was uncalled for. I'm sorry."

She looked embarrassed by what she said, staring down at the table like the day she told me about the baby. She was so scared that day, worrying about how I would take the news.

"That's ok, Khai. I know why you're so sensitive. You got good reason."

She nodded in agreement. Then she said, "You know, Fefe called the house a few minutes before I came." Unfuckingbelievable. Fefe was beyond comprehension.

"Don't ask me how she got the number. I think I have it listed under K. Roe in the phone book. She probably just matched the address with the name..."

I cut her off in anger, "She what! She done gone way too far Khai. Way too far. You know she really could get any information she wanted from the Internet too." The information highway gave away too much information about people. In this day and time, there's just no escaping psychos, no matter what you do.

"What did she say? Did she upset you?"

"Naw...actually she said she wanted to 'squash all this bullshit between us.' I really didn't know whether to believe her or not."

Poor Khaila she was so naive sometimes. She had a lot of book knowledge from college, but I was still training her on the street knowledge.

"I don't trust her Khai, and you shouldn't either. She came by the store about an hour ago, talking 'bout she wanted to be friends with me too."

I didn't want to tell her everything. I didn't want to mention that I had brought up the friend thing myself out of stupidity and desperation. What I had done was open up a door for Fefe to slither her snake ass through.

"Why didn't you tell me about her visit?"

"Cause I didn't want to worry you. I was gonna handle it myself."

Khaila was starting to get angry again. I could tell, 'cause her caramel complexion was turning blood red, and she was shaking like a seizure. Khaila was trying hard to not to cry, but it was a losing battle. She made such a big deal about everything. I'm not exaggerating when I say she even cried when her cereal got too soggy in the milk. I just hoped her stressing out wouldn't affect the baby. We still had another seven months to go.

I must say since her pregnancy news, I'd become more emotional myself, and supportive of her needs. I went over and gave her a warm hug right there in the restaurant booth. We never did care much about making a scene or getting a lot of attention in public. People looked, but

I kept holding her for a while. Then I walked her outside to calm down. We left most of our food on the table. I knew I would regret that shit later on in the workday- hungry as I was.

When we got outside my mind was on the baby. "You know Khaila I don't want you to be worrying about this stuff while you're carrying our baby. I'll take care of it. If she call or come by page me 911, I'll get Ray or the manager, John to cover for me. I know how to put Fefe in her place."

She said, "Or you could keep my car. Since I go to work before you and I get off after, it could work. I'm not gonna page you all the time though, it'll get you in trouble at work."

"John's cool. He'd let me leave for a few, and just take it away from my lunchtime. Or he would just have me work late. It's not like business is booming at Dickie's anyway."

"Ok, D.C. We can do that." She began to smile, "I'm feeling better let's go back inside and eat."

We hadn't been gone long so our food was still there. Of course, nosy people were staring at our every move. Khaila decided to go to the restroom to freshen up, making it less apparent she'd been crying. She came back to the table, beautiful as ever, with her make up and hair all done up.

I started thinking about our future together. "Khai, when you want to set the date?"

"Huh? What date?"

"For our wedding."

She smiled at me, and spoke slowly, "I thought we were gonna wait 'til I have the baby. You know I won't be able to fit into a nice dress until later on."

"Well I want you to be my wife now, before you change your mind." I joked with her.

"You don't have to worry about that D.C. I love you too much."

She made sure to say that loud enough for me and everyone else in the restaurant to hear. The nosy people across from us started to stare and whisper. I don't care what she say, it was apparent she enjoyed the attention.

"I love you too Khaila and I want you to be my wife. I'm serious about this." I reached for her hand and held it tightly. I wanted her to know how strongly I felt for her.

After about fifteen minutes of discussing the wedding thing, I decided I was fighting a losing battle. I had to remind myself that Khaila was a planner, and she probably wouldn't be ready to get married for at least another year. Khaila felt she needed to have the perfect wedding planned to a tee. The dress, the flowers, the ceremony, the reception- all had to be arranged and it would take time and money. She promised me, her dad would handle the finances of the wedding. That wasn't my concern. If I had to pick up another job I would to give Khaila the wedding she wanted. I guess I just wanted to marry her so bad. After three years of being uncertain, I was finally sure.

"You tell your mom about our marriage plans?"

"Yeah, I told her when I went over to tell her about the baby. I showed her the ring and everything. She was in complete shock."

"You tell your father yet?"

"Naw, I was too scared to do that. My mom told him for me. I haven't talked to him since I found out about the baby."

"Ok, so you're saying that you don't know how your father is handling the news, but you're sure he's gonna pay for the wedding." I laughed, because I couldn't believe her sometimes.

What I didn't know at the time was that Khaila's dad wasn't gonna speak to her period, because his angel had actually gotten pregnant, unmarried, with a "thug" at that. My thug days had been long gone, but her parents were both very judgmental. Her father never was crazy about me, but I knew he hated my guts after he received the news. I think her mother took it a little better than we both expected.

Thirty minutes later, we finished up our lunch, and went our separate ways. I went back to work, and Khaila went home to get some rest. The pregnancy was making her tired as usual.

## *Khaila*

When I left D.C., I went directly home. Walking up to my doorstep, I was welcomed by the most disgusting, horrific sight I had ever seen. I don't think I had ever screamed like that in my entire life. I stood there on the doorstep in perfect awe and confusion of what the hell was going on.

My neighbor, Cocoa came over to me in a hurry, trying to figure out why I was screaming like I had been stabbed with a knife 32 times.

"What is going on? You alright girl?"

"No, Cocoa I'm not. Did you see that shit on my porch?"

"Yeah, girl I was trying to figure out what that was. What is it, and where did it come from?"

"I don't know where it came from, but it looks like a dead baby chicken. Who the hell would put that on my doorstep?" I answered my own question without a thought, "that nut Fefe, that's who!!!! I'mma leave that shit right there so the police can see it!" My emotions were totally out of whack since I got pregnant, and Fefe's drama didn't help a thing.

"Look Khaila I want you to come over to my place for a few. Tell me what happened. I gotta' get back to the kids."

"A'ight."

I surveyed the area, before I left to make sure that bitch Fefe wasn't waiting for me somewhere, lurking in the bushes or something. I went over to Cocoa's place, and I let it all spill out. We weren't all that close, but I figured I had to talk to someone about it. My girl, Shante was working a lot lately so I couldn't disturb her sleep. Besides Cocoa was gonna find out about the drama on the streets anyway, so I told her the whole story from beginning to end.

After I finished, she was like, "Girl, you know you need to call the police, before that psycho does something else." Like I didn't know that much already.

"I have called them over and over. They say they need more evidence to arrest her, this should be more than enough evidence for them." I replied sarcastically. I was heated at the thought of them bullshitting me again.

"Yeah, I'd leave that shit right there 'til the police get here. Don't even touch it."

"Oh, you know I'm not touching that shit anyway. D.C. gonna have to move that. Where the hell did she get a bloody chicken from? It has the head and everything still attached."

"She's into that Voodoo stuff, Satanism, or something. Knowing her she probably killed the chicken with her bare hands."

"She's straight crazy, Cocoa, out of her mind. She needs to be in an institution, I'm telling you."

I called the police, and the same officer came out to the apartment to examine evidence. After he bagged the dead chicken, he told me he would dust for fingerprints and add the new evidence to a case file. The whole time I was thinking, where the hell would he get some fingerprints. No action would be taken to arrest Fefe. I knew he was shooting me the bull again, but I stood there and listened anyway.

Fefe had a record for assault and battery in the past and she only got a month in jail. She cut a girl real bad in her face over some dude years ago. She thought the girl was messing with her boyfriend. In reality, the girl and her boyfriend were only co-workers, not lovers.

Fefe showed up on the girl's job, waited for her to go to her car, then jumped from behind a nearby bush, and cut the girl. No questions asked, no conversation, no nothing. She just cut her and ran. A witness who was leaving the job around the same time called the police. They found Fefe a few minutes later running down the block looking for somewhere to hide out.

D.C. didn't have a clue about Fefe's past until six months after their relationship was over. Vey told him about it after he had heard the news in the streets. Mind you, the psycho was still stalking D.C., and terrorizing me at that time. Of course, D.C. was concerned Fefe would try to do the same thing to me, and you know I was more than concerned about it.

When the police left, I went back and told Cocoa what he said and what I thought about it.

"Girl they don't do nothing unless it gets real serious. Like I get hurt or killed then they may do something. D.C. was right. We gotta' handle it ourselves."

"You don't need to handle nothing. You pregnant."

"So what I'm supposed to do?"

"Move."

"I can't move or run away every time I have a problem. I've done too much of that."

"Yeah you right. But you not gonna fight her, you not gonna move, the police not doing nothing, so what other options do you have?"

"D.C. said he would handle it. I got faith that he will."

"D.C. not gonna always be there sweetie. Get you a gun to protect yourself."

"Hell, no. I don't want that in my house, especially now that I'm pregnant."

"That's why you need a gun, to protect you and your baby."

"Naw I can't do that. It's gonna be alright. We're all gonna be fine. I got faith."

"Faith? Faith is all good, but a gun would be better. Pop her ass before she reaches the doorstep." Cocoa was tripping me out. I just had to laugh.

"I got your back. If you need me girl I'll be right next door." She said in a serious, motherly tone. She gave me a hug and said, "And you know what? I gotta' gun. I'll pop her ass with no problem." We laughed as she walked me out the door.

"I'll see you later, Cocoa."

"You got my number, right?" She asked.

"Yeah I got it."

"Call me girl anytime you need or come by. It don't matter, day or night." I could tell she was genuine in what she was saying.

"Ok, I will."

I walked across to my apartment feeling nervous and full of frustration. Fefe had invaded my space, made me feel unsafe, and I was mad as hell.

I usually had severe headaches in the evening, which was a sure sign of a stressful day at work. It was a different kind of stress that day with Fefe's madness. I was starting to get one of those migraine headaches, feeling defenseless. Kinda like a trapped goldfish in a bowl without water. I knew D.C. would be there for me holding my hand making me feel free again. But telling him about the incident with Fefe could possibly make the situation worst.

I decided to lay down for a short nap, which turned into a long sleep. When I woke up it was already 4:15 pm. I was late picking up D.C. from work. His shift ended at 4' o clock. I looked at the caller ID and I saw that he had called a couple times. He left a message once at 1:33 pm. to check on me, I slept right through it.

I rushed to get over to Dickie's to pick up D.C. It took more than thirty minutes to get from the Southside to the Northside in rush hour traffic. D.C. was waiting inside when I walked up. He looked a little upset, so I knew I had to explain off top.

"I'm sorry, baby. I overslept."

"You a'ight babe, I just finished up. I've been helping John with his inventory. I'm just worn out Khai."

That explained his dead expression and blasé attitude.

"I think I might get a promotion."

You would think he would've been on top of the world with that news. He sounded deader than I did after sleeping all afternoon.

"That's good baby. Aren't you happy about it."

"Yeah. I'm just tired. Plus I don't know anything yet anyway."

"You know you'll get it, you work hard around here."

"Let's hope so, we really need the money now."

He patted my stomach and made me feel comfortable just like I thought he would. For a short moment, I decided to put the whole Fefe ordeal out of my mind. I conveniently neglected to tell him what happened at the apartment.

## *D.C.*

When we got home, Khaila went straight to bed to finish her nap. I was tired too, but I decided to wind down with a Black and Mild cigar on the doorstep. Nosy ass Cocoa, as predictable as ever, came outside at the exact same time. I'm telling you, she had way too much time on her hands. She lit her cigarette and sat in a chair in front of her doorstep. I started to retreat back inside, but it was too late.

"Hey D.C."

"Hey what's up?" I said real short and abrupt.

I wanted to let her know from my attitude that I wasn't much for talking that day. Not any day for that matter. I just really didn't like Cocoa. She was lazy and ghetto, and was getting way too close to Khaila for my comfort. I really didn't trust that. I was like, *why all of a sudden she start being buddy-buddy with Khaila?* I believed Cocoa had to be up to something.

"I'm alright. How are you and Khaila doing?" She had her fake concerned voice on.

I said, "We cool. Why?"

"I'm just asking. After what happened today, I figured you'd prob-

ably be pissed."
"I yelled, "What?"
"Khaila didn't tell you?"
"Naw what happened Cocoa?" Pissed off was an understatement for how I felt. I couldn't believe my girl was hiding shit from me but she felt free to tell the neighborhood. Telling Cocoa was like telling the neighborhood. She couldn't keep a secret if you paid her not to tell nobody.
"She should tell you then."
"Stop playing games with me Cocoa!" I was yelling so loud I knew I was waking up the neighborhood. I was so pissed I didn't care.
Cocoa must have been irritated, because she raised her voice as well. "That crazy girl done went off again, leaving a damn dead chicken on the doorstep!"
"She did what?"
I practically had steam coming from my ears. Not only was I mad, but I was also hurt. Khaila had shared her pain and grief with the town gossip instead of her soon-to-be-husband. *What kinda shit is that!* My pride was hurt too. I was supposed to protect her from harm, but I was too late. If I couldn't do that for her, then what purpose did I have as her husband?

## *Khaila*

I couldn't sleep because of all the yelling. Once I went downstairs, I could clearly hear every word Cocoa and D.C. were saying through the door.
*Cocoa and her big mouth!* I couldn't believe what she did. I didn't want D.C. to find out about the incident with Fefe, because I knew how he would react. Thanks to Cocoa, he was having another one of his childish temper tantrums. After his loud discussion with Cocoa, D.C. stormed in ready for war with me. I was hiding out in my room.
He stormed in, "Ughhhh!!!!!!! I'mma kill that bitch! She done took this shit too far!" "Khaila! Get yo' ass down here!" I took my time coming down the stairs. I guess I was stalling for answers. I decided to play the dummy role.

"What? What's wrong with you?"
"The question should be what's wrong with you. Don't play dumb with me Khaila. Why didn't you tell me what happened today?"
"Huh?"
"Khaila come on now! Stop playing!" Spit was flying all over the place. He was so mad at me, and I didn't blame him. I shouldn't have hidden anything from him after all we had been through. I still played diversion games to stall the inevitable outcome.
"You need to stop yelling at me like you're crazy."
There was brief silence. D.C. calmed down for a moment. He had his hands on his hips waiting for some information.
"I didn't want you to get upset and worry about me. You probably would have left the job to check on me. I was fine you know. Cocoa was there for me."
I knew those words were a mistake as soon as they left my mouth. He was getting upset all over again.
"How am I supposed to be there for you, if you don't tell me nothing? You marrying me, not Cocoa's ass!"
Oh, he had lost his mind for sure, he was not only yelling, but cussing at me too. I just stared at him for a minute- partly guilty, partly pissed.
He continued, "….It's my job to make sure you're ok. I told you to page me if something goes down, and you promised you would!"
"I can't talk to you when you're like this D.C."
"That's a'ight, Khai." He heads to the door about to pull it off the henges. He shouts back to me, "I'll take care of this shit with Fefe right now! You can do what you wanna do! You been doing that shit anyway! I'm out this piece!"
He stormed out, slamming the door behind him.
I found out he left to go see his best friend, Jyree's house, down the block to get a ride. He asked Jyree to take him to Fefe's place in the East End of Henrico. When they got there, it was obvious that she was home, because her car was out front. Fefe had the nerve to actually answer the door to D.C, knowing his state of mind. I had tried to avoid the whole scene from happening, but it play out anyway, one frame at a time.

After Khaila and I finished arguing, I roamed the neighborhood a while with my boy Jy, before confronting Fefe about the dead chicken incident. I just couldn't let that shit go. It was like she was making a threat to harm my unborn son.

I stood on Fefe's doorstep prepared for war.

Banging on the door demanding immediate attention, I said, "I'm telling you, you've gone way too far with this shit, Fefe! You testing me, I'm telling you for real!"

Fefe took a while to answer the door.

She blurted out, "What you talking 'bout D', I ain't did nothing."

She was holding back laughter, and I was trying my best to hold back my fist.

"Don't play with me. I'll slap the shit out of you, I swear."

"No, need for all the violence baby. Look come in and sit down a minute. Tell me what's wrong baby."

I stepped in the doorway, with absolutely no intentions of staying. I refused to sit down like she wanted. I was prepared for any tricks that *trick* had in her bag of tricks. All of her lies and deception, I was ready for it.

"You know, you can have a seat, 'D'."

"I'll stand. What made you want to do something so stupid?"

"What?"

She was gonna try to play me, but I was letting her know the game was over.

"Why did you put a fuckin' dead chicken on my doorstep! I want you to know we called the police. They took evidence. You didn't even hide your fuckin' fingerprints dumb ass! They found them all over the place."

I was lying my ass off, but she wasn't too bright, so I figured it would work.

"They ain't find no fingerprints from me, 'cause I won't there."

"Whatever Fefe! You slowly digging yourself a grave. I'm telling you if you do something else stupid, I'mma take care of your ass myself! Fuck calling the po-lice!"

"Are you threatening me 'D'?" She said nervously.

Fefe was starting to get riled up but I didn't care. Maybe she needed to get riled up to know I wasn't playing no more. I wanted her to know she was riding a thin line between life and death. A man can only take so much, before he starts considering homicide.

"No, I'm not threatening you. I'm promising you. Try me." I responded calmly, but I was dead serious.

"Get out of my muthafuckin' house, fo' I call the police on yo' ass! When you get yourself together maybe we can talk."

"Ughhhhh! Fefe…I ain't never gonna get myself together to be with you! You hear me!!!!! You can go straight to hell bitch!" With that said, I quickly left and got in my boy, Jyree's ride. I was breathing hard and acting funny, so he knew something had gone down. Of course he wanted the run down as soon as I got in the car.

"What happened man?" He said pulling off from the curb.

"I told her I'd fuck her up if she do some crazy mess like that again."

"I don't blame you after what you told me, man. I probably would have killed the bitch myself by now!"

"I've been trying to give her chances to……"

"Forget chances, man. You want me to off her, since you scare to." Jy was just talking shit. He wasn't gonna do nothing for real.

"Naw I got this son. I appreciate the offer though."

Even though Jy was a small time dealer in the 'hood, he wasn't the one for confrontation. Like myself, he had matured a lot over the years since I'd known him, and it just wasn't his style to "off" anyone. He was more likely to get someone else to do it first.

I remember the day we met at Dickie's. Off top, he was trying to get me in on a drug partnership with him. The job was used to cover up for the drug money he made. Back then he controlled most of the Southside drug action.

I used to sell here and there for a little extra cash myself, nothing heavy just a little weed. After my brother served two years in jail for selling heroin, I decided to get myself together and do the legal thing. I was determined not to go down for the same exact thing, so I happily declined Jy's offer. He kept trying to convince me for about a year or so, before he finally gave up.

Eventually, Jy decided to slow down on his of street pharmaceutical business, to live a more positive lifestyle. After one too many "close ones" and run ins with the cops, he decided it was safer to take it easy. I guess I'd influenced him more than he had influenced me over the years.

"A'ight, man. So what you gonna do? You know Fefe not finished. She gonna try to do something else to get at you."
"I don't know. The po-lice told us they connected her to the dead chicken incident. Said she would get a harassment charge, and be arrested soon."
"Uh-huh, whateva. You know they ain't doin' nothing for real. Ok, let's just say they do. What she gonna get? A few months in jail if that. Then what she gonna do when she get out? You know the answer to that one. I'm telling you kid, you better get her before she gets you. Survival of the fittest."
"I know. I just don't want things to get any worse. My girl's pregnant. I gotta' protect her you know."
"Yeah that's exactly why you gotta' get rid of Fefe- literally."
"And how am I supposed to protect her and my son in jail? I wanna be there when he's born."
"Son? So it's gonna be a boy?"
"Probably. I don't know yet. You know my sperm ain't making no sissies." We both laughed, which lightened up the mood for a moment.
"But on the real son, you won't have a son or daughter if you leave it up to five 'O to handle. You know what I'm saying." He said in a serious tone. "Fefe's probably gonna keep at Khaila hoping she'll get upset enough to lose the baby. She probably thinking with the baby out the picture you won't want to be with Khaila, you'll want her instead. Sick thinking, but you must think like a psycho to understand one. You know what I mean?"
I didn't wanna hear it, but he made a lot of sense when I really thought about it.
"Don't say that shit."
"'I'm for real, man. My cousin went through the same shit last year. The other woman he was messing around with, stabbed his pregnant girlfriend in the side. They a'ight now, but the girlfriend and her baby could have died." I couldn't respond for a minute, too deep in thought to speak.
"Well....I ain't gonna let that shit happen. You right it could happen, it could escalate into a very ugly situation, but I'm not gonna let it get to that point."
After riding around talking for close to two hours, Jy was ready to drop me off at my apartment. It was time for me to face an angry preg-

nant woman.

"Man, I ain't ready to go in there, me and my girl are beefin'."

"Why?"

"Oh...I forgot to tell you what happened. We got into an all out brawl before you picked me up. I was pissed she didn't tell me what had happened with Fefe this afternoon. She was trying to hide shit from me. I wouldn't even know about it if it wasn't for her nosy ass friend next door." I pulled out a philly and lit it. I only smoked when I got stressed. I had gave up weed years ago, and phillies were my only outlet.

"So I know she gonna give me the silent treatment tonight. That shit be getting on my damn nerves, son."

"Y'all gotta' squash all this shit man. You letting Fefe, Titi, or whateva her name is win. She want y'all to break up over this."

"Yeah, you right, you right. Let's do something before I go home. I gotta' get my head straight first."

"What you trying to do D'? You know I gotta' make runs tonight."

I knew exactly what he meant by runs. He either had drug transactions to make, or he needed to re-up on his product.

I mean, even though I no longer approved of what he did for a living, I wasn't gonna stop being his friend because of it. I just constantly tried to get him to change his ways instead.

"Oh you gotta' make runs..."

I started telling him about a job opening at Dickie's and some other spots 'round town, but he wasn't really interested.

He said, "A'ight man I'll check 'em out....I'll call 'em tomorrow......"

'Tomorrow' would never come for that nigga. The drug money just came too fast and too plentiful for him to give it up. It was like more addictive than the drugs he sold.

Jy told me on many occasions that he made more money in a couple months than most could make in a year working a regular 9-5. How could I argue with that kind of logic? It did make financial sense to work easy and make a lot of money, than bust your ass for a few bucks here and there.

Deep down I knew he was referring my situation. But I knew the repercussions of the fast money, and would remind him about it all the time. The jail time, the violence, you know all the stuff that came along with the game. He didn't care about any repercussions. So I decided to stop beating my head against the wall talking about it.

He'd say stuff like, "Man, you know I done time before, but now I got enough money to bail myself out of jail." He laughed. "Shit, most of the cops that arrest me, eventually make investments on my business. You know those cats not gonna take me in. Shit, remember I used to run most of the Southside back in the day, but I got enough money now to chill a little now. Maybe I'll do like you and settle down. Get me a girl or something one day."

I decided to change the subject about the job thing, a discussion that had grown old over the years. It usually led to a dead end argument that got us both nowhere. He just wasn't ready. Simple as that.

I told him, "A'ight, man. Let's hit the seafood spot over on Hull Street before you go on one of your runs. They got bum fish and chips."

Jy didn't look too enthusiastic about going out in public. He never did. I knew that deep down, he knew he was in a dangerous business and he couldn't just hang out anywhere. Being that he used to control much of that area back in the day, the last place he wanted to hang was on Hull Street.

He said, "Let's hit Gary's over there where you stay at. It's closer. It's almost eight now, I gotta' drop you off around ten, a'ight?"

"That's cool. I just gotta' get out for a minute. I need to relax, get a drink or something to release a little stress. Fefe really took me there tonight man, and you know Khaila is gonna take me there tonight too." We laughed.

He joked, "Well shit then maybe you need to go home then, since you trying to release some stress. That make up sex is the best sex."

We drove over to Gary's, for food and drinks. I even played a game of dominoes with the old heads. I really had the chance to take it easy for a while. Jy on the other hand, was looking at his watch every other second. I brought him two drinks, a Hennessey and coke and a shot of brandy to help loosen him up.

He was really feeling it, probably feeling it too much at that point. He started talking stupid like he usually did when he got toasted. He was the type to get real pitiful and depressed when he drank. He was beginning to be a real downer. Talking 'bout, "man, I'mma change, I promise…I'mma get my life together…." Crying and shit. Confessing like I was his man or something. I ain't gonna lie I was embarrassed. People was like, "what's wrong with that nigga."

I saw a spades game going across the room, and they needed two more players to replace the two losers that left the table. I talked Jy into playing a hand or two. We had them muthafuckas set! We beat 'em so bad they wasn't even trying to play for money.

\*\*\*

Jy dropped me off at the crib, and was out. He had to hit the spot at a certain time I guess. I took my time going in the apartment. I had to get ready for the Khaila's attitude. When I finally did get to the door, I couldn't get in. I was able to turn the deadbolt, but the chain lock was on too. Why was she double locking the door? To get under my skin, that's why!

"I can't believe this shit!" I said out loud. I banged on the door for about fifteen minutes, 'til Khaila finally opened the door.

She was half asleep. She mumbled through the door, "What?"

"Let me in Khai. Stop playing."

"I ain't playing. You ain't coming in here with same nasty attitude you left with earlier. I'll change the goddamn locks you keep playing with me, D.C."

"Ok, ok. I'm sorry, Khai. Let me in please."

"Where you been half the night? You gonna storm your ass out the door, and don't say shit!"

"I was wrong. Let me come in and we can talk about it."

I was hoping she would open the door, 'cause I felt real crazy talking to her through the chained door opening.

She opened the door and let me in, but she turned her back to go upstairs to bed.

I said, "Let's talk about this."

Most times, she was the one who wanted to do the talking and I wanted to do the forgetting. I learned that sleep overruled everything when you're pregnant. That's lesson #1- never wake a pregnant woman. They would rather sleep through a house fire than be disturbed from their sleep.

"I'm tired D.C. I'll talk to you later." She said in a slurred voice.

Khaila then walked blindly up the stairs eyes still half closed, and climbed in bed. Some kinda way she does that without tripping.

I was like, "See, that's what's wrong. You get mad and wanna give me the silent treatment."

"Whateva D.C.!" She turned her back to me. I tapped her gently on the shoulder and she turned around like she was ready to attack.

"Stop! Shit, D.C. I'm trying to get some sleep!" I held her from the back, she didn't resist. Could feel the round hardness of her stomach. My kid was growing inside her.

I calmly told her, "A'ight baby I'm sorry for walking out. The whole situation just had me buggin' for real. I went to Fefe's house and set her ass straight. She shouldn't be bothering you at least for a while." If she do, let me know. Don't hide nothing from me, ok?" Just page me."

Khaila told me, "I didn't tell you, 'cause I ain't want no more problems."

"I know. You was trying to keep me from killing the bitch."

"She is really crazy D.C. Don't do nothing to her though. I just want this to be over."

"Don't worry your head about it. A'ight?"

She nodded her head in agreement and turned over to sleep. We cuddled the rest of the night. I held her tight even while we slept. Sex crossed my mind, but I was satisfied with just holding her close to me.

## Chapter 11
## *Khaila*

D.C. woke up first, while I snoozed a few extra minutes. Fortunately I still had time off from work, although our vacation plans didn't pan out. Our trip to Virginia Beach wasn't gonna happen, especially since D.C. couldn't get the days off as expected, and I had a damaged car to be concerned with.

D.C. didn't have to work until noon, so he decided to treat me to breakfast at Chicken and Waffle Hut. I guess it was his peace offering for how he acted the night before.

I had just started on my pecan waffle and eggs platter, when my cell phone started singing a reggae tune. It was my sister. *Damn!* I really didn't feel like talking to her, but she would keep blowing up my cell if I didn't answer. I rarely talked to her 'cause she was ghetto-fabulous with a capital "G". Always had some drama going. Always.

Tracie blared in my ear, "Ho, why you ain't tell me 'bout the baby? I had to hear it from mama."

"I was trying to call you but I couldn't get through to you. So I asked mama to tell you, since I couldn't get you." I was never a good liar and Tracie knew me all too well.

She said, "Mmmhmm....whateva bitch. Anyway, what you doin'?"

"I'm eating. Let me call you back," I said in a hurry. She was starting to get on my nerves.

"A'ight then. I'm out. By the way, congratulations."

"Thanks, Tracie."

"Oh, I almost forgot. Can I be your baby Godmother?"

Was she kidding?

I had to get her delusional self off my phone in a hurry. I told her, "I'll talk to you about that later. Ok?"

"A'ight then. I'm gone." We finally hung up after the longest two minute call ever.

I didn't like lying, but I found myself lying to Tracie all the time. I had no intentions of talking to her later about being the Godmother of my child. I would ditch and dodge her everyday if I had to. She'd be pissed if she knew I had already made Shante the Godmother.

D.C. was eating his breakfast and barely heard my phone call. I stared down at my food, which I hadn't even touched yet.

"D.C., you know Tracie had the nerve to ask me if she could be the baby's Godmother."

"For real? Ha-ha, now that's funny." He laughed.

"Yeah, I ain't 'bout to make that hooch my baby's Godmother. I don't care if she is my sister. Shante's gonna be the Godmother. She's more responsible and sensible."

"Oh, really? Do I get a choice in the matter?" D.C. asked jokingly. "Ain't she going away to school soon though?"

"Yeah, really. I get to choose the Godmother. Shante is thinking about going to college in Maryland, but she'll still be there if we need her. She already agreed to be Godmother." I waited for his reaction. He didn't get upset like I thought he would. He just listened.

I continued, "You get to pick the godfather. I trust you to do that, you should trust my judgment too."

"Oh so, I can pick Jy right?"

"Hell naw, D.C.! You must be crazy. He'll have my son hanging on the corner with him everyday. Grooming my son to be a drug dealer someday. Oh hell no, I don't think so."

"Son? So the baby's gonna be a son like I thought, huh?"

"I don't know. I guess I want it to be a son too."

"Aw, that's sweet. We both want a boy. I can't wait 'til he gets here."

"A'ight now don't be shocked if the baby's a girl now."

"I would love her just the same. And when she got old enough, I could scare off all her boyfriends."

"Whateva, boy!" I playfully slapped his knee under the table, and he grabbed me around the waist. We kept playing back and forth for a while. You just can't take Black folks nowhere!

# Chapter 12
## *Cocoa*

A month or so passed by, and though I was concerned about Khaila's latest drama, I still had problems of my own to tend to. I had had five counseling sessions with my new therapist, Dr. Barker. At first, I felt kinda funny about going to a 57-year-old, white man to discuss my private business. Then I had to admit to myself he was really good at what he did, and my progress was amazing in such a short period of time. He was definitely the best no money could buy.

Dr. Barker was a licensed therapist who had been working in his field for over ten years. He was also a full-time college professor, teaching psychology courses. Part-time, he offered his services for free as part of an externship for school. He was working on his Ph.D. in Psychology, and told me he only had a year left in his studies. That was where I wanted to be in my life —successful and paid.

My therapist was very professional, but also a straight-from-the-hip kinda guy. He told it like it was, and I liked that. At the same time he listened very well, and understood how I felt about things. Sometimes he'd say what I was thinking before I could actually say it myself. He was harsh at times, but he always got to the heart of my problem by the end of each session. Unlike many therapists I had seen and heard about on TV., he wasn't into wasting a lot of time talking about your childhood and shit. He dealt with what was going on in the present, which made good sense to me.

I did my part as well. Dr. Barker told me in the first session that I would have to put in what I wanted to get out of therapy. It would require a lot of hard work for any real results. He told me he was not going to sit there and just listen or tell me what to do every session. I was the only one who would set my goals and work to achieve them. He would only be my "guide," as he put it, to help me get to the destination I wanted to be.

My first session was unbelievable. I looked at that man like he had the word STUPID written in bold red letters across his pale, white face. He told me off top I was being "resistant", and until I let down my guard, he could not help me. I was like, w*hoa, he really means business!*

In five weeks I had changed a lot of my negative thinking, and my whole attitude in general. I had discovered that I wanted to do something productive with my life, so I told Dr. Barker how I felt. He told me to bring in a list of three goals to accomplish as my first homework assignment.

The following week, I came in ready to discuss my list: (1) to start a career, (2) get more education, (3) learn to better care for my family and spend more quality time with them. I had even added some insignificant goals, which had nothing to do with nothing. My list was too long, with like a page of information. We decided to start with the first three goals on my list, as first assigned by Dr. Barker.

During the second session, we talked about how I would achieve the goals by developing "reasonable objectives." Of course, at first I made up excuses for why I couldn't achieve the goals, like I usually did with Reese. Dr. Barker let me put myself down for about fifteen minutes, allowing me to hear what I was saying. The only thing he did was listen, and confirm what I said by repeating it back to me.

He said stuff like, "So what I'm hearing is that you feel you can not go to school now because of the kids....," and "Cocoa, you seem to have a lot on your shoulders with caring for your family....how does that make you feel?" I mean the man was good with the psychobabble, I gotta' admit.

After my fifteen minute pity party, Dr. Barker shut it down like prison gates. He told me to stop making excuses and start building my confidence to achieve my goals. Otherwise there was no point in coming to therapy. He was serious about helping me, so I had to get serious too. By the third session I had my list of "reasonable objectives" to go with the "attainable goals." My plan was all set in motion. Well at least I thought so.

At home things weren't going so smoothly. Reese, who was once for me getting the help, was now dead set against it. All of a sudden he felt neglected, and he couldn't see any good coming from the counseling.

At first, I felt comfortable telling Reese about my sessions, but by the third session, Reese started to ignore me, and by the fifth, he was starting arguments on purpose. Instead of counseling bringing us closer together it was steadily pulling us apart. I thought about giving up the sessions, but that would be unfair to me. I mean whether he saw the progress or not, I saw it and felt I really deserved it. It wasn't just about the family, but it was about me getting my shit together.

Dr. Barker helped me to realize I couldn't help the family without first helping myself. I was finally feeling good about myself, and hopeful about my future. My mantra after every session was, *forget Reese, I'm gonna get mine*, while I soaked in a hot milk bath.

It got to the point where that muthafucka refused to pick me up from my counseling sessions, when he was obviously available to do it. I would have to ride the damn bus home every week in the dark.

One night I got home a little later than usual from my session. I think I missed my bus or something because our session went over by a few minutes. Even though I missed the bus, I was smiling from ear to ear when I got home. I had learned so much and I felt good about it. I was the only one in the house who shared my enthusiasm.

"Reese, where you at baby?"

He responded bitterly, "In the kitchen."

He had the day off, so he was probably pissed about having to watch the children again. My mom watched them the other days of the week, so what was he stressing for?

"At my session today, I worked on my life goals, and I decided I want to go back to college."

I had attended Richmond Community College for one semester three years ago. It was during the same time I got pregnant with my first child, Shayla. I had to drop out because I knew with child-care, baby food, diapers, clothes, and a ton of other things, I could not afford to go to school. It had been my plan to go back, but then my dad died and my second kid Reese Jr. was on the way. There was no way I could handle any extra stress, nor did I have the time. Finally after three years, I had the time and energy to really dedicate to finishing school.

"Cocoa, don't start talking that damn school shit again. Who's gonna watch the kids?"

I had that part covered. I was lucky my mom agreed to baby-sit for a few extra dollars here and there when I needed her. That was a pretty good deal, considering some grandmothers charge top dollar to watch they own damn grandkids!

My only problem was finding a part-time job to help pay for some of my school expenses. The government would pay for most of it through grants, but not all, and I also needed books, which didn't cost that much.

I explained, "My mama said she'd watch 'em for me most days. She only works a few hours a week. We can get a sitter for the few times she can't watch 'em."

"Who and what money is paying for a sitter?" He was heated. "And you all of a sudden got energy for counseling, a new job, and school. At first you couldn't even get off yo' ass and clean the house or take care of the kids!"

Oh so he was gonna go there with me. I kept my composure so I could get him to understand my view.

He continued bitching, "...and you gonna talk to mom about this shit before me, your husband. Now you want me...."

I cut him off. "To answer your question, I'll get the girl across the street to watch the kids for cheap. Just on the days my mama is busy."

"The girl across the street? Ain't she a crackhead?"

He was really getting on my last nerve. Did he really think I was sending the kids to a crackhead?

"No, Reese. That's Sandy. I'm talking about the Black-Asian girl that lives across the street, Kamerah. She drives the Gold Acura Legend. You know her. She usually speaks to us on the stoop and is always so friendly."

"We don't even know her Cocoa! Now come on. This is not gonna work. Just be real about it. You're just being silly." I was past through with his attitude. Disgusted is a better word to describe how I was feeling.

"Or is it that you don't want it to work Reese?"

"It's not that."

He was getting defensive. Boxed in a corner. He wouldn't admit it but he knew I was right about him not wanting it to work out for me. Little Shayla interrupted, "Stop!!!! Stop yelling ma!" She ran up to us crying, pleading for our argument to end.

"Ma's sorry, Sweet Pea."

She loved it when I called her Sweet Pea. It was her nickname, like Lil' Reesie was Reese Jr's nickname. I picked her up and gently place her in the playpen beside her brother.

Reese told me, "Cocoa, we need to talk about this later."

"Fine. Let me get the kids ready for bed then." I said nastily.

I showed him I could have attitude to match his.

Twenty minutes later, after the kids' bath and bedtime story, they were put to bed. I dreaded going to my own bedroom, but went anyway. I knew what was waiting for me on the other side of the door.

I said, "I'm all yours Reese. Ready for our next argument."

He ignored my sarcastic comment and asked calmly, "How are you gonna do all this stuff and take care of your family?"

"I told you before I'll have a sitter watch them while I am in school. Shayla's almost ready for the head start program, so that will help lower the daycare costs. I'll pay for all of it, ok?"

"The kids won't be able to adjust to not hardly seeing you. While you're enjoying school and your new job, I hope you know our kids will be raised without their mother."

He sounded real dumb. I said to myself, *they were without a damn father while you were working overtime every other night too.*

"No, Reese. It's yo' ass who can't adjust! The kids will be going off to school themselves pretty soon, so they will have to get used to me not being around all the time." Then I got real slick at the end, "They already used to not having their daddy around most of the time!"

Reese couldn't say shit. There was a long uncomfortable silence between us. He opened the paper to avoid dealing with the issue at hand, after he was the one who started it. I burned a hole right through him. After a few minutes of ignoring my evil looks, he finally spoke.

"It's cool. It'll probably be good for you. Don't let me hold you back from you dreams. I have to admit I was a little insecure about your plans, and I felt left out of your decision. That's why I was so dead set against it. You're right, it's not about the kids, it's about me and you."

For Reese to admit he was wrong was a big step. He didn't do that too often.

I believe he felt if I became too successful with my career and educational goals, it would make him feel less of a man. I'm sure he was also insecure, thinking that I wouldn't want him anymore. He felt I'd want another man who would have a high paying career and college education to match mine.

Reese only had a high school diploma, and I only had a semester of college. So to him we were equals. My going to school would all of a sudden change things. Dr. Barker warned me that my husband would probably be resistant about the change going on with me. I didn't believe him at first, but I learned he was right.

I said, "If you think about it honey, it would be good for the family. It means more money for our household. It could also mean we'll be able to move to the suburbs, get a real nice house and car. And finally get our credit straight too."

I joked about our credit 'cause it was past tore up. We probably had a −200 credit score, and I'm not sure if they actually go that low!

"Mm-hmm, we'll see." He said sounding quite depressed and defeated. He had lost our battle of wits.

## *Reese*

I thought for a minute about what my wife was saying and what it would mean. Only negative thoughts flooded my mind. She would probably meet a new professional man while she was going to school, one who could possibly care for her and the kids way better than myself.

While I dwelled in the land of self-pity, Cocoa blabbed on about her plans, "...and tomorrow, I'll go out and look for a part-time job. It'll have to be something on the busline....I'll just hit Broad Street and fill out as many applications as I can 'til I get tired."

"I gotta' be to work by eight in the morning, just drop me off and take the car."

"Really?" She squealed with excitement.

"Yeah."

She got up and kissed me on the cheek. She couldn't believe her ears, and I couldn't believe the words that were coming from my mouth. Offering the car would mean helping out her cause.

"Thank you baby." She hugged me tight. "You know I'd be worn out with all that walking up and down Broad."

"I'm tired, I'm going to sleep."

I turned my back to her with a little bit of an attitude. I guess she picked up on it, because she started squeezing me from the back. I tried to ignore her affections, but I couldn't ignore her once she kissed my neck- my spot. That was it for me.

"Why you messing with me woman, you know we gotta' get up early tomorrow."

"It's only ten pm. Reese, we got time." She said that real sexy like. It was about to be on. I took off my clothes in anticipation of some good loving. She did the same. Then….the goddamn phone rung, *who the hell is calling us this late.* Everybody we knew, knew not to call past nine, because of my work schedule and the kids' bedtime.

I answered the phone even though I didn't want to, mostly out of curiosity. I mumbled, "Hello."

"Hello. May I speak to Cocoa please?" It sounded like a white man.

"Who is this?" I replied with some attitude in my voice.

He replied, "Stan. Stan Barker."

I said, "Hold on."

I handed her the phone and gave her a suspicious glare. Then she got up and went to the bathroom with the phone. Like it was a private call. I said to myself, a*w hell naw, we don't have private calls around this muthafucka. Who the fuck is Stan?*

After she finished talking, she came out the bathroom to a tension-filled room. It was so thick you could cut it with a knife. I didn't say anything at first. She just looked at me, didn't say shit about who was on the phone.

"Who was that Cocoa? And why he calling here so late?"

I let my emotions rule over commonsense. I was so jealous and upset, I didn't think about what Cocoa had told me before. Her therapist's name was Barker.

"It was my therapist Reese don't you remember me telling you his name?"

"Oh, I guess I got thrown off by the first name. Y'all on a first name basis now, huh?" I said sarcastically.

"Yeah, as a matter-of-fact we do use first names, so we aren't so formal in our sessions. I do share my personal experiences with him you know."

"I don't know why you need a therapist anyway. You can talk to me, instead of some ole white man."

The temperature went up a few degrees in the room. She was fuming mad.

"No I can't! You don't even listen to me when I tell you about my sessions, Reese!"

She used some of her counselor's advice, and left the room. He had told her to walk away from arguments and just come back when things were a little calmer. She got dressed and went outside to smoke a cigarette.

I didn't like her smoking in the house with the kids. I hated the smoke myself, especially since I didn't smoke cigarettes anymore. I only drank occasionally on some weekends when I went out with the boys.

While she got herself together, I had decided to get a late night snack before going to bed. Another bad habit I'd picked up working the late shift. Eating was my way of unwinding too, like Cocoa's cigarette habit was for her.

## *Cocoa*

I went outside for a smoke to keep from strangling my husband to death. It was quiet outside, and there was a real nice cool breeze blowing across my face. I was in a zone for a minute, calm, cool, and collected, until I heard a car screech around the corner.

The car pulled to the curb right in front of Khaila and D.C.'s apartment. The driver looked around to see who was around. When she spotted me, she sped off. I didn't know who the woman was, but I remembered what Khaila had told me before. I wondered if the woman could have been Fefe. Who ever it was I knew she had something up her sleeve. She looked and acted too shady. So I went inside to call Khaila on the kitchen phone. Reese caught me, while stuffing his face with a tuna sandwich.

"You calling your boyfriend back?" He was acting so damned stupid. "Don't mind me, I'll be out of your way in a minute."

"I'm not calling another man, Reese."

"Then why you hesitating to make your phone call?"

"It's personal."

I didn't wanna tell him about it, because he would just say I was gossiping again. That wasn't it. I was really concerned for Khaila and her baby.

"Yeah....uh-huh....personal." He laughed and left the kitchen. I made the call to alert Khaila of what I'd seen.

## *Reese*

When I came upstairs to the bedroom, I couldn't even finish my sandwich. I was so busy trying to figure out who Cocoa was calling on the phone. In my mind, my worst nightmare was coming true. My wife was having an affair. I sat there hurt and angry at the same time, when a thought came to mind.

*Two can play that game. Old Wanda at work has been trying to holla at me for a while now. Maybe I'll give her a try. Cocoa's not taking care of business, not the way she should. Maybe it's time for someone else to fill her shoes.*

## Chapter 13
*Reese*

The alarm sounded, and we both woke up at the same time. I was sleeping on the floor, and Cocoa was still lying in bed. I refused to sleep next to Cocoa the night before. I guess it was my way of getting revenge. Cocoa sat up in bed looking for me, just realizing I wasn't sleeping next to her.

"Reese! Reese! Where you at?" She screamed my name out like I'd been abducted by aliens or something. My wife was always so loud, too loud especially for six in the morning. That only added to my irritation and disgust I felt for her.

"I'm right here." I mumbled half asleep, half awoke. I sat up slowly, rubbing my aching back.

"Why you on the floor Reese?" She glared down at me like I had lost my mind.

"I was leaving room for your new man to climb in with you."

"What are you talking about? I told you I talked to my counselor last night. You have no reason to be mad with me."

"Why he calling you late at night?"

"Reese, it was a little after ten, come on now."

"No professional is gonna call your house that late. Not even the worrisome ass telemarketers gonna call at ten."

"I guess he figured I would be up...." She was sounding more and more suspicious as she talked. "....we were discussing important things like our timeline for counseling.....and other stuff I needed to have ready for our next appointment....." She rambled on for a few minutes by herself. I didn't believe shit she was talking, and the more she talked the more she looked guilty to me. When she finished talking, I got up and sat next to her on the edge of the bed.

I said, "Well this is what I think. I think you and your counselor are getting too close. Counselors and clients aren't supposed to be buddy-buddy like you two. They have a professional relationship. What y'all gonna do, maintain contact after the counseling is over?"

She giggled, irritating me further, "What? You jealous, Reese? I don't want no damn old, white man. He's just there to help me, that's it."

"No Cocoa! I'm there for that!"

"Well, *you* didn't have time for me!"

That comment stung and she meant for it to sting. She kept repeating I wasn't there for her. Bullshit. I was there for her most of the time. I mean I have to admit I didn't always listen to her rambling about her sessions, but I listened when she was upset about stuff.

"Fuck it then! I'm getting ready for work, you do whatever."

"I'm looking for a job, Reese. That's it!"

I got up and slammed the bathroom door behind me. Fuming mad, I skinned my toe on the sink cabinet. She heard my painful moan through the door and laughed. Aw man, she was pissing me off so much, I can't even explain it with words. I got in the shower still preoccupied with our argument.

Under the warm water, I relaxed and thought about what she said. She was right. I was too busy to listen a lot of times. I thought about my insecurities. How I was trying to hold her back in her goals of school and a career. I thought about how I could not match her soon to be status. Then I started to get angry all over again.

I realized she was only focused on herself. She hadn't once mentioned me furthering my education and getting my life together. I wanted to get myself out of the dead end situation I was in as well. I had given up that dream years ago, because I felt it was just not possible to achieve them with my family responsibilities. I had to take care of them first. The family was always first in my life. It was usually second in Cocoa's.

I dried myself, and stepped out of the shower. I smelled a delicious food aroma in the air, and I instantly wanted to eat. After dressing I went downstairs to the kitchen in anticipation of having a good breakfast. Cocoa was serving the kids plate, but there was no plate ready for me.

I asked, "You making me a plate?"

She had the audacity to come back with, "You sleeping by yourself, you can cook for yourself."

I was sacrificing my sleep time and my car, so she could go job hunting and that was what she had to say to me.

She continued to rationalize her nastiness, "And I don't have the time anyway. I have to get the kids ready for my mom to watch them. She'll be here in a minute. I gotta' get in the shower myself and be ready by seven-thirty to get you to work on time."

"You made the kids' food, you could have cooked something for me as well. It would have only been a couple extra minutes to fry some eggs and bacon."

"I didn't even cook for myself. It would take twice as long for me to cook for all of us." She said all that bullshit with a straight face.

"I guess you're saving all your good cooking for your new man then." I said sarcastically.

"Whateva, Reese. I gotta' go wake the kids."

She got them up and came down with them a few minutes later.

Shayla asked, "Ma? Ma? Why daddy yelling at you ma'? Did you do something bad?"

It broke my heart to hear my little girl concerned about me yelling at her mother. It's amazing what young children hear and understand.

"No, sweetie. He wasn't yelling at me, he was just talking real loud."

I chimed in, "Yeah, you know how you and Lil' Reesie always talk loud to each other."

I felt bad lying to my little girl, but it was for her own good not to know what was really going on. Our scam worked, 'cause she forgot all about our yelling and move on to the food. I was glad she was only three years old, and was so easily distracted.

"Ma? Ma? What we gon' eat ma?"

"You and Reesie gonna have pancakes, bacon, eggs. Y'all hurry up and eat. Ma and daddy gotta' leave soon. Grandma gonna come over to visit you in a minute." Cocoa said in her sweetest voice.

"Yeaaay!" They both screamed in unison, and did the happy dance while they ate.

They loved it when their grandma came to visit. She took them to Kid's Playland and Mickey D's when they were "good." Which was almost every time she visited, so they knew the deal. Cocoa's mother spoiled our kids something terrible. It was nice though, because we seldom had time to go out as a family, with my long work hours.

My mother on the other hand seldom helped out. With her old drinking habit and new gambling habit, I really didn't want her to be involved in the family. She'd come by every now then, asking for money I didn't have to give her. She was best kept at a distance for occasional holiday visits only.

## *Cocoa*

I was already to leave for my job search, when there was a loud knock at the door. We all assumed it was my mother. I went to the door, peeped through the peephole, and I was surprised to see a strange woman instead. I opened the door to a large, stout woman, probably in her late forties, wearing what I call skank wear. She had on tight black stretch pants, hooker shoes, and a low cut leopard-designed top. She apparently had no real sense of style, and was in my opinion too damned old to be dressed like that.

I opened the door to find out what she wanted..

"Reese there?" She said real nasty, like she had a problem with me.

I responded, "Who are you?"

She shot back at me gritting her teeth, "I work with Reese. He called me and told me to pick him up for work. I told him I ain't have no problem with that. I live right down the street."

"He did what!!!"

I couldn't believe it. I didn't know what the hell she was talking about. Why would he do that when I was supposed to be taking him to work and keeping the car?

"That's what he told me lady!"

"Hold on."

I closed the door in her face, and raced to the kitchen. Reese had left the kids eating the table. I found him in the upstairs bathroom shaving. I think he fled the scene, 'cause he knew he was in trouble.

"You told some woman to pick you up for work? You taking rides to work now? I thought I was taking you to work today." My voice trembled, I was about to cry, but I was determined not to.

Reese was silent for a few seconds. I guess trying to get his lie together. After all his accusing, he had the nerve to have some strange woman knocking on my door looking for him. I knew he had set it up as a form of revenge, because he thought the damned counselor and I were lovers! Insanity.

"Oh...I forgot." He nonchalantly replied.

"You forgot? How you gonna offer me the car to look for a job, and then turn around and call another woman to pick you up and take you to work? I bet you called her after our argument, didn't you?"

"I told you, I forgot that I called her about the ride. Yeah I called after the argument, 'cause I figured you would be too *busy looking for a job*. I was gonna call her back to cancel, but I forgot."

"A'ight, so you wanna play the revenge game, huh? Ok, that's fine with me!"

"I'll get rid of her Cocoa."

He scrambled to get out the bathroom door. I blocked his pathway. Pointing in his face I said, "Naw go 'head with her. I don't even want to borrow yo' damn car now. Y'all can commute together or whateva. I'll catch the bus! That shit was real immature what you did. We been married for five years and you couldn't handle our issues no better than this!"

Before he knew it, I was gone without a trace. I whipped around and stormed down the stairs. I passed the kids, and didn't even give them their usual goodbye kiss. I passed my mother who came for the kids, probably confused as hell. I passed the hoochie waiting at the door, didn't even say a word. I went down the block to the bus stop, and I looked back to see what was going on. I could see him and the hoochie getting into his car. He'd taken my advice, they were commuting to work together like I suggested, and who knows what else. I guess that smart comment had backfired in my face.

Reese cruised passed the bus stop with a smirk on his face. The woman was in the passenger seat applying lipstick in the mirror. She never looked my way. It was obvious her ugly ass needed all the makeup she could get. She damned sho' needed it!

# **Chapter 14**
## *Cocoa*

By the time I caught the bus I calmed down a little, but I was still fuming. With all of the confusion, I forgot my resume' at home, tore my stockings up, and let's just say my hair was way past repair. My first stop was at the Midtown Inn on Broad Street I was so stressed out I couldn't fill out the first application right. I had to ask for another application which took me about fifteen minutes to complete. I wanted to be more prepared, because sometimes employers interview and hire on the spot. It had become obvious to me that I probably wouldn't be hired that day. Not only did I look like shit, but my attitude was nasty as hell too. I could feel it, but I couldn't change it.

I decided to go to the restroom before I turned in the second application. I fixed up my hair, and put on a little make-up. I took off the torn stockings and lotioned up my long, coffee-colored legs. Sexy legs can be assets on the job interview.

I turned in my application to the receptionist and requested to speak to the manager. She told me the manager was busy, and suggested I try calling him after two in the afternoon. I nodded and left without hesitation. I didn't have time to waste.

I proceeded with my search on the Broad St. bus line. I hit at least nine or ten businesses downtown. I had to apply for whatever positions were available, jobs like housekeeper, custodian, dishwasher, and cashier. I applied for positions with flexible, part-time hours. There would be no interviews on the spot like had I expected.

After several hours of walking up and down Broad Street, I was about to give up, and throw in the towel for the day. I staggered my tired ass over to the nearest bus stop bench. When I sat down I looked diagonally across the street and saw Jackson Loan and Trust. I walked closer and saw a Help Wanted sign in the window for a store clerk position. I figured I had a shot since I had a little retail experience from back in the day. It was worth a try. I thought about what Dr. Barker said at one of my counseling sessions. He said, "When you go out for that job, make sure you be assertive, think positive, and hold your head up high. Confidence must be coming from your pores." Before I went inside the pawn shop, I told myself, *I'm gonna to get this job.* I pepped up and put on my fake I'll-say-anything-to-get-this-job persona.

The older, white man inside appeared to be more worn out than I was. I was thinking, *this man really needs my help bad.* I guess the stress of the job had worn away his hair as well. He only had a few strands of hair in the back of his head that was too short to swoop to the front of his head. Why do white people just refuse to go bald? I think it's sexy, especially on Black men.

I greeted the man, "Good Evening, sir. I'm Cofina Harris. I am here to inquire about the job opening for store clerk."

"Hello, Mrs. Harris. I'm Todd Davis, the store manager. Yes, we are still desperately hiring for the store clerk position. Right now, I'm running everything in this store, literally by myself, twelve sometimes fourteen hours a day. I do all the managerial stuff, bookkeeping, administrative records, inventory, plus many store clerk duties." He paused while he rubbed his temples. He looked really pitiful.

He continued, "I have an evening store clerk who helps out after five, but I need help during the day as well. Do you have any retail experience?"

"Yes, sir I do. I worked at Klein Mart as lead cashier for a little over two years, from 2000-2002. As lead cashier I was familiar with cashiering, stocking, pricing, and I even helped out with inventory and other sales duties."

"That's nice, Mrs. Harris. Really nice. It seems that you are qualified for the position available. Mrs. Harris, please fill out this application, and then we can discuss the job duties further." As he passed me the job application, I realized two apparent facts: one, I was obviously hired, and two, my new boss was obviously desperate for help. He didn't even ask me about recent job experience. The only job experience I mentioned was from almost two years before. I was happy just the same, and it was impossible for me to hide how overjoyed I felt about the job offer.

I eagerly took the application, and said, "Thank you, I really appreciate the opportunity."

I was really laying it on thick. I was willing to say whatever I had to say in order to get what I needed and wanted. In the words of my father's immortal hero, Malcolm X, *by any means necessary.* Even though I was past exhausted, I was gonna do well during the formal interview. I knew I had the job in the bag. All I really needed was a little faith and a lot of confidence to win over my soon-to-be boss.

After I finished the application, he gave me some other forms to fill out like tax forms. That confirmed that I really had the job. I didn't wanna make assumptions you know, and get my feelings hurt, but I was sure at that point.

Mr. Davis reviewed the five or six forms I turned in, and then escorted me to his office for the interview. He asked me some hard questions, but I hung in there. I didn't let him see me sweat. I told him all the right things. His wide smile and constant nods let me know I was doing pretty good.

He left the room with my forms for about five minutes. Felt like it was longer. I was so nervous, I didn't know what to think. I even started doubting myself again, saying negative things to myself. *Wonder where he went? Why would he leave the room like that? I must've messed up something terrible for him to leave out like that. Probably trying to think of a reason not to hire me.* I must have looked real crazy when he came back to the room.

Mr. Davis had an unreadable facial expression. He took a long pause before speaking. *Here it goes- the rejection with a capital "R".* Who takes a pause before giving good news? No one I knew.

"You got the job, Mrs. Harris. My boss approved my recommendation to hire you. Now don't let me down." He winked at me.

"I won't let you down Mr. Davis." I smiled, feeling totally relieved.

I had actually gotten a new job with only one day of searching. Amazing.

"Come in on Friday at eight am., so I can show you the ropes. Although I'm sure you'll catch on fast with your qualifications. It'll probably be only a couple hours of training. Then you can start fresh next Monday, if you can start Monday."

"I'll be here Friday for training, and Monday to start. Thank you again, Mr. Davis."

"When you come in Friday make sure you bring your driver's license, social security card, or birth certificate. We arrange for criminal background checks and drug screenings, so you will have to be prepared to fill out a lot of paperwork. Dress casually on Friday also, because I will give you a tour of the stockroom, and other parts of the building. Hopefully, I can also show you the corporate offices in the West End. Do you have any questions, Mrs. Harris?"

"No, sir. I'm sure I'll have questions for you tomorrow, after I have had time to think."

He laughed, so I laughed too. "I guess I really threw you a curve ball today hiring you on the spot like that."

"Yeah, you did, but that was a good thing. I really needed this opportunity, and I'm happy it came through for me."

He smiled as he walked towards the door, and then said, "It's good to have you on board. Mrs. Harris."

"I'll be here Friday at eight. I'll see you then." I shook his hand and we said our goodbyes. I turned to leave out calmly, but I had to bust my ass to get to the bus stop in time for the next bus. It was colder than usual outside that night. I sat on the bench freezing. I guess Mr. Davis felt sorry for me, because he came out the store to catch me before the bus arrived.

"Mrs. Harris would you like a ride home?"

"No, sir. My bus is due to be here in a few minutes."

"It's getting dark out. You shouldn't be waiting for a bus this late. I mean, I understand you don't know me well, but you can trust me. I have no funny intentions, I just wanna make sure you get home safe."

I mean he was my new boss, and if he tried anything I'd pepper spray his ass real good and sue for sexual harassment. I decided to catch the ride home with Mr. Davis.

He quickly knocked down the wall I was getting ready to put up. He was such a friendly, down-to-earth kinda guy. He talked about the weather at first, but then moved on too more interesting topics. We discussed sports, he said he was a diehard Cowboys fan like me, and then we talked about the news we had both seen on Channel 8 the night before. Twenty-five minutes later I was pulling up to my apartment. I thanked Mr. Davis, and told him goodnight.

Reese still wasn't home yet. I was wondering what was going on with him and that hooch he left with earlier. I thought about calling, but I decided against it. It was his turn to feel unwanted, unappreciated, and unhappy like I had been feeling for months. I wasn't about to let him know I was concerned about the little games he played. I was gonna play like I could careless- careless about him, careless about his "friend", careless about his bullshit.

I decided to occupy my time so I didn't appear pressed when he came in from work at eleven-thirty. While I cleaned the kitchen, I listened to a little urban jazz and R & B on Smooth Soul 104. The kids were spending the night with my mom, so I just had to cook for myself. That was sure to piss off Reese. I chilled out on the couch with my late dinner and watched TV. Nothing was really on. The TV was watching me after about a half hour or so.

When I woke up it was one in the morning and Reese still wasn't home. I was starting to get upset. Not upset in the worried way, but a pissed like hell kinda way. I knew he was being spiteful, and I hated that shit. I called his phone, no answer. I'm boiling hot at this point. So I blew up his phone about 20 times in a row. Still no answer.

By two-thirty, Reese had finally strolled in drunk and loud. I could hear him messing around in the kitchen for a while looking for something to eat. You would think he would have gotten enough to eat while he was out getting drunk.

I was fuming.

He climbed the stairs about fifteen minutes later. He came in and laid beside me, assuming I was asleep. I let him get comfortable in his spot on the bed, before I laid into him good.

"So you out hanging out all night with your bitch, huh?"

"What? Don't question me after what I saw tonight."

"What you talking about Reese?" I was starting to feel uncomfortable. He was flipping things on me, so I didn't like where the conversation was headed.

"I saw you earlier when your man was dropping you off. You decided to start screwin' white men now, huh?"

"Reese what the hell…"

"I saw him drop you off. I was sitting in another car when you rolled through. I guess that's why you didn't realize I was watching you. I got off early tonight and was hanging out."

"You got nerve Reese! What about that bitch from this morning."

"That was a co-worker who was picking me up, so you could have the goddamn car to do your job hunting thing."

"Well that was my new boss dropping me off. He didn't want me riding the fuckin' bus home, which by the way I had to do this morning because of yo' ass."

"This shit is crazy. I'm going to take a shower and get in the bed. You can argue by yo' damn self." He said, as he took off his shirt and shoes.

I was at a loss for words, so I didn't say another word. I just laid there feeling hurt and frustrated. I had gotten the job I had been looking for and Reese could care less. He was too busy hanging after work with his female co-worker instead of me.

At that moment, I realized we were growing further and further apart. I was losing my husband trying so hard to find myself.

I didn't notice it until later, but there was a fresh red mark on his neck in plain view. He had even changed out of his work clothes. What a dumb ass! He must have thought I was stupid as he was. It was obvious he had been busy doing more than just hanging out after work.

When he finished his shower and came back to the room, I had almost drifted off to sleep. Reese came back with towel around his waist, dripping wet.

I tried to get my rest but he wasn't gonna let me. He stressed that the discussion was over before, but it wasn't really over.

"And you know what? I had offered your ass the car, but you didn't want it! I told you I forgot she was coming over to take me to work. I would have told her never mind and let you drop me off like we had planned, but you wanna run off and catch the bus instead. Now why would my wife choose to do that?"

"Why would my husband have a woman coming to the house offering him rides to work, when he has a goddamn car???"

"I called her last night so you would have the car to yourself for your job search. I figured you may not have time to get me to work. But then you woke up earlier than I thought, so I was gonna call her back and tell her never mind. She came over before I could. " Usually too much explaining means too many lies. His story just kept changing as he went along.

"You are trippin' Reese! I was really looking for a job and I found one, after walking up and down Broad Street for hours, I finally did. I start Friday with my orientation, and then Monday I start working."

"I was just trying to be considerate of your needs, so you could pursue *your dreams*." He was transparent enough to see through. Now he was concerned about my dreams!

"You could care less about my dreams Reese, you was just mad after last night, so you gonna call her over here to piss me off."

"Well, am I supposed to run this house while you're out pursuing your dreams? What about my dreams and the kids' dreams have you forgotten about them? "

"No, I told you the kids will be fine with my mama. They over there with her now, she be back with 'em in a few. Those few times she is not available, you could take care of them for me. I mean you are their damn daddy!" That hit a nerve.

"That's not right Cocoa." He sounded wounded.

"You not right Reese! That was wrong what you did this morning."

He walked out the room and went downstairs to sleep on the couch. That was fine with me. I didn't want his cheating ass sleeping next to me anyway. I felt relieved that I got out all the pent up anger from the course of the day and dropped it in his lap. I could finally rest.

## *Reese*

A couple hours later, around six am, there was a knock on the door. That aggravated me 'cause I had to be to work early that morning. I hadn't too long slipped off to sleep. Since Cocoa had pissed my off so bad, I had to watch a movie to fall asleep.

You won't believe who was at the door. I figured it was the kids' coming home from grandma's.

Wanda stood on my doorstep bold like it was her doorstep. I told her ass the night before to chill out on coming to my house. I opened the door with hesitation. I was determined to get rid of her before Cocoa woke up.

"What's up, Wanda?" You could hear the irritation in my voice. She motioned for me to come outside to talk with her. We stepped out to the curb.

"Hey."

"What you want Wanda?"

"I just wanted to see you. What's going on babe?"

"Nothing, it's six in the morning! I was asleep. My kids will be here soon, so you need to go."

"What about your wife?"

"She's upstairs asleep."

"Oh...so you wanna get some breakfast before work?"

"Did you hear me Wanda??? My kids coming home in a few. I gotta' fix them breakfast before I leave for work."

"Your wife is here, can't she do that?"

"Yeah...I guess."

I had been working on getting some of that brown sugar, instead of getting breakfast for real. Even though she was really a pain in the ass, I did find her sexy. Her face was a'ight, but the body was real tight. My conscious just wasn't there, and my sex drive was going into overdrive. I had my usual morning hard on too. I knew I wasn't gonna get none from Cocoa's evil ass, brown sugar was there throwing it at me.

"What we gonna do besides breakfast?" I said slyly.

"Whatever you wanna do, baby. We can call in sick and get a room if you like."

"Hold on a sec. I'll be back and let you know."

"A'ight I'll be in the car."

## *Cocoa*

My eyes had to be playing tricks on me. Reese and that hooch were getting in his car again, going who knows where to do who knows what. I screamed out, *oh, so he wanna play like that! I can't believe this shit! I got something for his ass when he gets back!*

When the kids came home, I fixed them some breakfast. After they finished, I let them watch their favorite cartoons in their room. Then I started packing up Reese's shit, stuffing his clothes in a duffle bag. I put his shoes and personal items in a trash bag. I threw all his stuff on the doorstep. I double locked the door, with the chain and deadbolt.

Reese didn't come home until that night in his work clothes like he had been working. It was about ten-thirty or so. I peeked outside for hours waiting for him to come home. He was on the front stoop, mouth hanging wide open. My first guess would be he was shocked to see his things on the porch stuffed in bags. I had never put him out before.

He tried to come in but the chain lock was on, and I guess he decided against breaking it off the hinges. So he just started banging on the door like he had lost it.

Then he yelled, "That's a'ight! I'll leave, but I want the rest of my shit first!"

Reese was loud enough to wake the kids. Which he did. I didn't want them to hear or see that, but he was getting the hell out of my house that night.

Shayla yelled from her room, "Ma, daddy outside!"

"I know baby. Go back to sleep baby."

"But Ma ..."

"But nothing Shayla. Do as you're told."

Lil' Reesie woke up with all the commotion and started crying. Shayla kept fussing, Lil Reesie kept crying, and Reese kept banging. It sounded like the Fourth of July up in there.

Eventually the knocking stopped. Reese left. Shayla and Lil' Reesie finally fell asleep after I read a bedtime story to them. We slept through the night without interruption.

The next morning I went along with business as usual, and got the kids up for breakfast. I wondered where Reese went that night, but I acted as if everything was normal in front of the kids. They sat patiently at the kitchen table waiting for their food.

They were used to their daddy going to work early and coming home late at night. Some days they didn't see him at all, so it wasn't a big deal that he wasn't there when they woke up.

Breakfast didn't go as planned. I burned the first batch of eggs, distracted by my thoughts. I started to cook them again, when there was a loud knock on the door. I turned off the stove and went to the door.

I could hear him yelling from the stoop, "Woman, you betta' open this damn door! This my goddamn house! I gotta' right to come in and get the rest of my shit!" Reese was drunk out of his mind. It wasn't like him to drink a lot especially in the morning. He probably was up drinking half the night with his new bitch. I knew he probably stayed there with her, since he had to stay somewhere that night.

He came in reeking of alcohol, looking a mess.

I asked, "So you want your shit?"

"If you want me out..."

"I don't want you out. I was just pissed. Why you leave out with your girlfriend, when you knew the kids were coming home? I was sleep, and you ain't leave no note or nothing Reese."

He slurred, "Well I'll do you a favor, and get out, since you wanna put my shit on the stoop. I got somewhere to stay."

"You gonna stay with that woman?"

He slurred, "Don't worry about where I'm gonna stay. You won't worried last night. I'm gonna be a'ight though. I'll come by to visit my kids."

"You leave and you won't be visiting no damn body."

"We'll see about that Cocoa!"

He stormed up the stairs to pack the rest of his things. He quickly put them in a trash bag without saying a word. The kids were screaming his name. He didn't respond he just kept going for the door. They knew something wasn't right.

I looked out the window to his car. There was the same hooch I'd seen twice before. I couldn't believe I was losing my husband to an old bitch. She was probably at least ten years older than I was.

I couldn't even finish breakfast for the kids. I just had to sit down a minute to have a good cry, which the kids noticed. They climbed out of their booster seats and ran over to me. Lil' Reesie climbed in my lap.

"You ok Ma?" He said.

"Yeah baby, I'm fine."

I told the kids we were going to Mickey D's for breakfast, and I threw out the half-cooked eggs. They were so excited. I called my mama and asked her to come over again to take the kids for breakfast. She was fussing at first, until I briefly told her what happened. She understood and came to pick us up. She told me she had to be to work, so we had to hurry up.

I quickly dressed myself and mama dressed the kids for me.

We went out to eat at Mickey D's and the kids played in the funland after they ate. Shayla barely ate or played. I waved her away to play on the jungle gym. Lil' Reesie had a ball on the hoppy-horse I put him on. I told my mom in code the full story, while holding my son on the ride. Shayla was listening nearby. She was really smart for a three year old, so I had to be slick on how I explained what happened. Of course, she already knew things weren't right between her parents. They wouldn't be right for quite sometime.

## Chapter 15
### *Khaila*

I strolled in Mickey D's to order breakfast after dropping D.C. off at work. Cocoa waved me down from across the room, in the play land area. She was with her kids and mother.
After grabbing my egg and cheese biscuit, I walked over to say "hello."
"Hey, Cocoa."
"Hey, Khaila. You remember my mother, right?"
"Yeah I remember. How you doin' today?" I said to her mother, who appeared to be past irritated.
She mumbled, "I'll be fine when I leave to get ready for work."
"Oh, ok. You're waiting for the kids to finish playing, huh?
"Yeah. They love it here. We shouldn't have come. They got plenty food in that house. They mother burned up their damn breakfast."
I glanced over at Cocoa who also looked irritated, probably by her mother's negative attitude.
I felt like I needed to save Cocoa from her mother's moaning and groaning. I said, "Well, I can take them home. You can go on to work if you want."
Cocoa's mother quickly took me up on my offer, "Thank you sweetheart. I appreciate that."
She was smiling ear to ear on the way to the car.
When her mother left, Cocoa was free to open up to me. She explained what all the noise was about next door. I had heard a lot of noise outside when I got up this morning. Though I didn't pay much attention to it, I wondered what it was.
She told me that Reese had left out with a woman from work twice in the last two days. He stayed out half the night prior trying to act like nothing had happened. The first night he did it, they got into it. The second night, she locked his ass out, and left all his stuff on the porch. I had to laugh at that. He came the next morning to pick up the rest of his belongings. While Reese was there, he pretty much told her it was through between them. It sounded like her plan backfired in her face. She never wanted him to leave for good.

Speak of the devil and he shall appear. We looked up and Reese and his mistress were sitting across the room eating. He spotted the kids playing in the play area, and tried to walk out without them recognizing him. It was way too late for that.

"Girl, there go Reese's ass right there with that hoochie. He got the nerve to come out in public with that skank!"

"Damn, girl what you gonna do?"

"Just act natural like you don't see him."

Reese and the other woman were trying to slip out door, when the kids ran up to him.

"Daddy!!!" They were excited to see him. Running up to him clinging to his legs and all.

Reese looked shocked that he was caught hanging out with the same woman. He didn't say a word. He just stood there looking stupid, with the children hanging on his legs.

Richmond is a really small place. If you cheated on your mate, somebody was gonna tell you about it, or you may even find out yourself by bumping into them in public. Some men could be so dumb. They can't even cheat right. Who the hell would be at a crowded neighborhood restaurant with the person they were cheating with? And you know the other woman ain't gonna care if the man get caught or not.

Cocoa finally decided to say something, instead of playing it cool. She asked me to take the kids to the car. Meanwhile, she had a couple words with "lover boy." I knew this, because I could see her neck rolling from side to side, and she was all up in their faces yelling.

Cocoa told me what happened when she came out. I immediately pulled off because I didn't know what had happened inside or what could follow her outside. I didn't need the extra drama in my life.

She explained, "Yeah, girl. I told that bitch, 'Reese may be with you now, but ain't no old skank gonna be able to satisfy any man that's been with me. Then I tossed her ice cold drink in her face. She jumped up like she was gonna do something, started cussing and shit. I left before she could do anything else."

Cocoa laughed like she had won a small victory. I was a little disgusted by the whole thing.

I told her seriously, "Cocoa you gotta' chill out. Your kids don't need to see you acting like that."

"You right girl, but you know the kids know what's going on. That bastard walked out on all of us. Why? Don't ask me. He's the one who did wrong, not me. You know what I'm saying?"

The kids must have been all played out, because they had drifted off to sleep in the back seat. We continued talking about what happened inside the restaurant.

"What would make him act like that? I mean y'all been married for a while now. I'm sure y'all had arguments before. And I'mma tell you, that woman don't have nothing on you Cocoa. I don't get it."

"Me either, girl. He's been acting strange every since I started therapy. He actually believes me and the therapist got something going on." We both laughed in unison, though there was nothing funny about her situation.

I replied, "That's crazy girl."

"So I guess he call himself playing the jealousy game. That shit ain't working though."

"But you'll miss him right?"

"Yeah, I'm gonna miss him, but I know he'll be back, because like you said, that woman don't got nothing on me."

"He acted like he didn't want to see you or the kids. He spotted the kids first, and he was gonna ignore them, 'til they made a scene practically attacking him in the middle of the floor."

"I know he still loves us, but he has to act like he don't need us no more."

"Why?"

"Cause he's a 36 year old child, who needs to grow up. It's that male ego that makes them act so stupid. He is not gonna risk losing his pride admitting he was wrong. And he's also the type who demands a lot of attention most of the time. If he doesn't get it, he acts immature like this."

"Has he ever done this before? I mean like packed up his stuff and left you and the kids."

"No."

I didn't want to hurt her feelings, but I had to say it. I bluntly said, "He may be serious this time. You could lose him to another woman. You gotta' do whatever necessary to get him back home to his family."

"I ain't doing nothing. He was the one who was wrong. Why can't he be the one to do what's necessary to keep his family together?"

I thought to myself. Part of me agreed with her. Why is it that the female is usually responsible for keeping the relationship together? The other part of me felt Cocoa had a bigger ego than her husband, and just didn't want to lose her pride asking him to come back.

It wasn't my business, so I decided not to press her about it. We drove in silence the remainder of the trip home. It was kinda an uncomfortable silence, but I didn't know what else to say.

Cocoa broke the silence. "So what you doing the rest of your day?"

"Nothing much. Me and D.C. were supposed to go to Virginia Beach, but he couldn't get the days off work. So we can't go on vacation this coming up weekend. I got a week and a half left off work, so I'll try to get some rest and relaxation in." I was feeling disappointed, but I smiled anyway.

"Well girl y'all will have other opportunities to go. Me and Reese have plans to go on a harbor cruise in Maryland next spring. We may be able to double date and go together."

I'm telling you, that woman was in some serious denial. I didn't say nothing, I just smiled. I wasn't too sure her and her husband would be together to go on any vacation with us, especially if she kept being stubborn about the whole thing. I mean she may need to take the first step for him to take the second.

I learned that with D.C. He was real bullheaded about things sometimes, but he loved me a lot and it showed. I think what he loved most was the fact that I was willing to bend sometimes to accommodate his stubborn ways. When I started doing a little of that for him, he started doing a lot of that for me.

We pulled in front of our apartments, and quickly parted ways. The cell phone was ringing inside my purse. I fumbled to answer it.

"Where you at baby?" D.C. asked.

"I been out for breakfast. I'm standing outside now. Gimme a minute I'll be in there."

I walked in and was greeted by a long, warm hug.

"So you said you went to breakfast? By yourself?"

"I bumped into Cocoa and her kids. We talked a little and I brought them home."

"You don't even like Cocoa."

"She's alright. She is growing on me a little. You're the one who really has a problem with her."

I tried to change the subject. "What you doing home already?"

"We had another short shift. They really didn't need me today. So I got Rayshaun to bring me home."

I looked at my phone. I noticed he tried to call for a ride home about fifteen minutes earlier.

"Oh ok."

"So what you eat?"

"I didn't eat much. Just a egg and cheese biscuit and some orange juice. I can't keep nothing down anyway."

"Khai, you know you gotta' eat right with the baby. Egg and cheese biscuits are not on the suggested diet menu the doctor gave you."

"I know, but I did have orange juice for Folic Acid. That is recommended by the doctor."

"You didn't have a balanced meal. He said you are supposed to have good balanced meals three times a day, plus healthy snacks in between. The first trimester is the mort important time...."

I wished and prayed silently for him to shut up. My prayer was not answered.

"The baby, the baby. All you think about is the baby. What about me? What about asking me how my day was, instead of what I ate for the baby?"

"You can't be on a damn diet with my baby in your stomach. You can do that diet thing when you have our son."

"Whatever D.C. The baby will be fine. My mother smoked all through her pregnancy with me and I'm ok."

"Yeah, but look what happened to your sister!" We both had a good laugh off of that one.

Suddenly my breakfast didn't feel like staying in my stomach. I ran to the bathroom to throw up in the toilet. Of course D.C. was at the door checking to see if I was ok.

"You a'ight."

"I told you I can't keep nothing down."

"You still gotta' eat right. Some of that food does make it down to the baby."

"Yeah, and the greasy egg and cheese biscuits from Mickey D's probably made the nausea worst." I came out the bathroom after washing my face and hands.

D.C. reached for my hand and walked me over to the bed. He told me to take off my shoes and socks. *Ok what is this all about?* He pulled out my goodie basket full of oils and lotions and placed them on the nightstand.

Then he went to work, kissing and licking on my toes. He vigorously rubbed his hands together to warm the coconut oil, and then gently massaged my feet. Slowly and gently, he massaged one foot at a time. It tickled so much I was wiggling all over the place.

"Ew, that tickles. Don't massage the bottom of my feet. I can't handle it."

He asked me to take off the rest of my clothes, and I did as told down to my panties. I was being pampered all over from head to toe. Pregnancy does have it's advantages- being spoiled.

"I'm enjoying this D.C"

"Don't enjoy it too much. My turn's coming up soon." He winked at me and laughed.

"Whateva boy. I ain't rubbing on those crusty dogs!" I joked.

"You dead wrong. You will be reciprocating all this one day, when you feel better."

"Yeah, 'cause the thought of touching your toes is making me nauseous all over again." I made a vomiting noise. "I'm just playing. I'll take care you in a minute."

"No, you'll get your rest after I'm done taking care of you."

D.C. picked me up, and carried me to the bathroom, straining like I was the heaviest thing he had ever carried.

"I'm too fat for you to carry now? Huh?"

"I think my back is broken."

He ran the bubble bath as I sat on the toilet waiting for the royal treatment. The warm water tingled as I got in the tub. D.C. bathed me all over. Kissing me and telling me how much he loved me in between each I got emotional and started crying tears of joy. I wasn't used to D.C. being so romantic and sweet.

I thought about my life a minute, and I realized that I was blessed. I had a sexy and loving fiancé', a baby on the way, a nice job, and school was going well. The only problem I had was Fefe and even she had chilled out for a couple days. I wondered where she was, probably needed time to plan her next stunt.

"D.C.?"

"What's up boo."

"Where has Fefe been these last couple days? I'm surprised she hasn't caused any more trouble."

"Oh I got her stupid ass straight the other day."

"I just don't understand why the police won't do nothing. The dead chicken thing was over the top."

"I keep telling you they don't care Khai."

"They got enough evidence..."

"I know, but don't worry about that shit. She ain't gonna do nothing else. I'll make sure of it."

I laid back in my bubble bath and relaxed with my eyes closed. D.C. left the bathroom to give me some "me time."

I came in to the bedroom dripping wet looking for a towel and clothes to put on. D.C. scooped me up and put me on the bed. And it was on. Or at least I thought it was on. In the middle of the kissing and groping, the phone rang. *Damn!*

"I can't even have my day off in peace!" I yelled. "Hello!"

"Hello, is this Ms. Roe?"

"Yes, it is."

"Ma'am, this is Sergeant Cooper. I have been working on your stalking case. We have arrested Ms. Feyona Jackson in connection with your case. We need you to come down to the station to identify her as the person who has been stalking and harassing you."

"That's good! Thank you for contacting me about this. I'll be there in less than an hour." I was so happy and relieved to hear the news. D.C. was looking at me like I was crazy.

"You'll be here for a while, Ms. Roe. After the identification process, you will need to complete paperwork. Then you will be issued a court date to bring legal action against Feyona Jackson. You will need to appear on your court date, and testify against her. I would recommend you consult with a lawyer for legal counsel prior to your court date."

"Ok, Sergeant Cooper. I will be there as soon as possible."

I got dressed in a hurry, telling D.C. what the officer said. He didn't say much. I think he was still skeptical about the police and doubted that anything would actually be done. Me being the optimist I had some hope.

I sped in and out of traffic to get to the station. I was so anxious to identify Fefe and put her crazy ass behind bars and out of my life for a while.

"Khai, slow down! We ain't gonna make it there to identify anybody if you get us in a car accident." D.C. compliained.

"Yeah I know. We don't want *the baby* to get hurt." I said with my most sarcastic voice.

""I don't want any of us to get hurt. I know you're excited about this, but take it easy. " He continued, "She betta' get some time for all the shit she's done to us. Make sure you got that restraining order in place. So when she's released she can't come within a certain amount of feet near you. Then she'll get locked up again...."

"Ok, ok D.C. I know what I need to do." I rolled my eyes, " I'm not a kid you know. I can handle this."

"I just don't want nothing to happen to my son...oh and you too." He laughed, trying to be a comedian. I swear I felt like slapping him in his mouth sometimes.

I pulled into the police station lot and left D.C. in the wind. He finally caught up with me inside at the reception area.

"I know you not mad at me for joking with you in the car."

"Naw, you just be getting on my nerves sometimes. I'm already worried about this bullshit."

"A'ight then I ain't gonna say nothing else then."

I ignored his ass and waited for the police officer at the front desk to help me. After waiting there for about five minutes, Sergeant Cooper came out to talk to me about my case. He then escorted us both to the line up room to identify Fefe. It was just like what I had seen in the movies and on TV. We stood in front of a special one-way glass wall. We were told that the suspects could not see on the other side of the glass, but we could see them clearly for identification.

I was still nervous, despite all of the officer's reassurance. Fefe was the first suspect in a line-up of five completely different looking women. She looked mean as hell. It felt like she could see right through the glass and right through me. I knew Fefe had connections on the outside. And I didn't need any more trouble. I thought I had drama then, it was really only beginning.

I quickly made friends with D.C., and reached for his hand. He was always my rock when I needed him.

We both identified Fefe for criminal charges. That was the day everything started to change - for good.

## **Chapter 16**

*Cocoa*

Four months had passed me by, it was November, and I still couldn't believe my husband was gone. When he would return home remained a mystery unsolved. I figured two, three days at the most, and he'd be back. We'd make love and everything would be back to normal again. I figured he'd realize he was just going through a phase and leave the other woman alone. After his little fling, he'd be back for sure. That was how it was supposed to happen, but it didn't.

He didn't even call to check on us until about a week or so had passed. Of course the kids didn't understand. They cried almost everyday for more than a month straight. Then I would cry also, because it was hurting me the most that my kids were hurting.

Eventually I had to find a sensitive way to explain to a two and three year old what had happened to their father. So, I told them that Reese was working out of town and wouldn't be back home for a while.

When he finally did call, he only spoke with the kids. The kids crying had calmed down, but it never stopped completely. I clued him in on the made up story I told the kids, so he would go along with it, and not upset them anymore than they already were.

He just responded, "mmhmm…yeah."

Reese finally talked with me over the phone back in September. Only to make arrangements to have the kids dropped off and picked up from my mom's house during the weekends. He agreed to make arrangements with me, because he really missed them. He never said anything about missing me. That hurt. I asked did he want to meet to discuss things or even get counseling, he refused to talk about it.

So then I explained to him that the family was really hurting financially as well as emotionally. Despite my new part time job, I could barely pay our bills. Reese only sent $500 a month the first three months to cover the rent, electric, food, phone, car note, and my old school loan payment. Five hundred dollars just didn't cover the expenses. Not to mention the money we needed for miscellaneous things like the kids fall clothes, and a lot of other stuff.

I never really knew financial burden until Reese left. My family had always supported me until I got married. Once I was married, my husband cared for our children and myself generously. I didn't even need to work, but I wanted to. When Reese left I needed to work either a full time job or two part-time gigs. I searched for another part-time job right after he left with no luck. I asked for more hours at my part-time, but Mr. Davis didn't need me to work the extra hours.

I finally called to ask him for money in October. I wasn't going to ask for the money up front. I was just gonna feel him out first, see what kind of mood he was in.

He answered with an attitude, "Hello?"

"Hey, Reese. How you been?"

"I'm fine. What do you want now Cocoa?" Reese said abruptly. He was gonna cut straight to the chase.

"I miss you Reese. I just wanted to hear your voice."

"Whateva, Cocoa. We both know what you really want...more money."

You'd have to call him psychic that day, because I rarely asked him for money. He probably realized $500 would not cover even half our bills.

"Reese I haven't asked you for shit. I just called because I miss you and want you to come back home."

"Well, you should have thought about that before you put me out. You were the one who fucked up, neglecting me and the kids to go to therapy and your new job. You were even talking about going to school too. When the hell were we gonna see you?"

"Well, therapy has helped me a lot, especially since you *left* me and your kids to be with your mistress."

"Whateva Cocoa. We both know the real deal." He paused. "You still going to see that therapist guy?"

"Yeah."

"Well then, we don't have shit to talk about! I mean we been married for over five years, and you gonna let someone you hardly know break up our family.

"What the hell are you talking about Reese? You were the one who was cheating. What the hell would I want with an old, white man. He is old enough to be my father Reese! Damn, you act so stupid sometimes!"

"Shit, at least Wanda is there for me. You won't hardly there.."

"Oh so that's the bitch's name, huh?"

"And she damn sho' don't need a therapist. She's here for me every night. Even when I work the late shift, she's at home waiting for me. And get this, she actually cooks a hot meal, which is also waiting for me when I get home."

I felt like crying when he said that, but I composed myself. I never thought he would go so low as to throw his affair up in my face.

All I could say was, "She's not taking care of your kids. And she don't love you like I do."

"Look Cocoa, you need to give up the extra shit and tend to your family. Maybe then we can talk."

I was silent for minute, thinking about what he said. Maybe I did need to do what I needed to do for my family. Then I heard a woman's voice in the background.

"Who's that, Reese?"

He put the phone down, but I could still hear him talking to the woman.

I couldn't make out what they were saying, except I heard Reese say, "Go back to bed and stay out of my business."

He came back to the phone like nothing happened.

"Hello?"

"Uh-huh. So that's Wanda, huh? You still sleeping with her Reese?"

"What you expect Cocoa? I mean we ain't made love in four, five months now."

"That was your decision when you decided to leave me."

"Well you know what…you know what you need to do. If you can't do it then maybe this marriage shit ain't gonna work. Simple as that."

He was so nonchalant and it was getting to me.

"We just going in circles. Let's talk about the kids. They need money Reese. I can't pay everything you left behind by myself."

"I thought that shit would come back around. I don't have no more money to give you this month. I got bills to pay too."

"If you stop paying your fuckin' girlfriend's bills, then maybe you can support your goddamn kids!" I screamed into the phone.

Then I lost it. I slammed the phone down on the base, before I burst into a river of tears. I didn't want him to hear me crying so I hung up.

When I calmed down, I thought about what he said. Even though he had said some hurtful things, I realized that he at least took the time to talk about our marriage. That was a good sign, because before he refused to even talk to me. It was also a good thing he was being nasty towards the other woman, telling her "to mind her own business." Even more encouraging was the fact that he didn't hang up on me like he'd grown used to doing since our separation

I dried my eyes and washed my face. I tried to spruce up a little before I leaving out to talk to Khaila next door. I needed to talk to someone right away, and my next scheduled therapy appointment wasn't for another few days.

Khaila was really the only close friend I had since I got married. I lost touch with a lot of my single friends who wanted to go out a lot and live the single life. I had one married friend who lived in North Carolina, so I couldn't talk with her often. Long distance charges were a bitch.

I knocked on the door and it took a while for Khaila to answer. I was getting ready to leave when she came to the door. She looked rushed, breathing real hard when she answered the door.

"Hey girl, what's up?"

I spoke faintly, "Hey. You busy?"

"Naw. Come on in. I'm just getting ready for this wedding, with my big pregnant self. How I'mma fit a dress?"

"Yeah girl you are getting big there."

"Well thanks a lot Cocoa!" She playfully slapped my arm.

"You are beautiful. Just glowing and all."

"Thanks but I feel like a fat whale."

"How far along are you now?"

"I am in my seventh month. I'm due January 15$^{th}$."

"You almost there girl. I know you can't wait. I kinda want another one, but I can't handle the two I got now."

I could feel the tears coming up again. I never could stand crying in front of people. Khaila could tell I was masking my pain with a smile.

"What's wrong, Cocoa?"

She reached for my hand, and that broke open the flood gates. I cried a river letting out all of my frustrations. I really didn't want to burden her, but I had no one else to turn to.

After a few minutes of crying, I felt a little better, and was ready to talk.

Khaila asked me. "What happened? Why are you upset?"

I...I don't need to worry you with all my issues. You don't need any extra stress while you're pregnant."

"Cocoa, you're my girl. You have been there for me the last six months with all my drama. The least I can do is be there for you. I ain't gonna do nothing but worry about you anyway, if you don't tell me what's wrong. You know how I do."

I decided to go ahead and tell her what had been weighing heavy on my mind. Things I hadn't shared with anyone outside the family. I told her about my therapy sessions, and my issues with my stepfather's death, my family situation, which all led up to how I was still upset about Reese leaving our family. I made sure to also inform her about the phone call with Reese, and Wanda's bitching in the background.

"Girl, I am so sorry. Men are such dogs! Except for my baby of course." She smiled proudly. "And Reese had the nerve to leave you with two kids. You betta' not call him back. Let the court do the talking for you. Make sure he pays spousal and child support and you know what else...?"

While she babbled about me divorcing my husband, I kept thinking about how much I wanted him back. I wanted my normal happy family life again. I knew we would at least need marital counseling to save our marriage, but I was willing to do it. I thought about how I would convince him to go to counseling. He hated the fact that I had individual therapy with my white "boyfriend." I doubt if he would want anything to do with counseling.

I had zoned out so long, Khaila was calling my name to get my attention again.

"Huh?"

"What are you day dreaming about?"

"I was just thinking about how I want my family back together."

"You are not actually thinking about getting back with that cheating dog are you?"

"Khaila, you talking about my husband, who I still love very much."

Logically, I knew she was right, I did need to move on. It was likely he'd cheat again. However, my heart usually made the decisions in my love life, and I knew I had to follow my heart.

# Chapter 17
## *Khaila*

I did what I promised Cocoa I would not do. I worried constantly. I was not only concerned about her situation, but I was also freaking out about my own. It was November and I was pondering over Fefe's next potential move. I knew she would make one, I just didn't know when. The last time we were in court was in August. Fefe had requested for a continuance until she could get a lawyer. It would be months before our next court date. We just had to wait until the time came for us to get it over with.

Fefe bailed out of jail in October. I was a nervous wreck. The Sergeant called to notify me of her release and told me to make sure my restraining order was still in place. It was. D.C. and I both knew restraining orders never stopped Fefe before, but I was gonna make sure I did what I could to deter her from constantly stalking us. I didn't need any more drama especially during my seventh month of pregnancy.

D.C. did what he could to calm my fears. He knew I was at high-risk of losing the baby if I didn't control my anxiety problem. Reminded me over and over again that Fefe had not done anything for several months, and that maybe she had learned her lesson. He didn't believe that mess any more than I did.

A lot of times he would try his best to keep my mind focused on the wedding, which was another kind of stress. I really enjoyed planning the wedding though. It was supposed to have been scheduled for December, a month before the baby was due. I made jokes about giving birth on the way down the aisle.

D.C. secretly got a second job to help finance the fancy wedding I had planned. I thought he was hanging out with his friends every day. It had even crossed my mind that maybe he was cheating with Fefe, until his second job at a restaurant called him in to work more hours. He didn't want me to know, because he knew I didn't want him working so hard. I would just plan a more simple type wedding. He was determined to give me the wedding I want, so I just let him be.

## D.C.

One day Fefe came out from hiding as I had expected, and called the house. She was impersonating a receptionist from the doctor's office. Fefe told Khaila that she needed to come down to the doctor's office right away. She said the doctor was concerned that Khaila was at risk of having a miscarriage, as shown by her irregular test results.

My poor naïve fiancé was on her way down to the doctor's office, when I came home from work. She told me about the phone call, and I almost pissed in pants laughing. I really fell out when Khaila said the receptionist mispronounced the word miscarriage.

It didn't make sense to me especially since Khaila had recently been to the doctor, and was told that she and our baby were healthy. Why would her doctor call back a week later saying something else?

Khaila wasn't quite sure, so she called the doctor's office back to make sure. She found out I was right. It was Fefe up to her usual shit. She was probably gonna do something to Khaila when she got to the doctor's office. I didn't put anything past Fefe.

Khaila pressed *69 and found out it was Fefe's cell number. She braced herself to call Fefe, when I took the phone from he hand. I told her I would talk Fefe myself.

Fefe answered the call, "Hey D.C. How you and your girl been doing?"

She was really unbelievable. It always tripped me out how she could wreak havoc and then later pretend like nothing happened.

"Fefe, don't try that shit ok."

"What are you talking about?"

"I'm talking about your phony call to Khaila, acting like you were calling from her doctor's office."

"What?"

"You were trying to get her down to her doctor's office to do something to her. You would think a few months in jail would have straightened your crazy ass out by now. You must need some more time."

"If I wanted to hurt yo' bitch I would come 'round yo' way and do something to her. Come on D.C. You know how I do it."

"Yeah, I know how you do it, all too fuckin' well! Leave my girl alone. Or I swear to God I'll…"

"You'll do what? Shit, I got peoples right around your way who would take care of you, your girl, and your retarded baby. Now try me muthafucka!"

She hung up the phone in my face. I sat there figuring out my next move. Was Fefe really worth it? Would she continue to destroy my family's happiness? I couldn't allow that. My son shouldn't have to deal with the bullshit me and Khaila had to deal with. That was for sure. Something had to be done, but what the hell was I gonna do about it?

## Chapter 18

*Cocoa*

I woke up in the warm arms of my husband, and it scared the hell out of me. I hadn't seen, felt, touched, or smelled him in four months and all of a sudden he was cuddled up next to me in bed. I slept so hard, I didn't even hear him come in. It had been about three days since our last hostile phone call.

I jumped up screaming. My heart was pounding hard against my chest.

I almost cut Reese with the switchblade I kept up under my mattress. I decided to buy a switchblade for protection when Reese left us to fend for ourselves.

I tossed the switchblade on the nightstand when I recognized Reese's voice and the scent of his cologne.

"Hey, babe. Calm down." He confirmed his identity with his sexy, romantic voice.

"Reese? I almost cut you, crazy man." I laughed. "What are you doing here?"

"Oh, you don't want your husband here?"

"Of course I do, but...."

"I know I haven't been there, babe." He took a deep breath, " Please forgive me. I know I was wrong."

He continued, "I didn't give you a chance to explain your position. I wouldn't hear you out at all. You keep doing your therapy thing. If it works for you, do it. Who am I to tell you not to get the help you need. I just hope you will forgive me for what I've done. We both probably need counseling now."

"Reese. I don't understand. What made you come back?" I said with tears in my eyes.

I wasn't sure if those tears were of joy or pain. I think it was a little of both.

He wiped my eyes, and said, "I woke up a few hours ago in my hotel bed and realized I was unhappy and alone. Even with another woman at my beck and call I wasn't happy at all. I haven't even talked to her in a while because she just couldn't replace you in way, shape, or form. She wasn't even close to taking your place in my heart..."

"But Reese the other day...you were upset with me."

"I still missed you...even though my pride kept getting in the way. I let my pride keep me from being happy." He lowered his head, and cried in his hands.

He continued, "When you called the other day, I was so happy to hear your beautiful voice. And my stupid pride wouldn't let me say I was sorry. I know I was being an asshole, and don't deserve you or our family."

He raised his head, looked me in my eyes, and said, "If you still will have me, I will go to counseling with you. And I promise you I won't ever leave our family again. I won't cheat on you again, because you are all I ever wanted and needed. Some kinda way I lost sight of that. I love you more than you will ever know, Cocoa."

He stood up and walked towards the door, "I'll be back. I just need a minute to get some air. Think about what I said."

## *Reese*

I was so overwhelmed by emotion that I needed some time to compose myself. I wept on the front stoop until my eyes burned. Cocoa eventually came to check on me a few minutes later. I couldn't even look her in the eyes I was so ashamed.

It was three in the morning and it was real quiet and romantic. There was a little fall chill in the air, but the cool breeze was soothing. Cocoa had brought some tea for the two of us. It was her special blend I loved so much, it had brown sugar, cinnamon, and a touch of rosemary.

I never appreciated the little special things she did like bringing my favorite tea or ironing my work clothes or making my lunch for work. I was gonna be committed to showing her my appreciation everyday.

"Thanks for the tea, babe."

"You're welcome. It's hot, so take your time with it. Last time you burned the hell out of your tongue trying to down it so fast!" She laughed. I had really missed her laugh as well. It was sweet music to my ears.

She didn't touch her tea, she just laid her head lightly on my right shoulder. I felt her tears through my t-shirt. I knew she was having an inner conflict. Not sure what to do. She didn't know whether to stay with the love of her life and risk further heartbreak. Or cut her losses and start over again. I would have cut my losses if I were in her shoes, so I would have understood if she made the decision to leave me. It would've hurt a lot but I knew I had messed up and I would have to deal with the consequences.

Cocoa's mind had to be going in circles since I magically appeared in her bed, after disappearing for months with another woman. Nothing was guaranteed. The only thing she could be sure of was the warmth of my body next to hers, shielding her from the cool November air.

## Chapter 19

*D.C.*

"...Come on now Khai. You gotta' stop worrying yourself. Everything will be cool, ok? Let me handle it, a'ight."

"So you wanna handle *all* of the wedding arrangements by yourself? Come on you can let me do something. The wedding is supposed to be for the bride you know."

"Ok, I got something for you to do."

"Yeah?"

"This is what you do right...you just show up... and look pretty. Now that's a big job especially with your face."

Khaila nudged me in the head. She had been doing a lot of that lately. It's kinda' funny that the things that usually annoy you about a person, are the same things you love so much.

"My dress will be huge you know?" She warned.

"You will be the most beautiful one in our little party of four."

"Six if you count little D.C. Jr., and the reverend." She giggled. "I know you wanted to give me a bigger wedding, but it's not the right time for all that, you know. We can have a big church wedding later on. " Khaila said.

"If a small private wedding is what you want, then that's what you'll get. If you're happy, I'm overjoyed. I just hope your trifling sister shows up on time. Now you know Shante or even ghetto-ass Cocoa would have been better choices for Maid of Honor, Khai."

"Yeah I know but she's my sister D.C. My mother would have a fit if she found out I picked Shante over Tracie for maid of honor. She was already mad at me because we're having a private ceremony in the Botanical Gardens. Here she go, 'I wait half my life for you to get married, and you don't even have the decency to get married in a church, in front of your family like Christians are supposed to.' Awwww, she really gets on my nerves."

"Are you getting married or is ya' moms? I mean it'll be our wedding and marriage, right? She just gonna have to deal with it, Khaila."

"I know."

"And look she can attend our church wedding as soon as we get straight financially. So please stop worrying about what your mom thinks. It will be all about you on December 20$^{th}$. Just get a dress big enough to fit your big, round belly! I don't want my son poking out the dress."

"I hate you." She laughed holding her pregnant stomach. She was no longer a petite, size five, but she was even lovelier than I could remember before.

"I know baby. I know."

I kissed her softly on her lips, which usually sparked off our romantic love sessions. What wasn't normal was the person watching us through our bedroom window that night.

## D.C.

Khaila called out my name, "D.C.?"

"Yeah, babe." I said, deep inside of erotic strokes with Khaila. Lost between heaven and earth.

"D.C. there is a bush shaking outside our window…" She moved from under me to peek out the window.

"Ok, Khai and…?" It's probably the wind. It is November you know." I said with irritation.

I gently slid her back into position, and kept going about my business. Khaila was about to cum, I could tell by her response and by the way I was hitting her spot.

"But…um….ew…shit! D.C……? D.C. you gotta' stop baby." She got up from under me again, pissing me off even more. "I think somebody's watching us."

"Good let them look."

"I'm serious."

"Damn Khai! Shit! You are always fucking up our groove with your neurotic self! Just chill out!"

"Go to hell D.C. I'm not being paranoid right now. There is someone or something peeping through the bushes. Look!"

Khaila got up to get a closer look at the window. The blinds were open, and they were up the windowpane halfway. I decided to humor her and look out the window too. The small bush in front of our window was shaking like a person or animal was behind it.

I put on my clothes and went to go check outside. Maybe I would get some more good loving after I searched and found nothing behind the bushes. Khaila slid under the covers naked, so there was some hope.

Khaila was disgusted by the thought of someone watching us have sex. I was just a little curious myself. Who was this freak? How long were they watching? And why?

I walked towards the bushes slowly. I didn't know who or what was there. Could be a cat or it could be a thief stalking the apartment to rob. I looked around the area for a few. Before I could reach the bushes, a woman ran off to the back of the apartment. I followed and yelled out a few choice words before she jumped into the passenger side of the car parked in the alley. It was hard to see a face since it was pitch black outside, but I was more than sure who it was when she ran to the car- Fefe. One of her friends was driving her car. They both sped off into darkness.

Enough was enough. How much can a man take? I had tried doing the right thing by, talking to her and warning her, but you can't rationalize or sympathize with a psycho. And fuck the police for real 'cause they had only caused grief in my life. They never solved anything for me.

I decided right then and there that it was time for Fefe to get reacquainted with the old D.C. who just didn't give a fuck. I had thought he was dead and gone for good. It was time for a resurrection.

## Chapter 20

### D.C.

"I'm sorry babe, but sometimes shit gotta' get worse to get better." I said aloud to myself, still standing there in the middle of the lawn. I knew from that moment on, things would never be the same.

I went inside knowing Khaila would be dead asleep. The combination of sex and pregnancy wore her out every time. I wrote her a note instead of waking her up.

> *Khai,*
>
> *I checked things out like you wanted, and like always you were right. There was someone watching us at the window, and I have no doubt who it was. I don't want you to worry yourself about it though. I will take care of everything for us, and little D.C. Junior too. It will be a boy you know.* ♥
>
> *I'm not sure how long it'll take me, but I'll be back soon. Please don't freak out. We both know it's your favorite thing to do. Or your second favorite. I'll give you your first favorite thing when I get back home. I'm returning with a vengeance since you ain't let me finish.* ♥
>
> *I love you boo,*
> *DC*
>
> *P.S. I can't wait to make you Mrs. Curry or Mrs. Roe-Curry, which ever name you like. I know you're so liberated and all.*

I left out to meet with Jy and my other boy, Q around the block where they scooped me to go to Jy's place. I had thought about inviting Vey to the meeting, but he was still mad and not talking to me since I moved in with Khaila back in June.

My boy, Q and me first became associates two years prior through Khaila's sister, Tracie. Q and Tracie had kinda an on-off love thing going. They were the perfect couple, because they were both thugged out and ghetto as hell.

Q was a short, small-framed dude, but he was also a live wire ready to set it off at anytime. He had been to jail several times before doing crazy shit. Robbing old ladies at gunpoint, drug possession, assault, the list goes on and on. When I met him, he had just finished serving a 24-month jail sentence. So he was trying to lay low and stay out of trouble after all that.

You may wonder how we became good friends being completely different men. Well, Q always had my back, through thick and thin, he was there.

I remember back in 2002 when I got jumped by at least four other niggas over on 18th Street in Churchill. Back then, I was on the block selling, making a lot of paper. Muthafuckas didn't like me moving in on their territory so they retaliated by jumping me. Kicking me in the ribs, stomping my head, I mean they were really fucking my ass up. Q and a couple of his boys were on the other end of the block and jumped in to have my back. I didn't even know him like that for him to do that for me, but he did and I never forgot it. He probably saved my life that day.

I had no reason to believe Q wouldn't have my back to help me handle my business with Fefe.

Now Jy, my best friend, was a lot more levelheaded than Q. We usually kept each other out of trouble. I needed to get his position on things too.

We were gonna design the solid plan at Jy's apartment, before doing anything stupid.

Jy repeated what he had told me before. "You may wanna move on the real, man."

"We ain't running from that crazy bitch. I told you that before. What we gonna move with anyway? We ain't got no money...."

Q cut me off, "You got money for a wedding, right?" He was just being a smart ass like usual.

"He do have a point there, D'," Jy said, "...but come on now Q their wedding is important to them though. Don't get mad 'cause Khaila's project sista, ain't the marrying type."

"Shit, you know me. I ain't marrying no chickenhead no way. I gotta' sew my wild oats nigga!" They slapped five.

I didn't find shit funny at the moment.

"I'm marrying Khaila next month in the way she wants at the Botanical Gardens. I don't care how much it costs or what it takes. We only got one real issue to deal with."

Q blurted out, "Well, what you want us to do? 'Cause you know me. I'll handle it for you. I don't give a fuck, I'm off parole now."

Jy said, "Youse a dumb muthafucka! We supposed calm this nigga down so he makes the right decision, and you over there hyping him up. You might not give a fuck what happens, but I know it's important to D' and his girl. When I represent my boy as best man at his wedding, I don't want your ass to be hemmed up in the joint for doing something stupid. How you gonna come to the wedding after party?"

I put everything on the table and said, "you know if he goes down for me, I'm going down with him."

"Man, you give me the right amount of money and I'll do it by myself. Just say the word and I'll do it." He paused and said, "It would be my pleasure, baby-boy, it would be my pleasure."

There was something really weird about the way Q said that last statement. Like he was actually serious.

"Ya'wl talking nonsense. What you gonna do alone Q, kill her?"

"If the price is right, then come on down nigga!" He laughed at his joke.

I knew Q was serious, even though he was making light of the whole thing. I was silent for a moment thinking about what he said, and I was actually considering making a deal. The whole thing was wild. I never imagined putting a hit out on somebody. Jy looked at me real strange like he knew exactly what I was thinking.

"D' now tell me how you gonna marry your bride locked up?"

"Well, Jy you know the plan is to not get locked up." I said sarcastically.

"You starting to sound just like that crazy fool." He motioned at Q.

I replied, "Ok, then. How 'bout we just put a little hurting on her. Enough to get her away from me and Khaila for a while."

Q snapped, "Now you know ghetto bitches, D'. Come on, don't be stupid! Listen to him Jy, and you calling me a dumb muthafucka."

Jy agreed, "He's right D' that would be dumber than killing her. She'll come back with so much shit you'll wish you had killed yourself instead. That's just not logical. You must be tired or stressed out for real, saying crazy shit like that."

They were right, I was talking out the side of my neck.

"Give me one of those forties you got in the fridge. I know you got some. I need to calm my nerves. This whole thing gotta' be resolved by the morning, so my girl won't worry."

Jy told me, "Hey, you know I gotta' joint in the room if you wanna calm your nerves."

"Naw, man you know I don't smoke that shit no more. I'll just take a beer."

"A'ight then."

Q told Jy jokingly, "I'll take the joint man. I think I might need to calm my nerves too." Q was acting dumb, tripping out about any and everything.

Still I found nothing funny about my situation.

We all headed to the kitchen to get beer from the fridge, and took them back to the front room. Jy and Q lit up a joint too.

Out of nowhere Q said, "What's wrong with her anyway. Your girl got some serious issues, always thinking somebody after her or you. When the baby's born, somebody's gonna be after him too." He took a pull of his blunt and passed it to Jy.

I shook my head, while those two clowns continued to laugh at my issues.

I thought to myself, *I can't believe them. Here I am going through a serious problem and they wanna make fun of it. They must think this is all one big joke.*

Jy must have sensed my irritation. He said with concern, "Seriously, D'. I'm here for you. What you wanna do?"

"I guess I only have one option. Since my other idea was dumb."

Jy said, "No you have another option. You could just leave her alone. Keep calling the police, file another charge against her. Eventually they will arrest her again. She's out on bail, right?"

"Yeah."

"Well she just added another charge to her long list of charges. When she goes back to court for sentencing, she'll have another charge on her record."

"We don't even know when we're going back to court. We haven't gotten the court papers yet." I was getting more and more frustrated. My head was starting to hurt.

I guess Q had heard enough, 'cause he yelled out, "You can't wait 'til then D.C. I can have her buried by your next court date. Just say the word." His face showed no sign of weakness or shame. Q was serious.

It was so still in the room for a minute you could hear pin drop. I didn't know what to say to Q, and Jy was getting upset with him.

Jy hollered out, "Man, have you ever killed anybody before? 'Cause I have, and it ain't no shit you wanna remember." He said staring Q down. Then we all fell silent again.

I knew Jy was probably thinking back to 2001 when he shot this young dealer on the block. Word on the street, the kid he shot had threatened to rid the block of Jy and his crew.

Dude was only sixteen years old, and he showed up alone ready to kill the leader first. He went straight to Jy, put a gun to his temple, and started talking shit. Big mistake. Street code: never talk shit, just do it. Of course Jy was strapped too. By pure instinct, Jy whipped around and pulled the trigger first. Shot little dude point blank in the chest, puncturing one of his lungs. About the same time another dude in Jy's crew shot the kid in the back, fucking up his whole spinal column. He hadn't even hit the ground good before Jy and his people bolted out of there.

Jy never forgave himself for leaving the kid for dead. He had never shot anyone before, and he never imagined shooting a kid around the same age as his little brother. We heard his story on the news a couple times. They were looking for anyone who could identify the gunmen to call this hotline number.

The kid surprisingly survived about a year, living in a wheel chair, hooked up constantly to a ventilator machine to breathe. He was in and out of the hospital due to complications from his wounds. The last month of his life he caught pneumonia, and died while sleeping in a hospital bed.

"Hey Jy, you ok?" I asked shaking him out of his trance. He was zoned out for a minute. I glanced over at Q who had this real stupid look on his face. He didn't know what to say.

"I'm cool. Just thinking that's all. You know it's been three years since I shot that kid. His name was Aaron Brooks."

Q said, "Man, that shit ain't all your fault. Another dude shot the kid too. How you know his bullet didn't kill the kid in the end?"

"I know 'cause he died of pneumonia, an infection of the lung. I shot him in the chest puncturing his right lung. I read the shit in the paper and heard it on the news." He took a deep breath. "For months they talked about catching his attempted murderers, who they mysteriously couldn't find. He knew it was me and this dude named Birdman from my crew, but he was afraid to testify against us. He was only 17 years old- dead because of me. I still haven't 'fessed up. That's real fowl man." He was a little teary eyed thinking about what he had done years ago.

The incident with the kid changed Jy a lot. He had even stopped selling for a couple months. He told me he had plans to go to school and get his life together, but those plans didn't last long. He was even talking shit about getting married to a good woman like I was. In many ways I knew he envied what me and Khaila had going on, even though we still had to deal with drama.

\*\*\*

## *Reese*

"Come here baby. Come and sit on daddy's lap."

After sipping our drinks on the patio, I successfully charmed my wife into bed for some action. It was the first time we made love since our separation. I took my time and savored the moment, holding her close to my body sitting Indian-style on our queen-size bed.

I wanted so much to start over with Cocoa the right way. However, my bitter ex-mistress thought otherwise. Wanda was determined to get me by any means necessary. She called my cell several times a day, at crazy hours of the night. I let it go straight to voicemail most of the time. She even stopped by the apartment a few times with no answer. Stayed in my face at work, I only ignored her. Even though I gave her no play, she just wouldn't stop. She kept trying to disrupt any happiness me and Cocoa were trying to build back in our lives.

Wanda assumed when I left her four days before that I went back home, but I actually stayed in a motel. I wasn't ready to go home and face Cocoa yet. I just needed to clear my head and muster up the courage to go home and talk with her.

I knew Cocoa was my lifetime soul mate, and I needed to stop denying it. No one was going to come between us if I could help it. Or would they?

## *Cocoa*

As I laid there on Reese's chest asleep, I could feel myself smiling. I dreamed good dreams about Reese, the kids, and myself enjoying each other as a nice, happy family. Of course I also had a few dreams starring my husband and me enjoying each other. Savoring each other's love the way we used to.

When I woke up to tinkle, I moved slowly away from Reese's chest to avoid waking him. On the way to the bathroom, I could hear his cell vibrating on the nightstand. I remember thinking, *Who would be calling Reese's phone at six-thirty the morning? It's probably his job calling him in again.*

I picked up the phone too late to answer. The call forwarded to his voicemail. I had the voicemail code previously from sharing the phone with Reese. Later on, I finally got my own cell, but I still remember his code. As I pressed the numbers I remember feeling nervous and guilty at the same time. I felt guilty because I never felt the need to invade his privacy before, at least not until his cheating. The nervousness came from a strange feeling that the message on his cell was not from the job. The twenty seconds it took to get through to his voicemail felt like hours.

The message went: "Hey baby. You still mad at me. I know I was wrong for accusing you of cheating on me. I thought you were getting back with your wife when you left, but I realized that you were just hurt and upset that I would accuse you like I did. I should have believed you when you said you were divorcing the bitch! I know she is not the woman for..." The message ended before she could finish talking.

I was insane with jealousy. I walked up to Reese while he was sleeping and threw the phone directly at his head. He woke up confused and unaware of what was going on, rubbing his throbbing head.

"You might wanna check your phone messages. Yo' bitch called!"

Reese figured out what was going on real fast when I said that. He sat there quiet for a minute. I was done. I'd said all that needed to be said.

I headed for the bathroom to calm down, the whole way running into things and knocking shit off the nightstand.

After finishing my cigarette, I peeked out to see what Reese was doing. He went outside on the patio with his cell phone in hand. I suspected he was returning his mistress' phone call. That only added fuel to the fire.

I rushed to the patio door slamming it open so hard I thought the glass would break. Though I was heated on the inside, the wind was blowing so hard outside I could barely stand the cold in my nightgown.

I yelled out, "Go 'head, call your trick in private. I don't give a fuck no more Reese!"

He turned around and told me, "Just calm down before you wake our neighbors."

"What the fuck I care about the neighbors right now. Khaila's the only neighbor I care about, and she's my girl. She'll understand exactly how I feel!"

"The kids are on the way home from your mom's. You don't wanna upset them do you? Just let me handle this. Wanda's just trying to cause problems between us." His whole aura remained calm while I was steadily freaking out. *How could he relax at a time like this?*

"Well if she's trying to cause more problems between us she's succeeding. Why is she still calling you anyway? I thought you said you were leaving her alone. You said you told her to 'get out of our lives and move on.' Why she still calling Reese??? Calling me yo' bitch, she the bitch!" I screamed at the top of my lungs in anger, masking the pain I felt to cry.

He said, "Cocoa! Just chill. Go back to bed, and let me handle this, ok?"

"You handle it or I'll handle it Reese. I mean that!"

I slammed the patio door shut. Then I continued to watch Reese through the glass door making the call to Wanda.

Insecurity and jealousy were growing in my gut. Deep down I felt he would cheat again. You know what they say, 'once a cheat, always a cheat.' My mind was going in a thousand circles. The whole situation was so mentally and emotionally draining. I laid down on the bed and cried myself to sleep. I was out within in a few minutes.

## *Reese*

Wanda pathetically begged in my ear. "Reese, baby come on, you know I love you. You gotta' come home, 'fore I go crazy."

I could care less if she went crazy. The only person I thought about when I was with her was Cocoa. The whole time. Even when I sexed her, I thought about my wife. I made that shit painfully clear to her, but she just didn't get it.

"Stop talking that bullshit! It won't work. I don't want you Wanda. And I don't give a fuck if you go crazy. Just-leave-us-alone!"

"Don't do this baby...I need you in my life or it's just not worth living."

"So you gonna kill yourself now Wanda?" I said with thick sarcasm in my voice. I knew she was talking shit and I wasn't falling for it. It was a sick play to get what she wanted.

"I don't know what I'll do without you. Come home baby. I need you...now!" She had really flipped her wig, screaming like crazy in my ear.

There was something eerie in her voice that made me all of a sudden worry that she would actually try to kill herself. I didn't need that shit on my conscience. It was the way she screamed, 'I need you...now!' that scared the hell out of me. She sounded possessed by the devil or something.

"I'll do whateva you want Reese. What ever it takes for you to come home...I need you..." Her voice trailed off as she began to cry hysterically into the phone receiver.

I had to get off the phone with Ms. Psychotic fast. I said, "Wanda, look, I gotta' go..."

"Noooooo!" She sounded more childlike this time. "You can't leave me!" She was crying uncontrollably in my ear, and all I had to do was hang up, but something kept me there.

For a minute or so all I could hear was sobbing. I yelled out her name, "Wanda? Wanda?" She didn't respond. She was so hysterical I don't even think she could heard me.

Part of me felt she was putting on an act. I found out later on that she was having another one of her chronic mental breakdowns. A co-worker told me she had been having stress related breakdowns ever since she was a teenager.

I hung up the phone when she didn't respond to me calling her name. I stayed on the patio thinking for a minute. Wondering if Wanda was really suicidal. Could she even be homicidal? Would she try to hurt my children or my wife to get back at me?

I felt a little hysterical myself when I thought about what Wanda could do. She knew where we lived and what my wife looked like. That was very damaging information for a psycho to possess. I mean look at what happened to Khaila and D.C. next door. A woman scorned can do some crazy things to get back at their exes. I didn't want my family to be the victim of her insanity.

The cell rang. It was Wanda again. I let it ring a couple times before I turned off the phone. I took a deep breath and prayed a short prayer to myself before I returned inside to face my wife. I knew I would have drama, but I had a feeling it would be much more than I could handle.

## Chapter 21

## D.C.

Jy, Q, and me set out to hunt a psycho and execute our plan as scheduled. Jy was still uneasy about the whole thing but he was out numbered, by me and Q. As my best friend he was expected to have my back regardless.

Before we left, Jy suggested that instead of killing Fefe, we use less extreme tactics. What we had planned was supposed to put the fear in her ass to make her want to leave town and leave us alone for good.

Now there was one thing about Jy's plan that made me uneasy. It was way too risky. She could rat us out to the po-lice. I thought about it though, and I figured it was really a win-win situation. Fefe wouldn't call the po-lice. With her violating the restraining order several times before, she would be turning herself in. Her calling the po-lice would definitely backfire in her face.

We pulled in front of Fefe's place, and exited Jy's car without saying a word. Everybody knew what they had to do, what their role was, and everything. No discussion required.

Both my boys were in position. I banged on the door first. No answer. Then I tapped the bedroom window. Nothing. I checked the front for her car and then the back. It was parked in the back parking lot. So I knew she was home. She didn't have many friends to take her anywhere. She only had one home girl named Tonda, and Tonda didn't have a car.

Fefe was probably hip to the fact I was outside looking for her. She probably figured I would just cuss her out again like before. I was on some new shit that night.

I got smart and decided to send a decoy instead. *Who was I gonna send?* The one close friend Fefe had, lived only five blocks down and two blocks over on Crenshaw Avenue. My plan B was to get her friend to go to the door and get her to come outside.

I knocked on Tonda's door alone, while Jy and Q remained in the car waiting for the signal. She didn't look through the peephole before opening the door. If she had, she would have never answered the door. Fefe's

home girl hated me ever since me and Fefe were together.
Tonda didn't see anyone outside so she stepped out further. Mouse in the trap, I grabbed her with ease. I covered her mouth and dragged her to the car. That bitch bit the hand covering her mouth, and tried to kick me in the balls. I overpowered Tonda, and she quickly realized there was no need fighting me. She had no chance of escape, especially with the three of us in the car with her.

After about a half an hour of threatening Tonda and her children, she was ready to do as told.

## *Tonda*

I quietly knocked on Fefe's door, feeling scared and guilty as hell. I couldn't believe what I was about to do, but what choice did I have. D.C. and his boys meant what they said. They made it clear they weren't joking about hurting me or my kids. The shortest one even gave me the gory details of how he would torture me before taking me out. Told me he would kill my kids while I watched.

They sat in the car watching as I walked up to Fefe's apartment. Just waiting for me to do or say something stupid before they "popped" my ass. I never saw a gun, but I wasn't gonna test them.

Fefe answered right away. She knew something wasn't right, 'cause I was usually in bed right after the kids fell asleep. I had left my six and eight year old at home alone. I supposedly walked seven blocks alone past midnight. That wasn't like me to do something like that unless something was wrong.

"Girl, what you doing here so late! What's the matter?"

"I'm cool, girl. I got something to tell you and it's kinda important. Walk with me to the apartment, so I can get back to the kids."

"Why didn't you just call me?"

I had to think fast with a lie. I blurted out, "I....I just wanted to...um... I just wanted to talk to you face to face about this."

"Tonda, girl, you need to come in a minute and tell me what's wrong, then I'll give you a ride back home. You know it's too damn late and cold outside to be taking a damn walk."

I giggled nervously, and said, "I can't. I gotta' get back to the kids Fefe."

I didn't know how convincing my lie was, but Fefe agreed to come out when she got dressed. I stood there on the doorstep, feeling like shit for hemming up my best friend like that. But like I said before I had to do what I had to do.

I can't say I didn't understand the rage D.C. had for Fefe. For years I watched the drama between them. They would make up and break up almost every day. For years I watched the cycle of their destructive relationship, until I guess D.C. had had enough. A small part of me felt sorry for him. Fefe had taken him through so much shit over the years. I told her over and over to get over him. He had successfully gotten over her with no problem.

After a while I got tired of preaching the gospel to her. I decided to just listen like good friends are supposed to do. She was my girl, so I was supposed to support her and be there for her, whether I agreed with her or not.

Still waiting for Fefe to get dressed, I thought again about what I was doing. I couldn't bail out if I wanted to. I hoped they would just talk shit to her, scare her a little bit or whateva. I knew better though. Would they really hurt my best friend?

Then I came to my senses. Shit, it was Fefe who got herself in that situation. She had done it to herself. I would be damned if I'd let her and D.C.'s confusion cause harm to my kids. Friends or not, my kids came first.

***

## *Cocoa*

I was trippin out for real by the time Reese got inside. He had finished his phone call with his little girlfriend or should I say fat ass girlfriend. I was like, *how dare he take his ass outside to talk to his mistress in private, right in front of my face.* He actually wanted privacy to talk with her.

I couldn't control my anger anymore. A big yellow pages went flying at his head. He ducked just in time.

"Whoa! Baby, come on now. Calm down." He was still being cool about everything. I couldn't believe him. "Everything is straight now baby. No more worries, ok?"

"Oh we got worries Reese...." The doorbell interrupted me in mid sentence.

He said, "That's probably the kids and your mother. Go 'head and get the door. Better yet, I'll get it. You just relax. Take a nice warm bath or something. I'll even take the kids to Kid's Playland for the afternoon. They can eat pizza and play games, while you chill out here.

"This shit ain't over Reese. I wanna know what you and *Wanda* had to discuss in private!"

He walked off to answer the door, so I went to the bathroom to take his advice. I ran a warm milk bath and lit another cigarette to calm my nerves. Funny thing, I had slowed down on my smoking when I had the kids. That stress with Reese had sparked my smoking habit again. I had kept an emergency box under the bed just in case.

With the bathroom door still open, I could hear Reese say, "Hey, mom, good to see you."

Reese and my mother always got along real good until she found out he cheated on me. Kissing up to her, was not gonna work for him anymore.

"Where's my baby? Cofina you up there?"

"She's taking a bath, mom. She'll probably be a while in there soaking. I'll let her know you wanted to talk with her."

"You ain't rushing me out of my own daughter's home, are you Reese? Something ain't right, and I ain't leaving 'til she come out!" I guess she could see through the charm.

She yelled up to me, "What's the matter? You a'ight Cofina?"

"Yes, mama. I'm fine." I said weakly.

"You don't sound fine. Don't lie to me chile. I know when something not right with my baby."

She was becoming irritating. I yelled, "I'm cool mama. Damn, can I take a bath in peace!"

"You watch your tone with me, Cofina Marie."

Reese interrupted, "Ma, you may wanna give her some relaxation time before she has to deal with the kids."

His plan to have her leave was not working. My mother plopped down on the sofa real comfy and turned on the TV.

"I ain't going no where Reese. What you scared she might tell me something you don't want me to know?"

She ruthlessly taunted Reese. I kinda felt sorry for him. My mother was known for being loud-mouthed and rude, always making scenes especially when it came to protecting me, her only child.

\*\*\*

## D.C.

Tonda decided to be smart and run as soon as Fefe got outside. She ran past the car like a bolt of lightening. She did as we asked, and she apparently didn't say anything to Fefe. So we let her live. We weren't concerned with her anyway. Our target was standing right there in front of us. Bulls Eye!

Instead of her following suit and running like her girl, she just stood there looking confused. We had her before she could react. We were all posted up behind the car ready to snatch her up. Jy and me pushed her inside her apartment and Q locked the door. It was time to execute Plan A – Torture!

\*\*\*

## Reese

I heard a loud Bang! Bang! Bang! at the door. I wondered who else wanted to make a surprise visit and not leave. Cocoa's mother finally left after she figured out that Cocoa was not coming out the bathroom. I was hoping it wasn't her coming back to finish her irate performance or even worst, Wanda putting on a freak show.

I peeked out the peephole first. Khaila from next door was crying like crazy on the doorstep. I hesitated, taking my sweet time opening the door. I didn't know what she wanted, but I knew what I wanted. I needed some quality time with my kids, and eventually my wife once I got in good with her again. We never even got the chance to go to Kid's Playland.

"Hey Khaila, what's up? You alright?"

"Noooo….Reese…..I'm not alright!" She screamed.

"What's wrong?"

"D.C.'s gone, and he left this letter behind and I....I don't know where he is...Reese...oh my god...what I'mma do..."

She was hyperventilating, having an attack or something. I didn't know what was going on. I remembered Cocoa telling me before she had nervous issues.

"Calm down, babe. Come on, have a seat. I'll get you something to drink. What you want? You want some hot chocolate, or tea?"

"I'll take some tea please…." Her breathing was getting heavier. I had to do something fast.

"Cocoa, get down here, your friend needs you!" I yelled upstairs. Then I told her "Ok, Khaila. I'm going to make your drink. You relax on the couch. Cocoa will be down in a minute."

"Get me a paper bag while you in there, Reese."

"What you need a bag for? What you having an asthma attack or something."

I realized how ignorant I sounded as soon as I said it.

"No…I'm a….I'm a… having another panic attack. I need the bag to help calm me down."

"A'ight, everything's gonna be ok. You chill out here, I'll be right back." At that moment, I thought I'd probably need a bag to breathe in myself. "Cocoa! Get down here now, your friend is upset!"

I gave Khaila the bag she asked for. She started rapidly breathing air into the paper bag. Cocoa finally made it downstairs a couple minutes later. She was greeted by Khaila's wheezing in a bag, like she was about to die.

"Khaila? What's wrong baby? Reese what the hell happened to her!"

"I don't know. She came over like that. She said something about D.C. and a letter he left her."

I brought out Khaila's tea. She had calmed down a little. Cocoa had been rubbing her back to help soothe her, like she did with the kids to get them to go to sleep. I guess that stuff worked with adults too.

Cocoa asked, "Khaila, what got you so upset?"

She handed Cocoa the letter from D.C. When Cocoa read the letter her face told it all. D.C. was in some serious mess. I just wanted to stay out of it, so I went back in the kitchen to "clean up." Curiosity wouldn't let me stay out of it though. I listened at the doorway.

I heard Khaila say, "I don't know where he is or what he is doing. He

said in the letter he'd be back soon. It's after noon. Where is he?"
She was starting to get worked up again. I peeked out the kitchen to check on things. I could see her sniffling and hear heavy breathing from the kitchen. *Women can be so damned emotional*, I thought to myself.
I said, "Everything a'ight out there?"
"She'll be a'ight." Cocoa yelled back to me. She turned to Khaila and said, "D.C. will be ok Khaila. Don't worry yourself. Drink your tea and relax for me."
"What do you think about the letter Cocoa? What does it mean?"
"I don't know honey."

Cocoa asked me to come in the living room She gave me a concerned look and handed me the letter. I just wanted to stay out it, but what could I do.

I read the letter and I understood why Khaila was freaking out. I didn't know what it meant but I knew it didn't sound good. D.C. didn't say anything about where he was going, what he was doing, or when he'd be back. I know most women freak out when their man disappears and he doesn't give any details. I suggested she call his cell phone, but she said it had been turned off. She told me she called the job and he wasn't there as scheduled. I remember thinking to myself, *dude ain't show up for work, he must be in some serious shit.*

* * *

## D.C.

I was homicidal, Q was psychotic, and Jy was still being neurotic. With different states of mind, we all had different ideas of torture for Fefe. I still wanted to kill the bitch, Q thought we should gang rape her, and Jy suggested we just threaten her with words and leave. With only a weak plan in place, there was no way we could turn back.

We grabbed Fefe up, knocking over a lamp and some other shit on one of her living room tables. It all went crashing to the floor. She struggled to get a loose cussing us out in the process.

When we got to her bedroom, we threw her on the bed kicking and screaming. Then we tied her squirming arms and legs to the bedpost from laces we pulled out of Jy's Timberlands.

That's where our plan came to a screeching halt. Q's sick ass was pulling at her clothes, trying to get her butt naked. Jy started talking shit to her. I was just ready to get rid of her.

She said, "What is wrong with you D.C.? Why you doing me like this?"

I answered her first with a bitch slap right 'cross her face. She tried to take it like a man, but the tears started welling up in her eyes.

"Shut the fuck up! I plan to fuck yo' ass up. That's why I'm doing you like this. I'm so threw with yo' crazy shit! You really don't have a fucking life, do you? Stalking me and my girl for years! Who's the stalker now? Or should I say your hostage taker and soon to be killer."

"I don't know what you talking 'bout D.C. Must be one of yo' other bitches stalking ya'wl. I got better things to do than mess with you or your ugly ass girlfriend!"

Q yelled out, "Fuck that! D.C. let's run a train on this bitch! Get a muffle and shut her the fuck up!"

Jy found two dirty socks and stuffed them in her mouth. She tried to bite his hand in the process. Then she tried to scream but no sound would come out. *Too damn late, dumb ass.* Fefe had always been slow to figure shit out.

I told Q, "I ain't running no train yo, especially on this skank'. Besides let me tell you son, I already had it before, and it's pretty much a dead fuck!" Me and Q laughed uncontrollably.

The phone rung. Me and Q didn't pay it no mind, but Jy stared a hole through the phone, looking scared as hell. My man was really bitching up I'm telling you. Bending over to the floor, fighting to get air. That's when I started getting nervous. *This nigga gonna get us hemmed up for real.*

He was freaking out, "Yo man, this shit has gone too far. Let's go man!"

Q noticed Jy's nervousness, and picked him apart, "Look, yo' bitch-ass can go 'head and leave then. I'm staying right here with my boy 'til we finish teaching this trick a lesson."

"I'm telling you man we need to go...now." He pointed towards the bedroom window frozen like ice.

We all turned facing the window, noticing the all too familiar red and blue lights. It was the po-lice! Q and Jy looked at each other, both with fear in their eyes. I imagine in those lights they saw flashing images of their soon-to-be fate. They both knew they couldn't afford another trip to jail. We had all done time before and knew the deal. Lockdown was no joke for real. Bad food and lack of freedom were the least of our concerns. Jail meant living in a jungle full of rapist and murderers. The same method of the street, also dwells in the jungle. You had to get "broken in", because you were "fresh meat." And unless you had peoples on the inside who gave a fuck about you, you were destined for the initiation process. Q stood to lose the most inside the jungle with Virginia's three strikes law in full effect. He knew more than any of us that he couldn't go back to jail. My boy could possibly get a life sentence with no chance of parole.

Before I could even say, "hold up," my so-called boys made a dash for the back door, while I stayed behind. I had unfinished business to take care of. I stood face to face with my enemy, and I had to finish what I had started.

Without a blink or a sigh I stared down at my victim, and said, "If we ever see or hear from you or your friend again, a court order will be the least of your worries. Do you hear me?" I approached closer hovering over the bed and said, "I promise you I-WILL-KILL-YOU-IF-I-SEE-YOUR-FUCKIN-FACE-AGAIN. You can quote me on that. Right now I don't give a fuck, and I ain't got shit to lose! I'd suggest you find a new place of residence....."

## Chapter 22

*Reese*

We rushed Khaila to the hospital after she had her second anxiety attack, plus painful cramps, and some bleeding. We were afraid something had gone wrong with the baby. My mother-in-law came back over to watch the children. Cocoa explained everything to her over the phone, and she had no problem babysitting while we took Khaila to the emergency room. At that moment, Khaila had a real reason to worry, with the risk of losing her baby to stress. The more she worried herself the worse her condition became. Cocoa sat in the back of the car with Khaila and tried to get her to relax. It was hopeless.

I drove as fast as I could to the hospital, glancing in the rearview mirror at every red light.

Cocoa rubbed Khaila's stomach in circles, and reassured her that everything would be fine. She even tried to keep Khaila's mind off things by talking about how nice their wedding would be and how proud D.C. would be to have a son. She accomplished her goal because Khaila calmed down a little by the time we reached the hospital.

When we went inside, we were immediately sent to the OB-GYN emergency room. Cocoa helped Khaila complete her paperwork. I turned it into the nurse, and she told me that they would need an insurance card to process the paperwork. I looked at her like she was nuts. We were in an emergency room, and they were more concerned with insurance information than the baby's health. I figured Khaila didn't have an insurance card on her after the way we rushed to the hospital, but I asked her anyway.

"You wouldn't happen to have your insurance card or number with you, would you?"

"No Reese, but they have to take me through anyway right? It is an emergency."

I told her, "Everybody's here for an emergency, but they'll need insurance information or they'll have to pay out-of-pocket."

"Damn! I left the card in my purse at home."

Cocoa said, "Call home and see if D.C. is back yet. Maybe he can come down here with your card."

Khaila called but no answer. She let it ring continuously until the voicemail picked up. She left a message about the whole situation.

"Cocoa, he ain't answering at home. I hope he's ok. He used to have a cell but it got turned off a while back. We really need it right about now."

"What about his friend's numbers?" I asked.

"I do have his friend, Jyree's number…shit….at home in my purse!" She screamed out helplessly.

Cocoa said, "Calm down Khaila. You have your key with you right?"

"Yeah, it's in my pocket." She took the key out of her pocket and handed it to Cocoa.

"Reese, can you go over to her apartment and get her purse for me?"

"Yeah, baby. Gimme the key."

"You can even call with the insurance number, so you don't have to come all the way back down here. The number is probably all they need. Then you can chill at home with the kids 'til I get home later on."

Reese replied, "A'ight, no problem. Khaila don't you worry, I'mma get the card number for you in a few.."

I kissed my wife on the lips and left in a hurry. It was amazing how Khaila's crisis had brought us together just that fast. It was a trip, that very same morning we were fighting like we were at war.

I drove over to Khaila's place in a hurry. When I got there I saw D.C.'s friend, Jyree on the doorstep. I didn't know dude that well but I recognized Jyree from the many times he hung out on the stoop with D.C. On occasion, I would greet him and exchange a few friendly words.

"Hey, Jyree man. What's going on?"

"Hey, what's up. I was just leaving a note for Khaila on the door. You seen her?"

"Yeah, man she's at Richmond General Hospital. She had a panic attack earlier and then she got sick as hell man. I hope she don't lose the baby. I gotta' get the insurance info. out the house now."

I headed for the apartment and then turned around to say, "You seen D.C.? She was so freaked out about him, she literally had a fit this morning."

Jyree got real quiet all of a sudden, and I didn't know what to say. He apparently knew what had happened to D.C., but he won't trying to tell it.

"I can't get into it with you Reese, but if you make sure she gets this I would appreciate it." He handed me the note D.C. wrote Khaila.

"A'ight man I'll do that."

"Thanks. I'm 'bout to be out. Peace."

Jy headed down the block and I went inside to find Khaila's purse. I was really curious and tempted to read the note, but I put it in my back pocket instead. I wasn't sure what it said, but I was sure it wasn't good news. My main priority was Khaila's baby. I searched frantically for her purse to get the card out.

## *Jyree*

I hit the streets hard to make some serious cash for my boy. I felt a little guilty for not having his back and running out on him like a bitch. I had to get $1500 to bail him out of jail. I only had like $900 stashed away, which was my re-up money for more weed. I had to make due with the product I already had to sell.

It's funny I didn't have the money to get my boy out of jail, because he wanted me to slow down hustling and get a real job. I never stopped, but I had taken a break from selling, until I had to sell to help bail him out. I figured he wouldn't really care about the drug money if it got his ass out of jail.

The news about Khaila disturbed me, and I felt even more guilty that I didn't stop my boy from winding up in jail. I'd left him alone to get hemmed up by the po-lice. Some best friend I was, but I was gonna make things right when I bailed him out. I knew Q really didn't give a fuck. He took a missing after that night at Fefe's.

## *Reese*

I jumped in the car when I got the card. I thought I would give Khaila the card and the letter at the same time. Then I thought about it, how could I give her a letter that I wasn't sure what it said in her condition? If it was bad news I had to protect her from it. So I had to read it.

It read:

> Khai,
>
> I know you're wondering what's going on. I took it upon myself to let you know what happened last night. Q, D.C., and me had a wild night. We got into a lotta shit I can't really get into, so I'll cut to the chase.
>
> D.C was sick of Fefe fucking with you and upsetting you, so he asked me and Q to help get rid of Fefe. I tried to reason with him, and talk him out of it, but he had his mind made up.
>
> We took Fefe in her apartment and tied her down to the bed. I can't even tell you what D.C. and Q wanted to do her. Good thing for Fefe the police showed up. Me and Q ran, but D.C. stayed. He got locked up last night. I'm trying to get the bail money together to get him out now. He's at the city jail on 14th street.
>
> I don't want you to worry about it Khai, I'll do what I gotta' do to get him out. I'll holla at you later. — Love, Jy
>
> P.S. You know if things don't work out for you and D.C., me and you can give it another try. I have grown a lot over the years, and I'm ready now.

I couldn't believe my eyes. None of the letter made any sense to me. I thought, *Khaila and Jyree had something going on? They all went out to 'take care' of Fefe? What? And why was Jyree stupid enough to write this shit and give it to a practical stranger to deliver? And most of all, why the hell would D.C.'s best friend leave him to face charges alone. What am I gon' do with this letter?*

I chickened out and called Cocoa with the card number. I'd let her deal with explaining the letter later.

## *Cocoa*

The morning after Khaila's crisis, I woke up in a hard, uncomfortable chair next to her bed. I pretended to be her sister, so I could talk with the doctors and stuff. The nurse told me the uterine bleeding had stopped and her condition had stabilized. They requested that she stay at least another night for observation and tests. I told them I would stay by her bedside and make sure she stayed another night.

The doctor explained that Khaila was to be on strict bed orders through the rest of her pregnancy. She could not return to work until after having the baby.

Reese never came back to the hospital, he stayed with the kids like I'd suggested. He called with the card number and the hospital was able to quickly process the paperwork.

I know we had been sitting in that waiting room for at least a half an hour before Khaila was finally seen by a doctor. Good thing she didn't have a gunshot wound or she would've bled to death.

When Khaila went into the emergency room, I got another call from Reese. He told me about a letter D.C.'s friend wrote to Khaila. At first, I fussed at him for being nosy, but when I heard what was in the letter I was glad he had read it. Khaila didn't need anything else making her upset.

I was in complete shock. I couldn't believe what Reese was telling me, especially the p.s. part of the letter. I thought to myself, *Jyree wanted to get back with Khaila. What's that about?*

I didn't tell Khaila anything about the letter. I decided to wait for the right time, whenever that was. If she didn't ask about D.C., it wasn't any reason for me to bring him up. She slept through most of the day, so I really didn't need to explain anything.

If I could hold out another couple days, I could help prolong another anxiety attack. I spent most of my time there watching TV., and trying to figure out how to buy some time to stall her. I needed to convince Reese to get D.C. out of jail fast or Khaila would surely lose that baby.

## *Reese*

"You must be out of your damn mind, Cocoa!" I protested through the phone.

"Come on baby. We got some money stashed away, we can afford to loan 'em the money."

"You don't even know how much this shit is gonna cost us. Come on, this is crazy! We have gotten wrapped up in their mess too much as it is." I said with bass in my voice, letting her know I was serious.

We had our own issues to deal with. We sure didn't need to get involved with other people's problems. My wife hadn't been home the whole day, and she seemed much more worried about Khaila and D.C's business, than her own family's business.

The hospital decided to keep Khaila an extra day, which was exactly what we were hoping for. Cocoa came home in the afternoon to eat, shower, and relax before checking back with the hospital.

When she arrived home, I made it clear we were not going to give away most of our savings for D.C.'s bail funds. I was still dead set against it, though my stubborn, close-minded attitude was short-lived.

Cocoa had a way of coaxing me into doing just about anything she wanted, with a seductive touch to my erogenous zones. That night, she was determined to use what she had to get what she wanted.

She gently kissed each of my earlobes, while massaging my nipples in small circles. I was growing and hardening with every touch of her soft, feminine hands, accompanied by her warm, full lips. Cocoa pleasured me orally to the point of insanity. Right before my climax, she mounted me with no hesitation, and rode me like a wild cowgirl in a rodeo show. Full of intensity, we made good love for more than an hour that night.

Cocoa knew like I knew, I was so weak when she threw it on me like that. There was nothing like good loving. No amount of money, no drug, no nothing could top it. Good loving usually resulted in poor judgment.

We agreed to take out the $1000 for D.C.'s bail. If we didn't have enough money, we would take out a bond to bail him out. The plan was to post bail before Khaila was discharged from the hospital, and had the chance to find out what happened to her man. That was the plan but sometimes things don't go exactly as planned.

## *Jyree*

For about two days straight, I put my foot to the pavement, hustling the strip, and I earned the extra $600 I needed for my boy's ticket out of jail. I decided I had a quick stop to make before I got him out. A much needed stop - by Richmond General Hospital.

She was sleeping like an angel when I walked in.

"Khai? Khai? Wake up baby." I whispered in her left ear.

"D.C.? Where you been baby?" She whispered back half-sleep.

I kissed her lips to wake her. She kissed me back still assuming I was D.C. I didn't feel any shame at the time, just a strong emotion I couldn't explain.

She quickly drifted away to sleep again. I tapped her shoulder to wake her again.

"It's me Khai. You would think you would recognize my voice after all these years."

She opened her eyes barely, and tried to focus on my face. I know she was like *what the hell is he doing here?* I prayed a short prayer, hoping she didn't know I had kissed her. I know it was wrong but I just couldn't resist.

I hadn't kissed her lips in so long. I missed it. We used to be a couple back in the day, and believe or not, I'd actually helped make Khaila and D.C. a couple.

Khaila and me were together for about a year back in 2000. We had an on and off again relationship. I liked her a lot, but she couldn't accept who I was. We constantly argued about my lifestyle. She said she didn't want a thug anymore she wanted a man who was the working type. Shit, I was working. Working the streets! Anyway, I tried to change for her, but the streets were in my blood.

Being that Khaila had planned to go to college soon, she felt she deserved an educated, professional man.

So what did I do? Tried to accommodate her. I even got a part-time job for her, but I was used to getting large amounts of fast money. We gradually grew apart day by day, and the separation period got longer and longer each time.

One day, Khaila came by the job to bring me lunch and I introduced them. Dumb right? I know. I think she instantly fell for D.C. 'cause he was all about working at that time. Getting to know D.C. later I learned he was an undercover thug himself. He just didn't let it be known. He tried to keep that shit hidden in his past.

D.C. quickly became my best boy. We hung out, and did everything together, except for hustle of course. He was always straight with me, and he always had a nigga's back.

About three months later, Khaila started showing up to the job more and more, openly flirting with D.C. I didn't really care, because I was ready to move on to other women myself. I figured if she couldn't accept me for me, then fuck her.

One day, Khaila called up to the job for D.C. and boldly asked for his number. By then, D.C. was my best friend, and he felt obligated to tell me what the deal was, and he asked me how I felt about it. I told him "go for it", and that I was over her anyway. I was lying to D.C. and myself, because I wasn't really over Khaila. Deep down I knew I was in love with her. I didn't know anything about love then, but looking back, I believe I really did love her. But my ego was way stronger than my love.

So I let my best friend get with my ex-girlfriend, and now they were about to get married and have a baby.

Lying there helplessly, Khaila turned to face me finally getting her eyes focused, and said, "Jyree? What…what are you doing here? What's going on? Where is D.C.?"

# Chapter 23

## *D.C.*

There I was rotting in a jail waiting for somebody, anybody to bail me out. I had only been in jail once before, and it was only for a few days. I didn't think I could handle any more than that. I couldn't believe one wild night of insanity would lead me to four cell walls and a toilet.

In a way, I was kinda relieved the po-lice showed up before my rage led to murder one. I would've gotten a lot more time for taking her out. And Q's crazy ass was gonna take the scare tactic too far by raping her. Even I didn't think she deserved to be gang raped.

Jy's punk ass came by to visit the day after I got locked up, talking 'bout he felt like shit and wanted to make it up to me. I told him, "Get me out of this shithole," which reeked of piss and some other shit I didn't wanna remember. I had seen things I wanted to forget.

I thought about my baby hoping she was doing ok. I wasn't able to get her when I called home, and nobody was telling me nothing. I told Jy he could also make it up to me by checking up on Khai.

I really didn't trust that snake to help me out for real. Jy had betrayed me once, he'd probably do it again. So I didn't really trust he would get me out of jail or check on Khai for me.

Q was really on my shit list. After years of having my back, I felt he had left me to the wolves. He hadn't even called or came by. Jyree said he'd disappeared. He wasn't even hanging on the block like usual.

The jail officer woke me up from a half-sleep. I could barely close my eyes in that place. I wanted to be prepared to defend my manhood at any time if necessary.

I had another unexpected visitor. It was Reese from next door. I was a little confused, but I was happy to see anybody I knew who could possibly free me. He did come to bail me out, and he came with some information too. Information I wasn't ready to receive. It was more screwed up than being in jail.

Reese slid me a letter written by Jy through the prison booth. It sounded ok 'til I got to the p.s. part, "You know if things don't work out for you and D.C., me and you can give it another try. I have grown a lot over the years, and I'm ready now. –Love, Jyree."

"What the....!"

Spit was flying from both sides of my mouth. I was fuming mad. I could not believe my eyes, so I read it again, which only made me hotter. I felt like putting my fist through the bulletproof glass.

Reese spoke through the booth phone, "Calm down man. Look I'm trying to get you out of here in a minute."

"He gave you this letter?"

"Yeah. I thought it was stupid for him to give it to me. I don't even know him like that. He gave it to me when I came home from the hospital."

"Hospital?"

"Yeah, Khaila's in the hospital, but...."

"Khaila's in the hospital? She a'ight? What about the baby?"

I felt the stinging sensation of tears forming in my eyes. Things couldn't have gotten any worst. I was in jail, my best friend betrayed me twice, and my pregnant girlfriend was in the hospital. I just couldn't take anymore.

"They're fine man. She just got real excited. They're releasing her today. That's why I gotta' get you out of here before she gets home."

"She in the hospital worrying about me man? Damn! I wanted to avoid all this shit. I knew if I didn't get home before the morning she'd wake up freaking out."

"Yeah, but everything is gonna be a'ight. She's fine and the baby is fine. Just let me post bail and I'll see you on the outside man."

"Thanks man I appreciate it."

## *Jyree*

After I left the hospital, I was ready to bail D.C. out like I'd promised. I still felt guilty about him being there, even though I wanted to get with his woman so bad I could taste it. I was gonna do one last good deed for him and that was it.

When I got to the jail, I found out D.C. wasn't there. Someone had already bailed him out. At first I thought maybe Q had done the same thing I had done to get D.C. out, but then I saw on the roster that a Reese Harris had signed in for him. *Shit!*

I put two and two together and got four. Reese gave D.C. the letter I gave him to give to Khaila. That would explain why Khaila didn't know where D.C. was earlier. What was I thinking? I wasn't thinking, I was just doing...some stupid shit. When I came to this conclusion, I knew it was about to be on between D' and me. *Damn, what did I get started?*

## *D.C.*

My release from jail was what I call bittersweet. I was happy I was free from jail, but I realized I was also free to deal with more issues than I could handle.

Fear and anger grew inside me as we headed towards home.

Out of nowhere I shouted, "I betcha' that nigga gave you that letter to give it to me on purpose. He wants drama. Well, you know what, I'mma give it to him!"

Reese looked at me like his patience was worn thin and said, "Come on man. I just paid $1000 plus $500 bond to get yo' ass outta jail. You need to chill. I shouldn't have shown you the letter, but I felt you needed to know about your boy and your woman. I mean you was 'bout to get married right?"

"I'm still getting married. I trust my girl a hundred percent, but Jy's been jealous of me and Khaila for a long time."

I conveniently left out the other details. It won't dude's business that Jy and Khaila were a couple before I got with her. He knew too much info about Khaila and me anyway, thanks to his nosy wife.

Reese said, "Man, you know I took a risk showing you the letter. I told Cocoa I would keep the letter 'til Khaila was feeling better. We knew it would mess her head up, you know."

I could see red at that point, "Uggh...wait 'til I get my hands on him man. He would be careless enough to write a letter to Khai right under my nose. Or maybe he thought I wouldn't get out so he could get back with her again. That's probably what he thought."

"Yeah, I know he must not be in his right mind. First he runs off leaving you with the criminal charges, and then he does this. That fool is crazy."

I paused a minute staring out the car window as we headed home. Then I said, "I wanna see my baby. Take me to the hospital man."

"Looking like that?" He laughed.

I looked down at my dirty clothes from the other day, and I saw what he meant. I hadn't shaved, maintained my locs, or anything. I was a fuckin' mess. Khaila would know something had happened if she saw me looking like that. I usually kept my appearance pretty tight.

"A'ight then, take me home first. Then I'll shower and shave. And if you don't mind, you can run me to the hospital. I gotta' see her."

Me and Khaila had only been apart one time before during our whole relationship. I had been accustomed to holding her on a regular, even when we argued. It had been two days, ten hours and fifteen minutes since I had last seen her angelic face, but whose counting?

## *Reese*

As requested, I took D.C. to his apartment to get dressed. I hung out in the car. In the rearview, I saw a tall, thin guy who looked a lot like Jyree. Dude all of a sudden turned and sprinted in the opposite direction. I guess he was avoiding trouble with D.C. at all cost. D.C. came back to the car, and I decided to keep quiet to avoid any more drama.

I couldn't drive to the hospital fast enough. I was uncomfortable with the whole thing and just wanted to get it over with. I was guilty of meddling in other's people's affairs, after I fussed at Cocoa for being the town gossip. If she found out about what I did she'd kill me dead. That was for sure.

I made a rash decision to give D.C. the letter. Dude should know his boy is living fowl.

D.C. ran slightly ahead of me to find Khaila. I directed him to her room on the 6$^{th}$ floor of the hospital.

He wasn't out of the hallway yet when he yelled, "You a'ight baby?"

"I'm ok now. How are you? You been gone so long baby."

They were having their moment, so I suggested to Cocoa we give them their space. We went to eat lunch in cafeteria.

## *Khaila*

D.C came in the room out of breath, desperately searching for me. I was still a little woozy from the medicine the hospital gave me to suppress my attacks. I had had a lot of excitement for one day, and really couldn't take anymore. D.C. immediately tried to explain himself. "I...I was..um..."

"You don't have to come up with a story or an explanation D.C. I know where you've been all weekend." I could feel I was about to cry. Jyree had told me the trouble they had gotten into when he stopped by. He told me everything would be fine and he would bail D.C. out for me. He was acting real strange, talking 'bout he still loved me and he wished we could get back together. I didn't pay him no mind. I just told him I wanted D.C. out of jail like yesterday. He left with his head down without another word.

D.C. said in shock, "But how you know..."
I interrupted, "I had a visitor a few hours ago."

## *Jyree*

I knew I had to lay low for a while. Messing with D.C.'s girl was grounds for murder. I decided to lay low with my great aunt on Rosewood Avenue in the West End for at least two or three weeks. I figured he would probably calm down by then. He wouldn't be able to track me down there.

I knew how much Khaila meant to D.C, anytime he was willing to kill Fefe to be with her. She meant a lot to me too, we had more history between us. But D.C. was my boy. I guess I just got caught up with my feelings for Khaila, it ruined my friendship with D.C.

I realized confessing my love for Khaila was a poor decision. Especially when she told me she didn't have any interest in getting back with me. *But what about our last fling, didn't that mean anything to her?*

\*\*\*

## *Cocoa*

After Reese's confession, I was pissed. We were officially not speaking for an undetermined span of time. He was always fussing about me being nosy, and told me I should mind my own business, and he goes and gives D.C. that damned letter. Even I wouldn't have done that shit.
We still had our own mess to deal with. Like his old mistress calling my house every other day. She called with more drama, which reminded us both we still had problems to hash through.
Reese was in the shower when I answered the phone.
"Hello?"
"Yeah, let me talk to Reese. I ain't for your shit today. I just gotta' tell him something. If *you* don't mind." Wanda said in a smart-ass sarcastic tone.
I said boldly, "He's busy. I'll take a message for him though."
She comes back with, "Naw I'd rather discuss this with him."
"I'm his wife, anything you gotta' tell him, you can tell me."
"A'ight, I was trying not to be nasty, but....I'm pregnant....3 months pregnant...and yes it's his baby."
For a moment I couldn't do or say a thing. I froze. Dropped the receiver, stood there, and stared in space. After about a minute of heavy breathing, increased blood pressure and heart rate, I gained my composure and picked up the receiver.
"Hello?" I said with a shaken voice, still in shock of what I'd just heard. Wanda, my enemy, was still there waiting to rub her news in my face.
"Yeah, bitch I'm still here. Put *my man* on the phone!" She screamed.
I hung up the phone without hesitation. I went straight to the bathroom to confront Reese head on. I rushed the bathroom door pissed off like usual whenever Wanda called. I walked in without knocking and told him we needed to talk.
He took his time coming out, 'cause he knew I had had enough of the constant phone calls from Wanda.
"I'm coming out babe, just about finished."
I grunted in a low voice to avoid waking the kids. "You need to be fucking finished right now."

I then went upstairs to the children's room where they were having a tea party with my mother. I asked my mother to take the kids out somewhere, and she wanted to know why. I whispered that Wanda had called, and explained the details of the phone call. After she got over her own shock she decided to take the kids out liked I asked.

With my kids gone, I impatiently waited for Reese to come out of the bathroom. When he finally did, I proceeded to slap his moist face as hard as I could.

"What was that for?" He asked while massaging his burning face.

"That was for your new bastard child, Reese!" I ran to the bedroom, and Reese followed only to have the door slammed in his face.

I screamed, "I thought we could start over Reese, but now I see it just won't happen. You done got some other woman pregnant! How could you be so careless?"

He didn't make a peep in the hallway for a minute. About ten minutes later he decides to make an appearance to explain himself.

## *Reese*

I was speechless, couldn't figure out what to say to Cocoa. Wanda had called the house blabbing to my wife that she was pregnant with my baby. What in the world?

I couldn't fathom how Wanda could be pregnant by me. I was always careful with her, using protection every time....except....one time. I had forgotten about the night at the Super 8, when we slept together. Both of us had been drinking. I got really drunk, trying to deal with the pain of missing my wife. I didn't' remember everything, but I did remember waking up naked beside that trick the next morning. Could she have impregnated herself as a ploy to get with me?

## Chapter 24
## *Khaila*

Two weeks passed since D.C.'s trouble, and we were still making plans for our wedding. The scheduled date was to be December 20th, right before Christmas. We were both ready to jump the broom, and I was more than ready to drop that baby. I was so relieved I made it through my anxiety attacks without losing my child. I couldn't have been more happy or at ease.

The wedding plans were just about done, with the exception of a few finishing touches. D.C. wasn't much on the wedding planning, but he was happy to share in my happiness. He kept saying he didn't care about the wedding details. He just wanted to marry me.

"Hey, D.C. What you think about putting these flowers on the gazebo?"

"Anything you want is cool with me. I just think you better order them now before it's too late, if you really want them."

"Yeah, I know I have been procrastinating on making the big decisions final. You know how I am about making important decisions."

"Yeah, I know. Any decision for real." He joked.

I responded, "Whateva man," and then I hit him with a nearby pillow.

Even though I was excited about the wedding and the baby, I was also nervous about much more. After Jyree's visit, I kept thinking, *what was he doing? Why did he come by the hospital confessing his love all of a sudden? Would he try to disrupt our wedding?*

He was supposed to be D.C.'s best man, but he mysteriously took a missing after the hospital visit. I had no idea why. D.C. all of a sudden acted real nonchalant like he could care less if Jyree was his best man. He said he would just replace him with his brother, Vey. I didn't like Vey as his choice for best man, because he deserted D.C. when he moved in with me.

I didn't tell D.C. all of what Jyree said at the hospital. I only explained that he told me about the trouble they'd been in. The last thing

I needed was D.C. getting jealous and doing something else crazy. As far as I knew he was just mad about Jyree and Quiante leaving him stranded while he went to jail for "harassing" Fefe.

D.C.'s version of the story was hard to believe, but I wanted to believe him. He told me the three of them went over to Fefe's house. They just so happened to be hanging together that night and decided to drop by. They waited in the car, while D.C. went to talk with Fefe. The talk escalated to a heated argument, and Fefe called the police. Jyree and Quiante drove off, leaving D.C. in the house to get arrested. I later found out that D.C. was definitely lying to me, and eventually got the real story.

## *D.C.*

We were in the middle of a pillow fight when the phone rang. We let the voicemail pick up the call, so we could continue enjoying each other. We missed each other so much those two days.

I decided to check the messages later on that night. One was from Khaila's mother just making sure she was ok. I skipped ahead to the most recent message.

It was Jy. His message went:

"I need to talk to you D', man-to-man, one-on-one. I gotta' talk to you now man. Before you get married, there are some things you need to know first. Meet me at the spot in an hour. I'll wait for you there in the back near the pool tables. A'ight. Peace."

I didn't know what was going on, but I needed to find out what the hell Jy was talking about. Even though I was clueless, I had a feeling it wasn't gonna be good. I jetted out the house in hurry, telling Khaila I was stopping by the store to get a few knickknacks for the house.

## Chapter 25

## *Wanda*

"Girl...I'mma go over there and talk to him 'bout this baby...he thinks he can avoid me...umhmm... I don't even think so! I'm going over there right now girl, and he gon' take care of this baby. I mean that! I'm too damn old to be raising a goddamn baby by myself." I ranted and raved to my girl, Francine on the phone.

I needed to confront Reese right then. I told Francine I'd call and fill her in on the details later. Then I got dressed and went straight to his place. I wasn't even thinking about his wife or his muthafuckin' kids. I was gonna straighten Reese's ass out. After reminding him of future child support payments, he'd come to his senses and marry me like he should.

When I pulled up to Reese's place, I saw his car, so I knew he was home. I pounded on the door for a minute. Then I saw his bitch peeking through the blinds, but she wouldn't open the door. I won't even falling for that shit. After about five minutes of non-stop banging, Reese opened the door, and quickly closed it behind him. He stepped to me aggressively.

"Wanda, come on now. Why you come popping up like this? I'm finally getting things somewhat settled in my house. I don't need you starting no shit! I'm serious I don't need this right now!"

Reese ranted on like he'd gone crazy. He was so close I could feel the warmth of his breath on my face.

"Well you know what? You got it now, Reese!"

He grabbed my arm and grunted, "Let's take a walk."

"Let go of my arm Reese.

"We not doing this here. Walk with me down the block."

"I don't care where we go, long as you gon' take care of your business with me and your child."

He kept pulling on my arm the whole way to this park a couple blocks down. He didn't say a word on the way, he just kept jacking me up 'til we reached Forest Hill Park. It was unseasonably warm that day.

I remember, because there was a nice, Indian summer breeze in the air The park had a really romantic feel to it, with a small lake surrounded by benches and decorative flowers. The whole scene was real pretty, but under the circumstances I wasn't feeling it at all.

Pregnancy had my emotions out of whack, so I wasn't surprised when I started crying. The anger I had felt before softened, and for the moment I felt vulnerable like a child. Reese was staring at me real stupid, like he believed I was crying fake crocodile tears for sympathy. The tears were real.

I started reminiscing about the times when we would come to that very park for sweet, romantic rendezvous. We'd make love in the grass, have red wine and cheese crackers, enjoy long walks in the park, and then we'd finish the evening by making love again. Reese would kiss and hold me, saying he loved me with such sincerity in his voice.

Experiencing the beautiful scenery of the park, while enjoying each other, was very special to me. It was never just a good screw. Whether Reese wanted to admit it or not, it was always much, much more between us.

So how did things fall apart for us? He wouldn't hear me out at all, and that hurt like a blunt knife being twisted deep in my gut. Treated me like I was some kind of whore or something, when he told me before he loved me. Promised to leave his wife for me, and he even described our future lives together.

Now I was carrying his child in my womb, and he was denying its existence. Well he was gonna learn to love me and our baby or he was gonna pay. One way or the other. It was his choice.

## D.C.

When I got to the pool hall, I couldn't find Jy at first. By this point, I was still confused about why I was asked to come there. He had nerve to even call me after the shit he pulled, visiting the hospital and writing a love letter to Khaila. I really didn't want to deal with Jy anymore period, but I admit I was curious to know what he had to tell me before the wedding. As if it wasn't enough, he had stabbed me in the back twice. I kept thinking on the way to the spot, *what is he 'bout to spring on me now?*

I walked to the back where the pool tables were, and he was there. He looked real rough, like someone had got to his ass before I had the chance. He wasn't well dressed as usual, and it was apparent he hadn't shaved in days.

"Jy, what's up?"

"Nothing man, just 'bout to rack up a game for us. How have things been?"

"It's a'ight I guess, considering...."

Jy interrupted. "I'm glad to see you out man."

I could tell he was trying to feel me out. I was in a cut-to-the-fuckin-chase kinda mood, and he knew it.

I said, "What's the deal man? Why you got me down here. If you haven't guessed, we ain't on it like that no more!" I was getting pumped up. I had to tell myself to tone it down before I revisited the city lock-up again.

"It's hard for me to tell you this D' but I'll just spit it out. You...you can't marry Khaila."

"Why you say that....?"

He blurted out, "'Cause I wanna marry her man."

"What? You wanna do what? You still got a fuckin' crush on my girl! I got the letter you wrote to her, talking 'bout y'all getting back together! That shit ain't gonna ever happen. Khaila don't want you no more, she wants me....I should fuckin'...."

I clenched my fist ready to strike.

"Man, hold on. I'm not finished. Let me finish. I hope you forgive me for what I'm about to say, but if you still wanna fight me, I'll understand."

"Yo, what are you talking about?" It was hard for me to control myself. I wanted to bust his shit right then, but curiosity held me back. The wait was killing me.

"Well, you know me and Khai were together before you guys became a couple. Back then me and you won't as close as we are now. I never knew then that you would be like a brother to me. You have had my back and I ..." He was getting emotional.

I preyed on his weakness. "Man, come on and spit the shit out already. Your story is very touching, but I got shit to do. Got a woman and child to get back to." I took a deep breath and said, "What do you have to tell me? What was so important for you to get me down here and confess your love for my girl. I mean I really don't care how you feel man, she don't want you. Khaila is gonna marry me and have..."

He completed my sentence, "My baby." Those words crushed me like a ton of bricks, falling out of nowhere.

"What! So what are you saying???"

"I think the baby Khaila's carrying is mine."

"You must be fuckin' kidding me. What?" I was in shock. I wanted to punch him in his nose, but I couldn't find the strength to lift my fist. I don't think I'd ever received such crushing news in my life, besides the news of my mother's terminal illness.

"We talked about it and everything. Khaila don't even know whose baby it is. She called me freaking out the same night she got the news from the doctor's office. I guess she figured she could confide in me. I wasn't gonna say nothing. I was trying to get over her, but the bigger she got with my baby growing inside of her the more I fell in love with her. Every time I saw her face I fell more and more in love with her. I was gonna keep her secret, but I was thinking the hospital scare would eventually reveal the truth. I was afraid a blood test would tell you what I'm telling you now. So I had to say something before someone else did. I felt I owed you that much. I know I punked out by hiding at my aunt's crib a few days, but I decided to do the right thing, and let you know who you were marrying. You shouldn't have to raise my seed. I should be the one to step up. Scared or not."

Still in shock of what I was hearing, I needed the stool behind me to hold me up. I had all kinds of thoughts going through my mind. One thought kept flashing repeatedly. I wanted to take one of those pool sticks, beat the fuck out of him, and then shove it up his ass. I fuckin' despised him at that point, and I didn't care what I did to him.

I still couldn't move an inch even to defend myself. It's amazing how your body can shut down when your soul is hurting. Jy gave me a minute to absorb it all. He went to the bathroom. That's when I came to my senses and followed him in there. Not a good idea to go to the bathroom after you just told your boy you fucked his woman and got her pregnant.

I caught him when he was about to walk out. "Jy? How you know it's your baby?"

"I just got a strong feeling. That was the other reason why I couldn't come back 'cause I couldn't be the best man at your wedding, living a lie."

"If Khaila don't even know, how…?"

"She got a feeling too though. Back in April, y'all had had another fight about Fefe. Khaila called to confide in me. She asked to meet in person. One thing lead to another, and I admit I took advantage of the situation…."

I stood there drunk with anger, pain, hate, and disbelief. With strong force, I swung at his head, but he ducked in time.

"Man, chill. Let me get all this off my chest before you knock my head off. I know I deserve it."

"That was low man, even for you."

"I know it was low. I guess I never really got over her. When y'all got together, I still had a thing for her, but you were my boy, so I told myself to move on. I felt stuck in the middle of what my mind wanted and my heart needed. I loved you as my boy, but I still felt something for her too."

"Earlier you said 'Khaila don't even know.' Why wouldn't she know?"

"Well, the condom broke."

"You didn't mess with the condom or nothing, did you?"

"Hell no, man I didn't put a hole in it or nothing. I didn't want to have a baby. I won't ready then and I still ain't ready."

I leaned against the bathroom sink covering my face with my hands. I was feeling faint again, like I was gonna pass out or something. The more I thought about it, the more pain I felt. *How could she do this to me? I can't believe after all we have been through, she could betray me like this. Lie to me like everything's ok between us.*

I said out loud to myself, "You know how many times I could have fucked Fefe with no problem. Would have gotten away with cheating on her like all those other bitches I used to mess around on. But I never cheated on Khaila, not once. I sat there waiting for the baby to come, when all the while she was hiding her little secret. She don't even know who the baby's father is? How skank."

Jy just stood listening, not really sure what to expect from me. He didn't know what I was gonna do next.

I surprised myself, and said, "I need some time to think man."

Then I walked out of the bathroom and then out of the pool hall.

Jy called my name from the door, but I just kept walking. I guess he had enough sense not to follow me in the street. He'd dodged one bullet in the bathroom.

For some strange reason, I hadn't punched him in the eye. I always said that if I caught my girl cheating, I'd leave her skank ass, and kill the nigga she was with. I never imagined the nigga would be my best friend and the skank would be my wifey.

## *Wanda*

I should have known it was a stupid idea, trying to talk with Reese about the baby. Of course he said what I thought he would. I was a "lying bitch" who just wanted to ruin his marriage. He said he knew the baby was not his because we were careful about using condoms every time. Then he said I manipulated him while he was intoxicated to get pregnant. Even though I denied it, he was right about the last part.

We were both tore down that night. Reese was laid out in the motel bed, passed out, looking all sexy. Even though I knew about his "no condom, no dick rule," I jumped on him raw that night. He was half-sleep when he came inside me, and fell back to sleep immediately after. Reese never knew what hit him.

It wasn't like it was premeditated or nothing. I was just faded and horny, and I wanted to have him raw. A small part of me wanted to have a baby too. I was unmarried and childless, and longed to have a family life someday. I felt like I had my opportunity and I was gonna to take it.

Now Reese not claiming the baby as his own was unfair, 'cause he knew he was the father. I hadn't had sex with anyone else in like two years. So I was on some - he gonna accept me and our baby or all hell was gonna break loose- type shit.

## *Reese*

Something deep in my gut told me that ho' was waiting in the wings to have my baby one day. I just didn't know she would get me caught up like that. Wanda always been a sneaky bitch, gold diggin' to get money. What the hell was I thinking, getting drunk around her? Knowing her, she probably poured my sperm from a condom down her pussy, so she could make sure to have my baby.

Cocoa and me were finally trying to make things work between us, when Wanda called with drama. How was I gonna feed another kid? I was having a hard time with the two I already had at home.

When I came through the door, after leaving the park, I found that Cocoa was gone. Sitting in her place on the sofa was her nosy mother staring me down. If looks could kill, I would have been a dead man on sight.

I asked her where Cocoa was. The old hag refused to say two words to me. I decided to bypass her, and check on my kids who were taking their scheduled afternoon nap.

They looked so peaceful and adorable sleeping, but I knew they were hell on wheels awake. I loved my kids a lot, but the thought of another noisy kid in the house made me cringe.

I stood there staring at my kids daydreaming about our used-to-be happy, family life. I had destroyed all of that for a useless affair with a woman I didn't even care for. Then I started wondering would Cocoa ever forgive me for what I had done. Getting another woman pregnant was unforgivable. It would have definitely been unforgivable if things were reversed.

*I* kept saying to myself, *Where is she anyway? How are we gonna work it out apart?*

Daylight turned to dusk and I was beginning to worry. After calling everybody we knew, I finally got some information from the old hag on the couch. She told me Cocoa said she needed to clear her head for a while. Her mother wouldn't tell me where she was, but I knew she knew all the details. She was too calm for anything to be wrong with her daughter.

I had unpleasant thoughts like, *was she leaving me and the kids to have an affair of her own? Would she try to do something crazy to Wanda?*

I shook those thoughts from my mind so I could think logically. I started thinking, *where would a scorned woman go to feel better? It's Saturday, maybe she went to the club or a bar for drinks.* That idea quickly exited my head. Going to the club and bar were not really her style. *Cocoa would probably be...in church. That's where she is. I bet.*

I drove over to Glory Baptist Church, her favorite church on the

East End. She loved to visit but never joined. There she was sitting in the middle of the last pew alone, praying and crying aloud. The last service had ended over an hour before. I wondered if they ever locked up the church at night.

Cocoa was hurting so bad with her head held down, she didn't even notice me sitting at the opposite end of the pew watching her. I walked down next to her in mid-prayer and touched her on the shoulder. She acted like I was the devil himself, because she started screaming to the Lord to deliver her from all the "evil" in her life. An older woman came out from nowhere when she heard all the commotion. I guess she was the person who locked up the church. She glared at me for a minute. The look on my face let her know that everything was fine, so she left the sanctuary.

I glanced back at my wife, who was still a basket case, and I realized her past bouts with depression were probably due to my stupidity and jealousy. I reached out to hold her close to my chest. She didn't resist. She just cried on my shoulder, saying, "Why? Why me Lord?" over and over again. I didn't say anything. There was nothing I could say.

## Chapter 26

## D.C.

The whole ride home I thought about what I was gonna say to the woman who betrayed me. Betrayal seemed to be the word of the day. I had mixed emotions about Khaila, and I really didn't know what to say, but I knew what I needed to do.

The only friend I really had to talk to was Q. I had gotten over what he'd done. Compared to Jy's crime, Q's was nothing. I believe I probably would've run myself if I had three strikes against me.

I wanted to know what he thought about everything, even though I knew he probably didn't have nothing positive to say.

He was hanging on the block down the street from his house, chillin' with his crew. They scattered like roaches, like I was the po-lice or something. To them, I looked so neat and professional looking, I guess I could have been an undercover detective or something. It was a good thing they left though 'cause I needed some one on one time with my boy. I gave him the up-to-the-minute version of the DC-Khaila-Jy saga. We had a love triangle going on for months, and I didn't even know about it.

What he said was classic for Q. "Man, I told you before, you need to quit the bitch and let that nigga raise the bastard."

I was like, "How you gonna come at me like that, son?" Then I thought about it, what did I really expect him to say.

"Shit, man you asked. I'm just telling you what you need to hear right now. You know that pigeon 'round the corner, claiming she pregnant by me too. Say what?" He laughed. "I gave her $250 to get rid of it, so she could get that bullshit out my face. She not getting this nigga caught up."

"She get it done?"

"I guess so. She took the money." Q didn't care for real.

"You may be in the same shit I'm in nine months from now. Only difference is I love my kid and baby mama. I want to take care of my responsibilities."

"Yada, yada. Now it's your baby again. Well you just gonna have to wait 'til the baby get here, and you can get a blood test when the baby's born. 'Til then you really can't do shit, but wait."

"Yeah...I know. You're right about that."

"I can't believe Jy's ass. He got balls. You want me to handle his ass, man? I always knew that muthafucka was a snake!" He was getting hyped. Drama and confusion gave him an adrenaline rush.

"Naw, I'll handle it."

"You ain't handling shit. You gonna confront 'em again, and talk about it like a female. Then he'll tell you how much he loved your girl for so many years like he did earlier. That's some mess."

"What was I supposed to do? I didn't expect that kinda' news. I was hurting man. I didn't know how to react."

"You react by bashing that muthafuckin' nigga's head in." He yelled out.

I was getting pissed all over again. Q always had a way of inciting anger in me, even when I wasn't upset. He'd done it again. Thoughts of Khaila and Jy together, not only having sex, but actually together in love, kept messing with my head. Of course Q added in his own theories about how Khaila was using me to take care of their baby. Since Jy didn't have a steady job anymore, Khaila would need me to be her baby's daddy instead. I wasn't sure if I was still willing to marry her, obligating myself to her and possibly another man's baby.

About an hour after talking to Q, I went hunting for Jy's ass. I found him hanging on the Brookland Park Blvd., one of his usual hangouts. It was obvious he'd been sipping on something since I'd seen him earlier, he looked tipsy as hell.

I guess he had a real guilty conscience, 'cause he was in confession mode, singing like a canary the whole day. He dropped another bombshell on me.

He explained that he recently found out he contracted Hepatitis C over a year ago. He didn't even know he had it until he went down to the clinic for a V.D. treatment back in July, and they ran other tests. This muthafucka gonna tell me Hepatitis is transmitted through sexual contact, and he won't even sure if he may have passed it to Khaila, or if the baby may be infected.

I had heard a little about Hepatitis before, and I knew it won't no joke. That shit starts shutting down organs like your liver, and you suffer a slow, fucked up death for some years. Who knew what else he had passed on to Khaila and the baby that could show up in lab tests later on.

Right then and there I lost it. I beat the shit out that nigga in the middle of the street on his own block. No one interfered either. His boys just watched the show. He was so pitiful he didn't even fight back. By the time I finished with him thirty minutes later, he was laying spread eagle on the ground half conscience, blood dripping from his bottom lip, and his left eye was swollen shut.

I grabbed him off the ground, threw him against a nearby car, and screamed on him, "Stay the fuck away from us muthafucka!"

Then I left to confront Khaila next. I still couldn't believe what I'd heard. It was too much shit for me to handle at one time. I didn't even know if the baby was mine, or if Khaila or the baby were sick with a contagious disease, or what. But one thing I was sure of- what I needed to do. I was prepared to take care of business with Khaila.

## *Khaila*

I almost had a heart attack when I heard the loud banging on the door. D.C. didn't use his key, which was weird, but that was the least of my concerns. I was not at all prepared for what he said to me. Everything was cool when he left earlier. We were playing and having a good time. Three hours later he comes back home livid.

"I just finished taking care of your boyfriend. Now I'm taking care of this fake ass relationship. We are threw, over wit', done, that's a wrap. I can't believe you would do that shit to me. I can believe him, but not..."

"D.C. What are you talking about?"

"I'm talking 'bout you and your new man, Jyree. You can be together now, 'cause I'm out of the picture."

"What?"

"Khai, don't act stupid. Jy told me everything. He felt he had to confess to me before we got married. I'm glad he did, 'cause you won't."

D.C. stopped talking, but I couldn't say a word. I was dumbfounded. D.C. was never supposed to find out. I should have known something was strange, when Jyree showed up at the hospital out of nowhere.

After our one-night stand, I thought it was over between us. Things were supposed to return to normal. I had no idea Jyree still had feelings for me. I figured he was just being supportive so he could get into my panties. At a weak point, I made the biggest damn mistake of my life. I had a sweet, romantic, caring man who loved me and my child, and I had probably ruined it for good.

Although I wanted the baby to be D.C.'s it was actually possible it was Jyree's baby. I didn't plan on the condom breaking and causing major issues in my relationship with D.C.

I knew I was wrong, but there was nothing I could say or do to fix things. Since I didn't deny it, D.C. packed his stuff in a bag, and left to stay with his brother. I laid there alone in bed crying myself to sleep.

## *Cocoa*

Early in the morning around six-thirty, Khaila called to tell me about what happened to her the night before. It may have been interesting to me, if I wasn't tired as hell from dealing with my own drama. I listened to the lowdown for about fifteen minutes. Then I told her I'd have to call her back, because I was exhausted. I really was tired because of a late night of sobbing and feeling sorry for myself.

I wanted to be sympathetic of Khaila's situation, but I had another woman causing problems in my marriage. A pregnant one at that. In my eyes, Khaila looked a lot like that woman to me. I never imagine her cheating with her man's best friend. She wasn't even sure who the father of her baby was. It was sickening.

Reese claimed Wanda's baby couldn't be his, but I had enough sense to know that anything is possible. I just kept thinking, *what if by small chance this baby really is his? What would I do? How would the kids understand it? How in the hell do you explain to your kids that their father has children with another woman?* Then I thought, *I'mma let his ass handle this shit. He made his mess, he gonna clean it up himself.*

Before I knew it I had fallen asleep dreaming about me and Reese and the kids. It was the same dream I'd had before. We were happier than ever, walking through a beautiful park, laughing and playing around with one another. While the kids played, Reese and me were alone to hold hands and cuddle under a big oak tree. We didn't have a care in the world, just concerned with how to enjoy our weekend relaxing with each other. Right when he kissed my lips, I suddenly jumped out of fantasyland back into reality.

The phone was ringing off the hook. I picked it up about the fifth ring. Damn if it wasn't Khaila calling again. I tried not to sound pissed off when I answered, but I was passed irritated. I never liked my sleep interrupted. Reese slept right through the constant ringing.

"What's up Khaila?"

"Hey Cocoa."

"What you need?"

"I'm sorry, did I wake you up?"

"Yeah, Khaila. I told you before I was exhausted. It has only been what an hour since you called."

"I'm sorry. Look I can call you back later. I just need someone to talk to about this mess I'm in. I can't tell my sister, Tracie or my girl, Shante. I would never hear the end of it from them. You and me have become so close lately, and I trust you. I know you won't judge me or spread my business around town. You're kinda like a sister to me now, you know?"

Boy was she laying it on thick. What could I say to that? So I just responded with "Yeah."

There was a silence for a minute, and then Khaila put the phone receiver down. I could hear her bawling in the background. I called her name over and over, but she couldn't hear me.

I figured, *Hey I'm up now, let me get up and console her. She needs me.* So I hung up the phone, got dressed, and went next door. She took a while to come to the door. When she finally opened the door she was shocked, but also relieved someone cared about her. I decided to leave my personal feelings at the door, and enter her place as a nonjudgmental friend. We sat and talked and laughed and cried together for hours, until we both fell asleep on the couch.

## Chapter 27

## D.C.

A week or so had passed since I left Khaila to stay with Vey. I'm not even gonna dwell on the hell he put a nigga through. I suddenly remembered when I came through the door why I wanted to leave in the first place. We really didn't get along. He started bitchin' and moanin' as soon as I got there. By the end of the week, I was ready to go home and check on Khaila.

She was due to have the baby any day and I had to check on her. Regardless of the who the baby daddy was, I had decided I was gonna raise him. He was my son. I was there since the beginning, and I wasn't about to bail out on him. Though I wasn't really sure about our future, I knew I had to be there for my son.

I walked through the door and got a surprise. Cocoa was in my spot on the sofa. I was trippin' like *damn are you taking my girl away from me too?* Cocoa cleared things up off top.

"I'm here 'cause Khaila has been very upset this past week about you leaving."

"Yeah, I came to check on her. She a'ight?"

"I guess. As well as can be expected. She doing real good for a woman whose about to have a baby by herself." I guess her smart comment was supposed to send me a message. She got up and left the room.

It did. I zoned out for a minute. I understood what she was saying and I felt bad about how I was acting. I left Khaila stranded when she needed me most. Even though I felt bad about things, I still felt like the victim. I wasn't even sure if the baby she carried in her belly was my kid.

Khaila walked into the room out of nowhere. "D.C..? What are you doing here?"

"I came to check on you and the baby." I paused. "I mean our baby."

"I really don't know what to say, D.C. I know you hate me. What decent man wouldn't in your situation."

"I don't hate you Khai. I'm just hurting right now."

In my mind, Khaila was an angel, my angel, who could do no wrong. I never imagined her having sex with my best friend of all people. The thought was making me angry all over again.

Then I thought about what Vey had told me before I left his place. He told me to either leave Khaila alone or forget the whole thing and move on. He was trying to be like a father figure. He told me we could never move on together until I truly forgave Khaila. Even though he never liked Khaila, he was able to put his feelings aside and give me the advice I needed.

I confessed that I loved her more than anyone and that I couldn't just leave her. Vey told me, "well then that means you have to do what you have to do to make it work." My brother really surprised me when he said we should try couple's counseling before getting married. He said we could do it through a church or professional counselor like Dr. Phil.

So I told Khaila what I thought we should do. "I think we need to get counseling services to get through this... for us and the baby."

"Our baby." She corrected me.

We smiled and held each other's gaze for a while. I was bitching up again. My eyes were beginning to water, and Khaila's were already flooded with tears.

When we got our composure, we sat down and talked about things. Khaila said, "You know, Cocoa knows a counselor who has sessions on a sliding scale. Based on our income it shouldn't cost much." She didn't want me to know that Cocoa had counseling herself. Then I would know she was a nutcase, like I always assumed anyway.

We kissed, and it was like nothing in our world was ever out of place.

Then I said without warning, "Why?"

"D.C., baby, I can only tell you I don't know what I was thinking. I was lonely and vulnerable when he came over to comfort me."

"To comfort you, huh?." I said in a sarcastic tone.

'That's why I invited him over. I never thought anything would happen. Plus, everything was supposed to be over between us after that big fight and a month of separation."

I admitted, "I can't even remember what that fight was about."

"I don't either." She said with an uncomfortable giggle.

"He tried to use our break ups to his advantage twice. He was probably hoping the same thing would happen this time."

"Well he did come by the apartment a couple days after you left, but I didn't let him inside. He was standing at the doorway saying we were meant to be. I told him that I was pissed with him for telling you, and causing us to break up because of it. Then I realized that he at least had the courage to tell you what I couldn't say for months..." She said with a sigh.

She started crying again, and I held her in a way that let her know everything would be ok…one day.

## Chapter 28

## *Khaila*

Our wedding was held as scheduled, shortly before the baby was born. We had a small ceremony at the Botanical Gardens. Only the five of us were there; D.C., Cocoa, Vey, the reverend, myself, and the baby. D.C. said he didn't care how many people were there, as long as I was there to marry him.

The whole scene was elegant with all the flowers and decorations in the theme colors, royal blue and silvery white. My satin textured dress was not expensive or over the top, but it was beautiful just the same. D.C. looked so handsome in his black tux with royal blue bow tie. Cocoa and Vey wore their clothes well too. It was a nice intimate wedding, minus the phony "ewws" and "ahhs" from people who came later that evening for the reception anyway.

It didn't surprise D.C. that I cried a river of happy tears. It did surprise me when he did too. He told me he loved me and forgave me for everything. He promised as part of his vows to not dwell in this painful point of our lives. Though we had been through so much this past year, he wanted to move forward with our new family. We were not married when I made my mistake, so in his eyes it didn't matter anymore. I promised him I would be faithful to him from that day forward, and never look back.

A month later, I delivered my baby boy right on time, 7 lbs, 5 oz. D.C. and I decided to name him, Khyon Akanke' Curry. His first name being a combination of both of our names. I found his middle name on a baby name internet site. It means "beloved" in Swahili. I thought it was such a beautiful and appropriate name for him because he was so beloved. It turned out his last name was appropriate as well, since we found out that D.C. was actually Khyon's father. Thank God. D.C. never denied our son. We talked it all out that night he came back. He told me then that he would take care of Khyon regardless of the blood test results.

Khyon looked just like D.C. There was definitely no denying he was D.C.'s child.

Don't get me wrong, things didn't just go back to normal. It took a lot for us to work through our issues like the help of a professional therapist. We were referred to a therapist from the same agency as Cocoa's therapist. Our therapist specialized in marriage/couple's counseling, instead of individual counseling. Cocoa had finally finished her sessions, but she was about to start family counseling with her church. I didn't feel they had much to be concerned about, since they were so in love. Even though the baby drama had torn them apart.

Cocoa was my girl, so she was not only named maid of honor, but Godmother too. I knew Tracie and Shante would be mad with me about it, but they'd get over it. Where were they when I really needed them? Throughout my whole pregnancy they were both missing in action. Too busy dealing with their own drama.

D.C. shocked the hell out of me, by naming Vey as the best man and Godfather!

## *Cocoa*

Things were finally looking up for Reese and me. We were closer than ever. Every now and then I would think about him with Wanda, and I would have to pray on it to feel better again. The trust thing would take a while to establish, but I was willing to wait it out. I didn't have an alternative as far as my family was concerned.

It turned out Wanda lost the baby after carrying it only three and a half months. We will never know whose baby it was, but I really didn't care anymore. It's wrong to say but things had worked out for the best for our family.

Reese was a little upset, because there was a chance the child was his. I knew he was bothered by the lost of the baby, but he really didn't care about Wanda though.

That woman continued to call the house and his cell constantly, and he constantly hung up on her. She had to leave messages about the baby, because he would rarely let her calls through. When they did talk, Reese cut the conversation short. He agreed to only talk about baby-related stuff like her doctor's appointments. He went with her to one appointment to the doctor. I had to trust he would do the right thing, and it was hard.

Reese made sure to come home directly after the appointment. When he came back from the appointment, he told me how Wanda was still trying to tear our family apart, so she could have him. I joked that I would make sure to come to the next appointment with him. We laughed, but part of me was still a little jealous and needed the reassurance. Eventually, God worked out the situation for us, and provided the reassurance I needed to have faith in our relationship.

Our only road block was my mother. She of course believed Reese was the scum of the earth, but she was not married to him, I was. She didn't have a family at stake like I did. I loved my mother, but I had to keep her out of my personal business from then on.

## Chapter 29

## D.C

Over the past three months my life seemed like something out of the *Loves Jones* movie. I had a beautiful wife and son, a promotion on my job as store manager, and a nice new townhouse for my family.

We had moved out of our small apartment to a larger two-bedroom townhouse to fit our new family size. It was in the same area where we were before. We saved for months for the move. Khaila broke down like a baby when we moved out, like it was some kind of bombshell. She said she would miss Cocoa and Reese, who lived a whole ten blocks away!

Everything was cool, except my ugly past came back to haunt me. I was served with court papers in March almost four months after the incident with Fefe. I still had to face what I had done to Fefe in court.

A few days prior to my arraignment, I thought about the fact I could possibly face five to ten years in jail. I wasn't only scared about the time in jail, but the time away from Khaila and Khyon. I was willing to do whatever I had to do to avoid that. I had a fake-ass lawyer, court appointed, who didn't care what happened to me. So I was gonna be up shit creek literally.

My lawyer tried to get me to plead guilty for a lesser charge. I was like hell no, they don't have a real case against me. Who the hell was I kidding? They caught me red-handed leaving Fefe's apartment. She was tied to the bedposts with cuts and bruises all over her body.

I decided to fire the fake-ass lawyer and hire a well-known defense attorney. He was a brother too so I knew he probably cared more about my fate. It was gonna cost me but it was worth it.

I also called Q and asked him to take care of things before my court date. After a long talk I convinced his crazy-ass not to kill Fefe and Tonda, but to only put fear in them. Let's just say, they would not be showing up to court to testify for shit. The state of Virginia would throw out the case without them present.

Q and Jy had both left me to take the full rap for all the shit. What if the prosecution brought up fingerprints for all three of us? Then Q and Jy would both be in position to turn states evidence on me so that they could walk. I really didn't trust them niggas, especially Jy. They were both self-serving muthafuckas and would do anything to save their own ass before trying to save mine. For this reason I was buggin' out for real. What was I gonna do?

.

# Chapter 30

## D.C.

The day of the arraignment hearing, I was sweating bullets, and Khaila.... let's just say, she was freaked out even worst. Khaila and her family sat with me in the busy, crowded waiting area. It was a packed house. Nervously, Khaila sat there on my right, with poor Khyon shivering on her trembling lap. I glanced over every so often to reassure Khaila that everything would be ok.

She was a special kind a woman to marry me after I had committed such a violent crime. I told her the true story about what really happened when we made up. I guess she felt that if I could forgive her for what she had done, she could definitely forgive me.

For the first time in a very long time I prayed a long, silent prayer. I closed my eyes before the hearing. I was being sentenced for five counts, with a possibly of ten years over my head.

Since my own family didn't care about my fate, I had Khaila's mom and sister there for emotional support as well. Even though we didn't always get along, they were like family. Khaila was the one that needed them most. She had to have Tracie hold Khyon, because she couldn't hold it together.

When my name was called, I took my time leaving the seat to enter the courtroom. Mrs. Roe walked in beside Khaila, holding her up from fainting to the floor. They sat two rows behind me. I had to brave my destiny alone in the defendant's chair, next to my well-paid lawyer. Tracie and Khyon stayed behind in the waiting room area, since babies were not allowed in the courtroom.

The jury found me not guilty of one count of attempted murder and two counts of kidnapping. They dropped the serious felony charges due to lack of evidence. I was so relieved. I figured the court believed it was just a lover's quarrel between Fefe and me.

My lawyer and new homeboy had gotten me off the big charges. I made a good choice picking him to defend me instead of the phony lawyer I had before.

But I was still found guilty on one count of breaking and entering and get this…..one count of stalking. I laughed out loud in court when they said that. Judge banged the gavel for order in the court.

I ended up with only two years of probation time, which to me was a piece of cake. I could swing that. I just couldn't go out of state, and I had to report to a probation officer weekly. I think what also helped me was the fact that I only had a short record of misdemeanor crimes. So I guess the White judge was trying to give a Black man a chance for once.

Of course Fefe and Tonda never showed up to the court hearing. They did make an appearance though.

Afterwards, I walked my lawyer to his car to talk over business. After he left I glanced at the car and I noticed a note on the windshield. I laughed and said to myself, *will this bitch ever learn? Don't she know that at the snap of my fingers I could have her taken out?* Before balling the note up I decided to read it.

The note was a lot more humble than the others. She was just writing a guilt trip about me getting what I deserved, and "God don't like ugly…" *Whateva hooch!*

After I read the note, I waited in the car for Khaila and her family to come out. About five minutes later Khaila came out looking spaced out like a zombie. I noticed Khaila also didn't have Khyon. At first, I figured he was with Tracie inside, but Khaila's facial expression just didn't look right.

I asked, "Khai? Where is Khyon?" I paused for a response. Nothing. "Where is he?" I asked her over and over again where Khyon was and she acted like she didn't hear me. She just started crying. I was like, *aw lord, there she go again having one of her fits. She probably just upset about me being found guilty and having to serve probation time. Khyon's probably with Tracie or her mother.*

I shook her shoulders to snap her out of it, which made her cry even louder. Then she came through, "He's gone…he's gone…oh…my…God!" She screamed at the top of her lungs like I had never heard before.

Finally Tracie and Mrs. Roe came out the court building. I thought maybe they could tell me what was going on. I knew something was wrong when neither one of them had the baby in their hands.

"What do you mean he's gone, Khai? Somebody tell me where the fuck is my son???"

Tracie broke in, "Khyon's gone. This what happened: I went to the bathroom to change his diaper. This light-skin chic I ain't never seen before came in behind me. I didn't think nothing of it, but then a dark skin chic I had seen once before came in right behind her. I can't remember where I'd seen her before. Anyway, they started talking shit. The dark-skin chic said something to the other chic 'bout fixing Khaila's ass for good. I was like 'that's my sister you talking 'bout bitch! You ain't 'bout to do shit!' So I started beating the shit out the dark-skin chic, even though she was trying to fight back. I even had her head in the toilet. By the time I was finished with the dark-skin chic, the light-skin chic was gone and so was the baby. I ran out the bathroom and started looking for the light-skin chic and the baby, but I couldn't find 'em. Then I told my mama and she reported it to the po-lice. They still in there now questioning people."

I was spaced out like Khaila by the time she finished her story. *What the hell was going on?*

I knew exactly who the "chics" were and why they had done what they'd done. Fefe and Tonda both wanted revenge. I didn't think Fefe would stoop that low. They wanted to turn things into an all out war for real. Taking my son was definitely grounds for murder.

"I know who they were Tracie. It was Fefe, you know the crazy bitch I've been dealing with over this charge. Fefe and her friend, Tonda want revenge. I got a note on my windshield and everything."

I picked it up off the ground and gave it to her to read aloud. We all stood there spaced out for a minute.

I'm not quite sure what exactly happened and when it happened that day, but the Fefe-Tonda-Tracie bathroom incident had to take place during the time I was outside with my lawyer. Khaila and her mother were casually looking for Tracie and my son. They figured Khyon just got restless, and Tracie took him to the car to calm down. Tracie caught up with them heading for the door, and that's when she explained everything. How ghetto can you be? Fighting, while my son was being taken right from under her nose. I've never heard of anything so bizarre in my life with all my years of hanging in the streets and watching the evening news.

Mrs. Roe explained that she reported the incident, but the sheriff only checked people at the door and took a report. No shutting down the court for a full investigation was done. They told Mrs. Roe to report it to the local authorities, because it was out of court jurisdiction once they left the building. So she called the po-lice as instructed, and they did what they always did- nothing.

Tracie's dumb ass talking 'bout, "Wait 'til I catch them bitches in the street!"

I knew Fefe wasn't that dumb. If she took my son she was definitely leaving town for good. And that bitch Tonda had successfully walked out of the court building probably real casual like the baby was hers.

I thought to myself, *That's it! I'm putting out a hit tonight. Q would be more than happy to follow through.* As he had told me once before, "It would be my pleasure, baby-boy, it would be my pleasure."

# Catch the Upcoming Thrilling Sequel

# Venomous

### by Kharisma

*(Brief preview on next page)*

# Chapter 1
## *Khaila*

More than two months had passed since my world had been turned completely upside down. My baby boy was gone, just like that, and with him a part of me was gone as well.

Things never were the same after the kidnapping. Although D.C. and I were still together, we were both hurt and depressed, and we made sure to take it out on each other daily. The arguing increased as time went by. We kept playing the blame game, blaming each other for what happened to Khyon.

I would blame him for having us in court that day, and he would blame me for letting Tracie handle the baby. I blamed myself for that too, because she wasn't the most responsible person I knew. We both knew how stupid and ghetto she was.

D.C. and I realized eventually that we were acting out of anger and grief. We both knew Fefe would have found an opportunity to get at us one way on the other. She had found the perfect opportunity to hurt us, by taking our son.

Fefe disappeared with Khyon without a trace immediately after the court incident. We knew she had to have the whole thing planned for a long time. When we went by her apartment about twenty minutes after we discovered Khyon missing, she had moved all her stuff out Same deal with Tonda. Nobody knew where they went, or least they weren't saying if they did. Most of Fefe's family lived up north like New Jersey and New York, so it was hard to pinpoint exactly where they were with Khyon.

D.C. contacted his friends in Jersey and New York right after the kidnapping, but we didn't get any word on where she was. She was probably laying low with a new identity and everything.

We all lost all faith in the legal system. The police and court hadn't done anything to help us with our situation. I mean talk about evidence, how much more evidence do you need to convict, and put her away for a long time? My sister could positively identify both of them since she had seen them both in the court bathroom. The only thing the police did was put Khyon's name on the national missing children's registry.

The whole thing was especially hard for me in the beginning. I requested a leave of absence from work with no pay or benefits, so I could try to deal with the stress of losing my son everyday. I'd do nothing but cry, lay around the house, eat everything in sight, and then cry some more. I had always been a slim person, but I gained more than thirty extra pounds two months after Khyon's disappearance.

D.C. basically took care of bills, working two jobs, his full-time job at Dickie's, and a part-time job at Roses as stock clerk. Of course, his working so hard and me not working at all took a toll on our relationship. Although he knew I had issues with anxiety and stress, I believe he felt I was being lazy, while he worked like a dog. Our bills were out of control. Even though we didn't have the baby we still had baby-related bills, like the hospital bill, a rent-to-own crib, and a layaway of some other stuff we thought we needed. We didn't get rid of the stuff because we kept hope that Khyon would return home someday.

Cocoa tried to be the best support she could, but her and Reese had to get their own family issues straight. Even though they went through spiritual counseling, Cocoa never did fully trust Reese after his affair with Wanda.

D.C. didn't really have any support other than myself. His brother went back to being an asshole. He was more concerned with himself, than his own nephew. At first he played the angry role, talking about he was gonna 'hunt the crazy bitch down.' He wasn't going to do nothing.

Then of course "Q" was talking about violence too, but he landed himself in jail a few days after Khyon's disappearance for some other stuff he did.

Jyree and D.C. would never be the same after their falling out. In D.C.'s eyes, Jyree could have been in on the whole kidnapping scheme. He was really acting strange. He was especially bitter, because he couldn't be in the wedding. He couldn't understand why D.C. wouldn't forgive him, but he would forgive me. He found out the baby was D.C.'s instead of his, so he was really upset about that too. Every now and then we would bump into Jyree at the store or on the street. You could just see the bitterness in his eyes, hear it his tone, and feel it coming from his pores. He wouldn't say anything out the way though, because he knew he was the one in the wrong by coming on to me. He didn't like the fact we were married and at one time were a happy family. He was probably happy to hear about our family tragedy, although he tried to act concerned about the baby.

## *D.C.*

You know I never was much for drinking and I rarely cried, but I found myself doing a lot of both when my first-born left me. I thought Khaila's cheating hurt, but you can never know pain like losing a child. Even with all the stuff I had been through in my life, I had been though it all, living with circumstances like having no father in my life, a mother who suddenly died young, running the streets ducking bullets, Fefe and her bullshit, having a best man who fucked my soon-to-be wife, the list could go on and on.

At the age of just 27, I was going through what some people hadn't dealt with in their entire lives. Never did I imagine losing my son. I still believed he was alive somewhere, but it felt like I had lost him forever.

There was some hope though. Fefe called from a blocked number out of the blue one day. Of course she said she had Khyon and was holding him for ransom. Not a monetary ransom, but an emotional ransom. She still wanted to be with me. Talking crazy shit about us being a happy family. Just her, the baby, and me. You know I played along to get my son back but she got hip and hung up the phone. I guess it was the desperate tone of my voice or Khaila's in the background tipped her to what was going on.

That was about a month and a half after she took Khyon. She never called back. We didn't see or hear from her again until....

*Stay tuned for the sequel:* <u>*Venomous*</u>
*Email: miller_publishing@yahoo.com, for more information about purchasing any of Kharisma's work.*

Miller Publishing Enterprises

## Featuring Author: Kharisma

Website: www.millerpublishingkharisma.com
Email: millerbusiness2000@yahoo.com

## Order Form

NAME: _____
ADDRESS: _____
CITY:_____/ STATE:_____/ ZIP CODE:_____
PHONE: (home)_____other)_____
EMAIL: _____
ADDRESS: _____

| Quantity | Product | Price | Total |
|---|---|---|---|
| | Novel: <u>A Taste of BitterSweet Fruit</u> (comb-bound) | $10 | |
| | Novel: <u>A Taste of BitterSweet Fruit</u> (perfect bound) | $12 | |
| | "<u>Book Thongs</u>" <br> Extra Small <br> Small <br> Medium <br> Large | $.25 <br> $.50 <br> $.75 <br> $1.00 | |
| | Total Order | $ | |
| | Shipping & Handling | $ | |
| | VA Sales Taxes (5%) | $ | |
| | Grand Total | $ | |

**METHOD OF PAYMENT:** ☐ CASH     ☐ CHECK     ☐ MONEY ORDER